The Ones We Loved

TARISAI NGANGURA

HARPERCOLLINS PUBLISHERS LTD

The Ones We Loved
Copyright © 2025 by Tarisai Ngangura.
All rights reserved.

Published by HarperCollins Publishers Ltd

First Canadian edition

No part of this book may be used or reproduced in any manner
whatsoever without written permission.

Without limiting the author's and publisher's exclusive rights,
any unauthorized use of this publication to train generative
artificial intelligence (AI) technologies is expressly prohibited.

HarperCollins books may be purchased for educational, business,
or sales promotional use through our Special Markets Department.

HarperCollins Publishers Ltd
Bay Adelaide Centre, East Tower
22 Adelaide Street West, 41st Floor
Toronto, Ontario, Canada
M5H 4E3

www.harpercollins.ca

Library and Archives Canada Cataloguing in Publication

Title: The ones we loved / Tarisai Ngangura.
Names: Ngangura, Tarisai, author.
Identifiers: Canadiana (print) 20240535340 | Canadiana (ebook) 20240537645 |
ISBN 9781443467742 (softcover) | ISBN 9781443467759 (Ebook)
Subjects: LCGFT: Novels.
Classification: LCC PR9390.9.N43 O54 2025 | DDC 823/.92—dc23

Printed and bound in the United States of America
25 26 27 28 29 LBC 5 4 3 2 1

*Undoubtedly this is for my family because
I could not have started without them.
And for the people who couldn't speak love,
so they stayed quiet. I heard you.*

*How exquisitely human was the wish for permanent happiness,
and how thin human imagination became trying to achieve it.*
—Toni Morrison, *Paradise*

0.

WHEN THE GUNSHOTS rang out across Waterfall, the first before the fire started and the final one after the scream, startled feet surged towards the sound, like a wasp swarm, roused and unnerved. The women who collected money to build new homes. The preacher who spent it and the schoolteachers. The neighbor who sold the good sweets and lollipops. The builders and the secret drunks. The children who made a game of pushing each other in wheelbarrows. The men who raised their voices for love and fear.

Everyone hesitated after seeing a woman on the ground with hair spotted red, and She nearby clenching a gun, chest heaving and back straight. Beads of sweat bloomed on She's temples, dampening her hair, which had been pulled into six diamond-shaped plaits tied just below the nape. People who had often moved calmly now gathered recklessly, grabbing on to each other, not knowing what was skin or fabric, what was tight and what was too much—only caring that something was held. They looked at one of their own, then back at the stilled body. They had seen that first, but its blood would seep into the ground for a full day before they remembered that one of their own was gone. And *She* was gone, because a body was bleeding into the ground and smoke was ascending. They buried the woman on the second day and waited.

Gasping for breath, the girl thought she heard her friends, but couldn't be sure if their voices were in the air outside the church or cries in her head. The people of the town placed bread, fruit and water in her hands because they had left their homes knowing a deadly thing had visited and someone would be in need of food for the escape. As the crowd grew bigger, a hand clamped around She's wrist and dragged her away. Stifling panic made her stomach feel unyielding, hardened by grief and memory like a tombstone fitted between eyes that couldn't see and stiff feet. How many endings would be carved out of this catastrophe? Her own, the town, the woman whose body was on the ground.

Their pace slowed abruptly when the hand twisted her around and used its twin to lift up her face. A gentle touch wiped her eyes. She hadn't known there were tears and blinked twice to see who had moved her out of the noise.

"You have to leave," said the hand.

Her eyes traveled up the tight grip, noticed full veins, lines of fine hair on parched skin disappearing under frayed sleeves, and landed on a face. She saw red flecks, then blinked again. The girl's knees buckled and her muscles trembled like reeds in the river. She began to sob, voice dry and cracking from the smoke. It felt deliberately passive to crumble while she was being rescued. A selfish demand for attention when so many people had already given her their eyes. Her mind wanted to stand upright but her legs refused to listen. Her mouth demanded a scream but chose to hide the blood drawn by her teeth biting down on her tongue. She quickly felt guilty for failing to cry. For not knowing how to do it peacefully.

"I've killed us all. We are done. We are finished," She mumbled, tasting iron and what remained after choking on smoke and coughing up life.

THE ONES WE LOVED

The hand knelt in front of She, dropping the white purse that had been squeezed inside the folds of its familiar body wrap loosely gathered around a waist. Pulling She close, tears appeared in its own eyes. "They will kill you, so you have to leave now. Do you hear me? Now!"

Placing the girl onto its back like a baby, and snatching up the purse, the hand moved desperately towards the bus stop. One came by every few hours and the two arrived just in time. The hand helped She stand steady, the task made difficult by jostling food parcels. The girl's arms were weak and aching, but she hauled herself onto the bus while the hand turned to talk to the driver.

Stumbling down the aisle, unkempt and dusty, with traces and splatters of dirt on her school shirt, She ignored the stares from the passengers. The pleats on her skirt no longer pristine. Her socks limp around her ankles. Slumping into a back seat, she slid over to the end so she could lean her head against the dirty windowpane. There were cigarette stubs jammed in the corner. She pressed further into the blue seat marked with the indents of many and their baggage. A bored traveler had taken a knife to the headrest, shredding the leather to reveal tufts of brown underneath. Another had left a faded stain along the sewn edges, tinting the white threads with a yellow that looked like oil residue from a once-hot stew. She knew this ugly seat was not the only reason her journey would be a solo one. People rarely sit next to the person with red in their eyes. The hand walked over and looked at her close.

"You are going to a place I trust. It's far, nothing like you're used to and a little riotous for people with tender soles. But you'll be safe there if you just listen and help."

"I don't have any money," She whispered.

"That's fine. This driver has been to the church and he knows me. We worked out an arrangement."

The girl tried to say a thought of gratitude. For leading her away, for carrying her part of the way.

"I am sorry," said the hand, who was now crying.

"I killed her," said She.

"You did the right thing."

"What will I do?"

The hand whispered in her ear and brushed She's hair with her fingers, flattening the rising curls.

"Will you come see me?" She asked.

The hand didn't hear.

"You can't ever come back," it said. "Stay gone."

The bus made ready to depart, its engine sputtering and belching white blasts of smoke and bits of gravel as the driver rolled down his window and spat out a bullet of phlegm. The girl felt heat from the seat rise through her skirt, and the smell of fuel grew. Gripping the purse as though it were the only thing that now mattered, the hand looked at the girl one more time, then rushed off the bus, standing to the side and waving. The girl knew as her eyes peered through the window that the wave was one without expectations. It was a clearing of ghosts. An expulsion of a dark thought. A prayer. There would be no reunions.

As the wheels moved forward, the waving grew smaller and smaller. Looking at her own hands that had pulled a trigger and dropped a gun, She noticed scrapings of someone else's skin burrowed under her nails and the black stains on her fingertips, almost like soot covering the pots that sat over the fire. These hands had killed someone, and this was all they had to show. With each groan and clearing of the pipes, she felt her geography fall from her body.

Who was She now?

I.

THE BUCKET SMACKED against the side of the well hard as She hurriedly pulled it up. Usually she was awake before the birds started to flit and fuss, but sleep had kept her underneath the blankets heavy-eyed, even after Mama called out twice. On less urgent days when her mornings were timely, She would crane her neck over the window ledge close to their bed and watch the day's colors start to bleed, colors that seemed to steep and soak inside the wideness of the sky, using its length to stretch out and breathe: deep blues that became violets darker than the night, a gray that could be white and that spread faster because there was nothing it needed to be but pale. And after, a yellow that turned orange on the end dipped furthest into the sky, while the other side, the one held up by the hand that kept it all above them, looked golden. All this she would watch if she woke up early trying to decide which of the colors would anchor her day. Today there was none of it. She was late. And she was rushing.

She started to chew her tongue, feeling her upper teeth pressing into its flesh. People always said it looked like she was eating, and some said it was funny seeing one side of her face moving in such a way.

"Come on, girl, quickly! You don't need all that water!"

Mama was growing irritated. The woman didn't like being late. It meant you were not someone to be taken seriously, and to not be a serious woman was almost as bad as not being a devout one. Mama, with her worn smile and tender eyes, could do without any type of indulgence and had lived with never enough to make her feel settled but just the right amount to foster a grateful heart for the smallest necessities. Somehow, in a life shaped by scarcity, this woman whose hands kept a record of all the things she had clutched and cut had raised a daughter who craved and needed a costly bliss—a full tub. Lowering into the water, which She liked painfully hot, she would feel the sensation of pricking needles on skin as her body adjusted to the extreme. She would sit with her knees tightly pressed against her chest and water spilling over the rim. Three buckets of boiled water were usually enough, but today, only cold would have to do. She ran into the house, the bucket splashing on her way towards the washing room. If She wasn't careful, she would barely have enough to cup in her hands and run over her legs.

While clenching a rubber band with her teeth and long twigs for the sweeping stick between her legs, sorting the strongest from the weakest, Mama called out from the doorway. "Watch you don't fall, that water is dripping everywhere. Do you want to eat your porridge? I received some ground peanuts from the Reverend so it's not maize today."

"No, I won't have enough time. If I rush it down, then run to school, I'll probably not feel well on the road."

"I will put some in a jar for you. Eat it when you can."

"It's all right, Mama, I have my lunch. I'll eat that when it's time."

Her tongue danced in anticipation of the fiery sweetness. Last night Mama had cooked her favorite dish over a wood fire: stewed tripe, with generous amounts of mhiripiri, the alarmingly red tubes with bright green stems that grew outside their home, on the left section of the front yard. Buried next to the leafy covo, sprawling tomato veins and delicate shallots, they were the first thing people noticed through the short fence while walking by. A favored part of their every meal. You could easily reach over and pluck a few, but there was never any need. Mama gave to anyone who would accept, and to those who hid their need in effusive compliments. On the other side of the yard was a mango tree, and it was this that had first caught Mama's eye when she saw the land.

"What was it about the tree?" She had once asked.

"Your father would have loved it," Mama answered, the first and only time he would make an appearance in their home as a verbal recollection. Over the years, She would tread around Mama's life with him, probing for a way into that time. After several sly attempts and a few tense outbursts fermented in frustration, She convinced her mind to leave her father as a mystery. Mama once told She that stories had kept her alive when she was a young girl, yet the woman resisted every impulse to give her daughter any kind of souvenir to understand their current life. Something to cradle, or brighten with longing. The girl had questions about their journey, if her father had known about her and why it was just the two of them who came from where they had been.

But he loved mango trees. That much She had been told.

There weren't many people in Waterfall who came from elsewhere, and when they arrived, Mama found a place that was putting itself straight after a great loss, a little like her own life. There had been several redbrick houses uniformly placed along the main road for neatness and to make practical favors easy. These homes were also the town stores, and each family had or made something that could be bought and used by the rest. Bars of soap, slabs of butter, bags of chicken gizzards, bowls of maize meal, a cup of salt, an armful of mangoes. The money spent was collected every three months to pay for more bricks and tools so another home could be built for the next family looking for a place to stay.

Neighbors had told She that some of the other women had sent their husbands to help Mama build their house because she had no husband of her own. When the last brick was laid, She had crawled for the first time on the new floor, bruised her knees in the shared bedroom and pulled herself onto her feet in the kitchen where they cooked and ate.

Now grown, the girl's body flinched when her feet touched the bathwater, cool on skin used to heat. It was probably for the best; the colder it was, the quicker she'd be done and on her way towards Eastern Farms.

Ten minutes later, She was kissing Mama on the cheek. "Let me pray for you before you go," the woman said, reaching for her hand. Her daughter pulled away and moved towards the door.

"There's no time. I will see you when I come back."

2.

ON THE ROAD to Eastern Farms, past the white flowers with yellow centers that let out milky sap when plucked, past the house with the hedge turned a yellowy-green by huddling grasshoppers and before the bougainvillea where the neighbors sold colored sugar drinks frozen in the shape of short sticks wrapped in plastic, were the first sightings of sunflowers. The red-hatted landowner had planted them for his wife, who wanted a garden to fortify her ease and make her feel something besides languor and heat. When the wife saw the delicate stems, instead of towering stalks, her enthusiasm shriveled. The buds needed work and attention before becoming desirable, and the duty of walking back and forth between every row and tending equally to each did not coax her spirits, so Mama offered her hands, which could draw life out of any spent creature and plant.

Growing into their fifth season, the swaying blooms were an unexpected radiance in a land filled with so much green. Mama made no money for this labor. Her payment was in things that were discarded and threadbare after the landowners were done with them—shirts ripped open that Mama stitched into curtains, a broken bucket that she made into a tool that kept her wild seeds, socks with holes that became cleaning rags. Once the red-hatted landowner's wife had given Mama a pile of undergarments, and she'd wondered out loud to her daughter what use she was expected to make of that, shortly realizing that all she was given was not meant to be useful. It was being tossed out, into her hands.

Eastern Farms owed its new name to the arrival of the landowners. The girl couldn't remember what it was called before the change, but she'd heard it from someone longing for the old name's return. Then, it had been a red expanse inside Waterfall, with unevenly sized scrubs hiding rabbits, mice, bird nests and field snakes. On hot days, the soil crumbled like dried leaves, and when wet, it formed itself into something that had the strength of a brick, locking everything that flowed below its surface. Now the area looked like a filled notebook, every open line spoken for and filled with seeds. There were several stables, larger than her home, that also owed their presence to the new arrivals who had seen this land and treated it like it had always been their own. It was now almost impossible to find small creatures here, who'd retreated when the sounds of hoofs and turning soil took over the sanctuary. Nothing tiny could survive after this change. She had never seen a rabbit, and her oldest neighbors spoke of those they saw back when they ran like children, without worrying about breaking any bones.

The landowners and their families all lived near the farms, by Waterfall's namesake, a little piece of nature that She's neighbors and the people before them would stand under to wash off the history of an ending year and flow into a new one, clean and ready. It was in the center of town, and after the landowners arrived, She's neighbors were never allowed close to the falling water, which was saved for the horses. The people were told to wade into the river but that was not enough. So every year passed heavy on the skin, sinking into their backs, until their bodies felt like shells covering

THE ONES WE LOVED

the fruit inside. No one had ever told her that this was how it felt. She just imagined it.

From the road, you could see glimpses of the landowners' houses painted a white coat. There had been five when She had started walking around the town with Mama, practicing her first steps beyond their house and learning the names of her surroundings. *Sunflowers* for the tallest plants she'd ever seen. *Gates* for the bars that closed off the houses and the gardens from the rest of the town. *Bus* for what came and took the landowners' children to a school that was closer than the one she was now walking towards. She tried to leave home early enough so their children couldn't wave at her as she walked. It wasn't that She minded, she just didn't like stepping off the road so the bus could pass.

Today there were at least fifteen houses, and just as many horses. She rushed along the road. Glancing at the sky, She saw dark clouds starting to cluster, and a breeze had begun picking up the morning smells from her neighbors, who were frying eggs and green onions in too much oil, brewing strong tea and baking round cakes. She kept walking—running, really—but not too fast because she didn't want to sweat through her uniform and loosen the friction that kept her shirt tucked into her skirt. When that happened, her clothes would start to slip out of place. *Unkempt* is what the teachers called it, and she knew it was only allowed for the children on the bus who didn't wear their uniforms like She and her classmates. Those children on the bus wore white shirts with three embroidered leaves on the right-side pocket. As long as the leaf was visible, the shirt could be long-sleeved, short, even sleeveless for those who ripped off the arms. Their shorts, skirts or pants had to be blue, and for the girls it was suggested they wear skirts long enough to fall to their knees. Many rolled the waist up until the skirts skimmed their thighs. The socks were white, inside black shoes. They could wear their uniform as freely as they wore other clothes. But for She and her friends, the uniform wasn't about freedom, it taught discipline.

Her neighbors had chosen this uniform after they decided to build a school to teach their children. Every weekend Mama washed the set and made sure that her hands left no creases on the black shirt after rinsing, that the gold threads embroidered on the left-side pocket in the shape of a cross never came undone. The skirt, which was long enough to rest four fingers from the lower part of her knee to the hem, was the color of too-ripe mulberries with imperceptible pleats, so primly pressed only rapid swerving made the eye notice the detail and appreciate the patience of the fingers that had made them. And that of the children who wore the lines so finely. Her socks were a pale brown and folded once first, then again for the right length. This is what the parents wanted. The leather shoes, which Mama made She polish every Sunday, were brown and severe, the heel too thick to be beautiful but somehow still unreasonable, and laces that could not give any slack, no matter the pulling and fidgeting. Even with thick socks on her feet, the heel cap cut into her ankles. As she walked fast, while trying to run slowly, she remembered what the parents had told all of her classmates on their first day: To never look unkempt in their uniforms. To never be seen acting wild in their uniforms. To never be heard disrespecting God in their uniforms.

She rounded the corner, and as she prepared herself for the climb up the hill, she saw her large tree on the side of the trail. She didn't know the name, and Mr. Miles, the science professor, had no idea. She knew it was older than everyone in the town, and on days when she was early, she would carefully climb all the way to the top, sit behind the shading leaves and hide. From there, she could see the men who were headed off to Eastern Farms, the late risers who missed the first sun but caught it on its way up. They moved heavy, like their bodies weighed more than skin and nails and tears and blood and sweat and

THE ONES WE LOVED

hair. She was interested in their tellings, which reached her ears when the wind was agreeable. She especially liked the one who always kept his lunch swaddled inside the crook of his elbow like a small baby—a hunk of soft bread, a cup of soup wrapped in plastic—and she would pretend to join the conversation as they drew closer and then left her behind, playing a small part in their smuggled leisure.

They worked for the landowners, going out to the farms every day to count the seeds that the people from the other town threw into the ground. This was the job of men in Waterfall, to count the maize, the sorghum and the pumpkins while following behind the other men, the women and the children who planted it. To see the men leaving in the morning and returning after sunset, you would think their lives were built around options and time. Sometimes they went to church, and other times they didn't. They would go to the fields all day, but unlike the people who lived in the other town, they didn't have to work until their backs tightened and their hands split open. For She, something in the way they always set off on this journey from town to the farms told her that they found peace in this moment and pulled at it slowly, making it last as long as their walking. They could be loud, let their clothes rumple, and their bodies could sweat. They were given permission to show that the sun was beating down a bit too hard. *They can look unkempt and no one will be mad*, She thought to herself.

It was unusual work they did, still. In their own yards, the men could work on the soil, quickly stirring seeds in their palms so they slid between fingers and landed in the holes, which would be quickly covered by fast-moving feet. Yet in Eastern Farms, they were useless, tasked only with keeping their eyes open until the day passed, like small children who couldn't be left alone and were handed duties that worked the limbs while keeping the mind in a stupor. That's probably why they walked without rushing. The seeds would be planted

13

whether they arrived late or early, but their presence was necessary. The landowners demanded it.

As She entered the school gates and made her way to class, she peeped under her armpits and saw there were no growing stains, sniffed and smelled only the soap she used, before patting her shirt that was fitted into her skirt. She looked down at her feet, where her socks were folded over neatly, right above her ankles. The bell rang and she did not look unkempt.

3.

AFTER A DAY in the fields, the people of Spilling River would walk into the alley to drop off the day while holding their breath and their children. Consistently enough that it became ordinary. There were two rows of sheds, and in one, the townspeople left the hoes they took to the fields. They weren't allowed to take anything past the alley, which smelled even worse on the days it rained. None of them minded leaving the tools behind and tossed everything into a pile, closing the door each night. At least they could leave this part before returning to their homes and the bits of land they tilled for themselves, with their own deceptively crude tools that could slice through thick roots, dredge up soil and hold up a slanted table. It was hard work, but they had enough.

These sheds were the midway point between their homes and the landowners' estates. In several were bags of seeds that would be planted each season. Bigger bags held the sugarcane brought in from distant towns. The landowners wanted these seeds to turn into white gold, no matter how often the townspeople told them that sugarcane needed more water than could be spared. That it turned the other crops into scavengers.

The boy had been running fast when his foot stumbled on something large in the street and twisted to the right. Lying face-up in the dirt with his ankle throbbing, his mind returned to what He had seen. This regular alley, a place that could always fall to the rear, had now become permanent in his mind. His eyes would see it, his legs always walk through and his hands always leave empty. He felt the tears start to run into his mouth, tasted salt mixed with grains of sand. The smell clung to his skin, and He shifted onto his side so the vomit could land on the ground.

He didn't know how much time had passed, but when he got up, the night had crossed its darkest period and streams of light were starting to break through the clouds. He felt his knees shake as he staggered forward, trailing his leg behind him. Then he stopped. There was something that needed to be done.

By the time He arrived at the shared home, his neighbors were preparing to go to the fields. Their bodies stuttered when they saw him and struggled to find the right action: a small step forward, a hand rushing to cover the mouth so no sound could be heard, faltering fingers dropping a clean shirt into the mud. The children who approached him to see if that was really blood on his body were pulled away by their fathers. And the women who had tilled the soil next to him in the fields cast their eyes down while they swept their doorways. These were people who had known his grandparents and grown up with his parents. They understood what had happened. Later they would wonder why they had stayed so quiet.

There were four streets in Spilling River, all narrow enough to walk along and visit any of the six houses lining each side. Commotion littered their changing lives; laughter, sneezing, yawns, screams and cries could not be uttered without reaching several pairs of ears. His grandparents had lived in the third house to the left, on the fourth

THE ONES WE LOVED

street. After they died, that's where He'd remained. The neighbors had known his boy's voice, heard it break when he got older, and listened in now to the faint sobbing.

He picked up the bag he sometimes took to the fields and always left by the door. He did not go inside to recenter the floor mat and take a final look at the mud-plastered walls, the carefully carved bench, and incomplete baskets. There was no letter or message for his friends, so they could find him again when they were ready, and after they forgave him for not offering a proper farewell. He didn't know where he was going so he walked and walked until he forgot the pain. And kept walking until the blood became so caked that when he wiped at it, the remains of last night floated down like dust.

He passed the fields and looked at the rows where, with the drenching rain now absent, stalks of sorghum and maize stood tall and days away from picking. He had been praying over the harvest right before he held his breath. In these fields he had talked to the sky about his life, the yields he hoped would be plentiful, and listened for assurance that the peace he built would not be taken. The sky had rarely talked back but He had trusted it. Nothing was worth more to a god than a trust. If there was something, He would have given that. Whatever it took to keep his peace.

When He finally reached the bus stop, the only one that brought few people to his town and took even fewer away, he lowered himself to the ground and waited for a bus that would take him. The last time, he had been just a boy arriving in the place his parents had left and where his grandparents had stayed. The town was supposed to be a friend. Now, he was leaving with nothing but bruised palms and a bruised leg. Would his journeys always start because he was alone?

An hour passed before the bus rolled by, and when He boarded, he fell into the nearest seat and shut his eyes. The next time he looked

17

up, he saw a girl pass him with blood on her shirt and terror in her wide eyes. He turned his head slightly, but she disappeared into her seat at the back.

Closing his eyes again, He hoped for death. Maybe this time, he wouldn't be left behind.

4.

MAMA WAS WATCHING She walk in the direction of the farms towards school. Her braided head down, the girl was moving briskly. From the back, the woman could tell that after a couple of steps, She would skim her hands down her skirt and shirt. Her daughter was good that way, as a God intended. When they had first arrived, young woman and newborn, the people of Waterfall had worshipped outside. This was something that needed to be remembered. Praise could happen anywhere, but their bodies yearned for a place they wouldn't be watched. A house to let tears flow and raised voices echo, with no fear their instinctive responses would make them look dangerous or strange when seen by those used to them restrained.

It took work to keep a body still when it wanted to expand out of fury. In church they could release their rehearsed composures. So that the yelling they felt sitting in their throats became the ecstatic singing that shook the door, and the hands that wanted to take a life lifted to receive grace and grab hold of faith.

Nothing in Mama's life had ever felt more auspicious than having a church built shortly after they had arrived in Waterfall. Everyone had dug into the ground and followed the foundation laid by the neighbor who knew the most about such things. Even She, who had been too young to help, had buried her little hands into the mud and pulled out what she could. The townspeople carved pews from the dying trees flanking the landowners' homes, chiseled a cross into the largest branch, added polish and placed it in front of the wide room with a floor that made the children walk light because God was listening, and more importantly, so they wouldn't trip and risk splinters piercing through their clothes—their skin could better handle the unsightly marks left by the haphazard pricks.

To use the rotting wood, which would become the most sacred object in their town, the people had promised the landowners better crops, had given money and had begged. Even then, for some time after the church was complete, the congregants brought to the doors distress, clenched in their hands. What if, they agonized, when coming to pray, they arrived and the building was destroyed? How would their minds and bodies keep that story? They imagined holding vengeance in their memories and nestling it close. Considered training their feet to walk in step to the sound of forgiveness—remembering that each foot going ahead of the next was proof they were still beloved because their bodies remained moving, and so did those of their children. So that even if the church was gone and they were pressed down, their bodies were unharmed. They considered anger, and then a surrender without end. Is that what freedom entailed? The right to pray ceaselessly and the right to destroy ceaselessly?

Yet days became more. And their pews were left alone. So their hands relaxed.

Later this morning, the small house would be left empty as Mama took the same path as her daughter. Instead of continuing down the road, her stop would be the large sunflower garden where she worked, usually uninterrupted. This was where most of her time would pass before returning to prepare her afternoon meal and then dinner for

THE ONES WE LOVED

her daughter, who came right before the sun slept. She saw a lot of the town's women at this hour, also leaving for the landowners' homes, which they filled their every weeks cleaning and righting into order. On their walks, they would talk about the coming Sunday service and plan beatitudes for the home visits that always happened in her house because the neighbors loved how she made her chicken: skin dangling off the bone and melting into the mouth, placed next to a well-shaped bed of smoothly ground maize and over fried spinach sitting in a soup that didn't drip but clung to the chicken, the bone, the lips and the fingertips, needing to be licked and lapped up. All while feeding over thirty mouths. Any cook could feed a family of three and four and uncomfortably five. But only a person who understood how to serve people and portions, and split time and seasoning, could feed a party.

Mama tended the garden and kept the sunflowers blooming because she had asked to, and the landowner's wife kept her out of the house because she didn't want hands that touched dirt cleaning her walls and furniture. In her daily prayers, Mama was thankful for this reality that had come out of spite. She had not wanted to clean the landowners' houses—making them places of warmth and reliable assurance—this she did at the church, sweeping its floors often, alone on weekdays and sometimes before Sunday's service if her mind needed the comfort. Working outside made her feel like someone doing family work, larger than seeing to the needs of a few. Mama was attentive to the sunflowers because she wanted her neighbors to be touched. For her daughter to be stunned by something lovely whenever she left the house. The landowner's wife wanted to stoke envy while Mama wanted to give joy.

In the far town of her old life, Mama's husband had spent his boyhood peering through the windows of landowners' homes and jumping to see above the school gates where he was not allowed. He grew into a man sent to farm and harvest, and with each year that passed, couldn't understand why no one refused the commands that were always uttered like reason. Landowners were not mountains; they could be toppled. "Why can't the children who work in the fields also learn in school?" he asked Mama when they were young and still not quite useful enough to be tormented.

"It's because our houses are not big enough," she'd told him, while planting butternuts in the small patch her mother had cleared for her.

"We can make them big," he answered.

"No, we can't. Only the landowners have big homes."

"We built their big homes."

She had looked at him and knew then that they would live together like her mother lived with her father. When they became lovers and her stomach began to grow, he couldn't imagine his child pondering the same questions. "Those who till should join those who learn," he told the growing belly. He had already known they would have a girl, and this girl, his daughter, would find her way to school. She would not be stopped at the gate or peer through windows or follow a command without reason.

But he pushed too hard, so that when the bullet found his back and brought him to his hands and knees, all that touched him were the flapping pants of the townspeople who rushed past. They had been struck by his words, and grief had fallen from their eyes, which they kept low so the landowners wouldn't mistake it for anger, yet they did not help him. Losing her husband had shown Mama that their wants did not count for anything more than a shotgun fired once, then placed gently over the shoulder. Mama felt She coming in that moment, kneeling next to the man who was supposed to be her father and whose hand never left his wife's embrace. No, the landowners were not mountains. They were water. And her husband drowned while trying to breathe and died even slower because he fought to live. That same week, the next month or still that year and at some hour in

THE ONES WE LOVED

the day, Mama knew they would come for her and She. And for the
parents who raised the woman who loved the man who asked for too
much. Not because they were dangerous but because they were still
here. So the two had left, to protect those who remained. That was the
only choice to make.

On their journey from her old home to this one, Mama had felt
hauntings biting at her skin, taking the meat off her ribs, which
became easy to count and painful to rest her new child on. Waterfall
had pulled her like it knew her past was filled with lack. The decades-
old trees that swept the ground, heavy with fruit, the houses that were
sometimes washed away by a river spreading its home and the red
soil that looked black when saturated with rain. Life existed in such
abundance, it hid some of the heaviest burdens. You couldn't help but
be consumed by this town with a name that could be a happening or
a plea. Waterfall brought fat and muscles back into her body so that
her baby could squeeze and touch without causing injury. It fed her
dreams and ripened an obsessive faith that had been seeded out of a
tragedy.

During their first month here, it was not apparent that this beginning was meant to look like their lost life: building a house to raise
their daughter, clearing a patch for her garden and a place to pray.
Church didn't mean much when her husband was the one to believe
in. He had been as constant as daybreak, delivering love and filling
cracks in the mundane with enough light to soothe. The Sundays of
her youth were for them to wander and find new plants for her garden.
She had never joined the women and children who knelt in prayer,
their private asks and proclamations seeming unnecessary in a place
that never changed. But that's where she'd turned when the bullet
hit her husband. Before letting go of his hand, Mama had promised
that if her feet safely departed the town, and their child arrived with
enough breath to face new life, her trust would fall to the one that

23

guided the path. She needed something else to believe in. A thing that could join her as she wandered and didn't need her body like a child. A thing that was strong enough to hold her, so she could begin again.

"I'll take her to church this Sunday," Mama told herself while lifting the tub her daughter had used and tossing the water into their yard.

The woman who loved her husband never let go of his hand. The one who arrived in Waterfall understood the landowners of this place so much better because of those from her lost years. Although the geography was different, the landowners were the same because servility was what they desired. The servility kept the townspeople of Waterfall safe. They practiced so they could do it without pain or thought, and so it became a part of their bodies, like breathing, but not a part of their living, like love.

Landowners needed to be handled, their hearts made to feel generous. Like a door locked shut for seasons, any opening took time. There needed first to be a nudge, a small push, then another nudge, stronger this time. Over and over until the lock loosened and the door opened, barely broken, never knowing it had been closed. The first nudge was building houses for all who came seeking life, and not solely Waterfall's earliest people. That push had happened before Mama arrived, a bartering from an older time when the people of Waterfall and the landowners saw each other, not eye to eye, but clearly.

Having a church, Mama told the landowners as she handled them with care, meant the townspeople would be able to remember, without effort, all they had been given. And be grateful for how they were spared. A church would make them solemn and turn their joy into a serious matter. They became so sensitive, the townspeople, to the movements of the landowners—hearing footsteps before they landed and changing directions because of it. The church gave them a place to head after pivoting. She's father would not have gone to a service, and an uneasy part of Mama knew neither would the woman who had been his wife. But that woman no longer had a husband.

These landowners were not angry, the woman mulled, only afraid. Those she fled had wanted to break people down, stamp them into the ground until their bodies were sanded by the gravel, removing any friction or grit. She's father had refused to become something as painless and easy to grasp as a pebble. Mama had fought too. Her words only changed when she realized they held consequences for more than herself. Mothering love had sanded the sharper points that formed her rage, and he hadn't understood.

Church was her gift to the one who led her here, and to the townspeople. The school was her answer to the nightmares that had followed after she ran, judging her for leaving him alone, without sending any notice to the deceased. This had been another nudge, another push, another nudge and delicate handling. Mama had held her breath. A school was for the man whom she'd left, so he could know that she had listened when they were children, heard him still when they were loving and older, and kept him on her heart after she ran.

Sometimes, when the sadness claimed her sleep and the ghosts hovered above her ears, she would swing her fists and speak her grief.

He died and took everything. Even the memories of our life are his alone. If I had taken them, every happy moment would lead to him lying in the dirt. He made demands. I'm the one who gave her a new beginning.

Closing the door, Mama placed her head into the palms of her hands and knelt on the floor. The same words floated in the air over and over again. Mama prayed. And prayed and prayed. She wondered if charity could turn malevolent. And prayed again. The red-hatted landowner's wife would be waiting for her to care for the large garden and listen while she wallowed in the wretches of being a woman living in a big house. So Mama prayed even more. The garden would have to wait a little longer.

5.

It was raining again. Thunder rumbled in the distance like an old uncle muffling bad lungs. Rain came every year in Spilling River, but this time it was different. In the past, it landed in short spells broken up by high heat. For the last three weeks, it had rained every day for hours, never stopping, only slowing to fool their expectations, then resuming. There had been rough days, and a feeling He couldn't rid told him they'd not yet seen the worst of the season. He squatted and placed his head between his knees, letting the rain run down his back.

He looked up resignedly, imploring in silence for somebody to make the rain stop just long enough for him to plant the maize and then be on his way. If it continued, they would never finish planting the crops. He put his hoe to the side and lay flat on the ground. He closed his eyes, and the rain trickled down his face, lightly tapping him on the forehead.

"What is going on?" He asked. "Why is there so much rain this time? Is something wrong?"

He listened.

"Would you tell me if something was not well?"

Inhaling deeply, he let the questions sit on his shoulders before flowing into his stomach and then resting in his legs.

"Do not let me hope if there's no reason. I know there's more to come, but once it's done, will we be all right?"

He listened.

"I don't want to be disappointed."

He waited.

"You promised," the boy said, dropping a hint that he hoped didn't sound like a scold. "A voice said it would be different and I know it wasn't mine."

He listened.

Impatient yelling forced him to rise and see his friends waving from the field's perimeter, motioning that they wanted to return home. This was that wait-a-while kind of rain, and their neighbors were already walking back. The boy saw one of the men from Waterfall speedily moving through the rows, pointing an index finger at the mounds so he wouldn't count one as two and have to start over. When he reached the end, he would call out a number to the other two waiting, and if it was the same, their work would be done. Raking his scalp with his blunt nails, He picked up his hoe and headed for the pine trees.

"You looked like you were half-asleep out there. The rain bringing you down?" said Kind Eyes, looking at him teasingly.

"It's going to be falling for some time."

"It came fast today," said Blink and Miss. "I didn't even have time to finish one row before I smelt it."

"By then it had probably been coming down for an hour, but your eyes were shut the whole time," Kind Eyes added. Blink and Miss was known for the languid, almost lazy way he blinked. His eyes didn't stay open for an uncomfortably long time, and when you looked at him, they always moved as if they were in no rush to catch anything

THE ONES WE LOVED

in front of them. The girls found it arousing and the boys found it unsettling, until they realized he wasn't trying to seduce them. After a while they would start to think about him. Not unkindly.

"I could have opened my eyes as fast as a bee's wing and that rain would have still come out of nowhere," Blink and Miss retorted, squinting at Kind Eyes, the only other person allowed to tease. As untroubled as he looked, Blink and Miss carried a heavy punch. If the jokes ever went too far, nobody wanted to be on the other side of his fist. The boys stood under the trees for a moment, watching each other as friends did when something unexpected cut through a familiar activity. There wasn't any self-consciousness, just a slow appraisal to understand how this change would affect their moods and what their day would now become.

"How many did they count?" asked Kind Eyes.

"I heard fifty," answered He.

"Me too"—his friend nodded—"from the one who was closer to me. That's good for just the morning."

"We still need to plant more just so we can get the same amount as last season."

The landowners had brought in sugarcane from a town that was several rivers away, and the people in Spilling River shuddered. They had told the men from Waterfall about the extra work that would need to be done and the harvests that would suffer. Could they not pass on that news? The same way they sent over the numbers each day? The men had just looked and kept counting.

"They should have come earlier," Blink and Miss chided. "Now they have to rush before the rain interrupts."

"Who cares? This could make them work harder and not just stroll and count like people trying to fall asleep while standing."

"If they move too fast and count wrong, the landowners will come for us." Blink and Miss sighed.

29

In unison they turned to observe this work, which the boys and their neighbors occasionally mocked—in the flick of their wrists as they tossed seeds while imitating the men from Waterfall and the exaggerated way they raised their hoes when their day was done—so the counting men would know they looked silly while trying to be busy.

"What were you looking at up there?" Kind Eyes asked He, bringing the boys back into their day.

"I don't know. Nothing really," He answered.

"You talking to the sky again?"

He looked at Kind Eyes, searching for ridicule, but his face was blank.

"There's no one talking to me right now."

"Are you asking the right question?" his friend asked him.

"Who said I have questions?"

"Why else would you look to the sky if not for answers?" Kind Eyes quipped.

"It could be that I just need someone to talk to."

"We're always next to you."

"You can't be the ones who accept what I need to give."

"Why? How do you know that if you never open your hand to us?"

"Because some things can't be given to the people around you. Only the sky is able," He finished, his voice unassailable, but sounding distracted. They could have gone on with this way of talking. He and Kind Eyes. Questions piling over more, until the beginning itself became dubious. No one understood it and Blink and Miss would sit back, dizzy from the spinning.

A streak of lightning cut across the sky, marking its path with a jagged line. Kind Eyes shook his head, kissing his teeth in annoyance. "Is that what you were asking the sky about? To stop this rain?"

THE ONES WE LOVED

"It's rained every day since the beginning of the season," He answered, exasperated and anxious. "If that's what I was asking the sky, then it looks like it hasn't been listening."

Pushing his hat down, He picked up his hoe and slung it over his shoulder. The other two lifted the little they'd brought and started walking back to town. They hadn't made it ten steps before the rain started beating against the dust road, forcing the boys to bow their heads low and break into a sprint. Their minds wandered, one worrying if the windows had been shut before leaving home this morning, the other remembering his clothes hanging on a line outside no longer dry, and another thinking of dinner and a meal that would make them smile. All three worried about the land and the crops. Puddles were quick forming, and as their feet splashed in muddy water and gravel clung to their pants and legs, Blink and Miss slowed down and looked up.

"Come on, what are you doing?" yelled Kind Eyes.

Blink and Miss came to a stop and looked at his two friends ahead of him, both trying not to run and leave him behind.

"What are you doing?" repeated Kind Eyes. He felt the rain spill into his broken-down shoes and make streams between his toes, sending fits of cold up his leg.

"Why are we running?" Blink and Miss yelled back, his arms outstretched and his face gradually letting a smile take over.

"Blink and Miss, I don't know what it is you are trying to say, but whatever it is, neither one of us understands," He replied.

"It doesn't matter if we run," Blink and Miss answered, raising his hands to the sky and looking at the road. "We are not going to be dry any faster." He placed his tool bag onto the ground, lowered himself next to it and lay down.

"Blink and Miss, stop acting like someone is whispering magic into your ears!" He yelled hoarsely.

31

"Odd words from someone who speaks to the sky," said Kind Eyes, smoothing down his brows as if to press them deeper into his head.

"What are you doing now?" the boy asked as Kind Eyes walked over to Blink and Miss, whose eyes were now slivers on his face and whose hands were flat at his sides as his face pointed to the sky.

"What will happen to us if we stay?" Kind Eyes asked He.

"So we make ourselves sick?"

"No," yelled Blink and Miss, above the rain. "We make ourselves water."

Kind Eyes lay down next to his friend, and their heads formed a shape that became a bridge. Uncertain whether to join or wait until they were done, He looked at his friends. Kind Eyes was right, there was nowhere they needed to be, and out here it was just them, cold but together. He walked towards the disappearing two and stood over them, before dropping down and placing his head next to the bridge. He could no longer tell how strong the rain was, and his clothes were now fighting with his skin to become one with his body. Water ran into the openings of his ears and down the corners of his closed mouth. He tried to open his eyes to see the state of the sky, but his vision was blurry.

Blink and Miss let out a loud laugh, head slightly lifting. He laughed and laughed until the others joined in, unable to resist the euphoria clearing out of their friend and into their own bodies.

"What is wrong with you?" Kind Eyes asked between giggles.

"I just thought that if the sky was talking, we wouldn't be able to hear anything now because our ears are half drowning."

Blink and Miss released a loud shout, and the boys started hollering, every sound carrying them higher and farther, far from here, three always. Then He lifted his head, and through his wet eyes saw three girls splashing through while running towards the small town beyond Eastern Farms. They must have run by while his ears were submerged

THE ONES WE LOVED

in puddles. He couldn't see clearly, but he could tell they went to that school with the blood skirts.

"I wonder what they think of us," He said just loud enough for his friends to know he was speaking.

"Who?"

"The girls."

"Why?"

"The girls."

"Who?!"

"You are both going in circles again!" yelled Blink and Miss, cackling at the missed attempts.

"I don't know what he's talking about," said Kind Eyes, roughly cleaning his ears with his finger before propping his head on his palm. "What are you saying?"

"The girls who ran by us. Didn't you see them?" He said, still looking in the direction they had gone. "I wonder what they thought of us."

"What girls? And what does it matter. I thought you were talking about the sky," said Kind Eyes, letting out a long breath that shuddered as his body shivered, finally aware of the damp. He tilted his head to the left to see if Blink and Miss was listening, but the boy had a silly expression on his face. It looked like his mind was visiting someplace else. "Maybe they were also coming to help count, and when they saw us, they realized how useless it was for them to be running," Kind Eyes added.

"I doubt that they work on the land," He answered, shaking his head.

"Neither do the men who count," answered Kind Eyes, happy to state what he solidly believed. He shared this thought often with his friends and they, more than him, knew he said it because doing the work felt better when he did. "However they spend their time," he

33

continued, "it's nothing that can help us here. It's your voice in the sky you should be thinking about."

Kind Eyes had never understood his interest in the acts of the sky, He knew. It was there, and that alone was enough for almost everyone to be sufficiently awed by its power and reluctant to find meaning in its existence. That was not enough for He, and since they were children, his eyes had spent more time looking at the sky than watching his step. For someone who was inclined to run everywhere, there was an effortless trust in his belief that his feet would always touch solid ground.

"The sky wants to talk to us," He said. "It's always here, so why would it come back unless there was something it needed."

"And you think what it needs is us?" Kind Eyes asked, a little incredulous but more intrigued by the wisps and turns of his friend's mind that regularly found a way to make their being, as people and friends, a much larger thing. He made it seem so important. Their walking and eating, even the smallest part, their seeing. Kind Eyes never said, but this made him feel good, like someone who was a part of a row that would be incomplete if he was missing.

"Perhaps. I just need to find out how to listen."

Kind Eyes playfully rubbed the top of his friend's head. "When you find out, keep nothing to yourself except pride. Let us know too."

"What questions do you have for it?" He asked quizzically.

Kind Eyes shrugged, trying not to seem too dependent on this sky ritual. "Whatever comes to mind when it finally answers you."

"I think it's a woman," said Blink and Miss. "A young one too."

"Boy, we thought you were sleeping," He said, chuckling.

"I tried to drift but your ramblings brought me back."

"How young?" Kind Eyes asked curiously.

"Not much older than us, I think," said Blink and Miss confidently.

"Why do you think that?" He asked.

THE ONES WE LOVED

"It seems obvious doesn't it?" answered Blink and Miss, sitting up to look at his friends, who had both shifted to face him. Their dazed looks made it apparent it was not, and he grinned like a satisfied uncle when he realized that he had asked a question neither of them could answer.

"Only a woman, a young woman, would spend so much time act-ing out of character and then say absolutely nothing when asked to explain," said Blink and Miss. "It's clear that there is a reason, but every-one has to wait until she's ready to talk, or they've figured out how to hear her answers to the questions they have not asked."

The two sat in silence with doubts and rebuttals jostling in their minds. Blink and Miss gave a pleasant grin, happy that his answer had been unexpected, and from his own consideration, quite wise. The rain had slowed, and now it was coming down in steady drops, large enough to keep you in the house but not so strong that it was difficult to walk.

"Have you tried not looking at it for a while and seeing if anything changes?" asked Kind Eyes. "If the sky is a young woman like Blink and Miss said, she'll make herself known when you step back."

As He looked at his friends, a smile opened up his face. "I never planned to learn about women from you both." Just as he expected, Kind Eyes looked away, while Blink and Miss jumped up and faced him.

"I'm not wrong. You'll see." Kind Eyes clapped in agreement, and they looked at He, who was still sitting down.

"All right?"

"All right."

6.

"... And every day that we learn and pray,
We listen to our teachers who keep evil at bay,
And to our parents who know and guide,
We ask that (a) God is always on their side."

EVERYONE RECITED THE daily prayer at Samson's Cross: the children who had been walking for some years, those who were old enough to start families but too young to care for them and all the teachers. The first group spoke passionately, not paying attention to the meaning but determinedly working to show how well they could enunciate. The older students were less fervent, the prayer dulled by a plainness that made it easy to recall but too weightless to inspire action. She had added that extra word in the last line because Mama always said "a God" whenever the girl heard her talking alone. It made the God feel closer, She thought, as she joined the lines going to class.

Rising from the first hill that welcomed eyes into Waterfall, Samson's Cross was a better school than most. Shaped like a garden fork with four stone-gray buildings about three meters apart connected by short hallways, each room for different students depending on their age and the subject. There was more than one teacher, multiple classes a day, and the books were shared only between two people.

Unlike schools in the far-off towns you only heard about after something terrible happened to the people, there was not much that placed them in a state of panic. It helped that Waterfall was far from those places, but by the time news of a disaster finally passed over the hill—first reaching Reverend Mr. Shoko, who would encase it in the gospel, before passing it on to parents, who told their children—the affected town would have swallowed the remnants of whatever had poisoned their lives, while the people in Waterfall were just starting to understand the depths of the contamination. Everything for them took time. Bad news to arrive. Bad news to settle.

At Samson's, whenever you entered a new grade, you would find someone who lived close so you could take the books to their house when you were done. Some schools had five or six children sharing one textbook, and sometimes it didn't have all the pages inside. If one of them lost it, they would go without for the rest of the school year. Because She read so much slower than her classmates, she was one of the only students who had her own textbooks. Her teachers assumed that words were difficult for her to grasp, and so while others had to read several pages a day, She was given no time limit. "Do what you can," they said. So she did, stretching the pages over a period of weeks, one day for herself, and the rest to teach Mama. If the teachers knew she was actually the quickest reader, she worried they would have her give the books to her classmates. And then Mama wouldn't have time to learn. Sometimes She felt guilty for the lies, until she reasoned that she did share the book with one person.

The classrooms at Samson's Cross were big, making them cool in the summer and cooler in the winter, but that was fine. It meant the students couldn't sleep while the teacher was talking. They were either too busy rubbing their hands to stay warm or basking in the crisp air before leaving for homes that sweltered because of the asbestos overhead.

All but one of the teachers had left Waterfall and gone to where they could learn everything they needed to know about how to work with children. After two or three years, they came back so they could share what they had been taught. This year they even had a teacher, Mrs. Maynard, who wasn't born in the town and was now here with her husband. It had been less than two months, and already she was talking to some of the men about building a house at Gethsemane's Point, a place with only a few families because it was too high up, farther than the school. Hauling bricks was tiresome and the air got thinner as you ascended, but after you arrived at the top, somehow breathing became easier. As if nothing was in the way. Until it was finished, Mrs. Maynard and her husband lived in the shack right next to the school, where all the extra bricks and building tools were stored. It had been cleaned out, the bricks and tools pushed into a corner and a mattress and stove brought inside. Samson's Cross was a good school, better than most but not quite as lofty as the one for the landowners' children.

Who wants that type of school anyway? She thought as she looked outside, where showers were starting to fall, hitting the ground like a titter that was anxious about distracting the children from Mrs. Maynard's numbers problem. You couldn't possibly learn anything in a school where you had too much of everything. People needed to learn how to make do with little. That's the only way they would know how to wait and be grateful. She couldn't imagine a life where she didn't know how to be patient. All the things around her needed time. The water she boiled over their old paraffin stove to warm up her bath, the iron they heated up over coals to smooth the pleats on her uniform, the church services that went on too long, the humid days that refused to become cool nights, the sunflowers that sprouted at their own willing, under good care. She knew what it meant to wait. Those who didn't wouldn't know how to survive in her world. How to live according to the patterns of everything around them.

"I think the landowners and their children would lose their minds," She said aloud, forgetting she wasn't talking to anyone.

"You know the answer, dear?" asked Mrs. Maynard.

She looked at the teacher, who was patiently waiting for a response.

"Umm, no, I'm sorry. I thought I did, but I was thinking of the wrong problem."

She quickly looked down, hoping Mrs. Maynard would move on. The answer was simple, but she didn't want to say. If she answered the question correctly, Mrs. Maynard would look at her for the rest of the lesson, like it was just the two of them in the classroom, and try to build a rapport. Mrs. Maynard had mentioned that phrase a few weeks ago, and She had looked up the word she didn't understand in the giant dictionary at the front of the class down the hall.

Rapport: a close and harmonious relationship in which the people or groups concerned understand each other's feelings or ideas and communicate well.

Such a strange word. She had played with it on her tongue, testing it out, but it did not feel true. How do you build harmony? That seemed like something you lived with on the inside and which you couldn't make brick by brick. When you build something, every tool you pick, and those you leave out, are all decisions you make. And no one can make a decision that, today, they are going to live in harmony. That they are going to understand someone's feelings and talk to them well. You're either born in harmony or outside of it. But it can't be made. If it were that simple, then everyone around her would have made it. They built everything else on their own, the homes, the church and this school, with scarcely enough to use. If it were possible, they could most certainly build harmony. Mrs. Maynard was a

40

THE ONES WE LOVED

nice teacher, might even be kind, but her intentions were not sensible. Especially in Waterfall.

Still looking out, She trained her eyes on her tree beyond the school. One of the branches seemed to be touching the clouds that floated like clothes on a tight line. She wondered who had first seen the tree in the beginning, and if they had climbed it. There were some markings she had seen a while back that looked like the bark had been scratched on the way up. Or maybe down. They weren't recent, and so they couldn't have been made by anyone she knew. No one paid attention to the tree. Adults never leaned against it on their way back from work, and children never looked up to see its towering reach. It was as if she was the only one who knew it was there. She started to chew her tongue.

The small clock by Mrs. Maynard's desk made a rapid ringing sound, as if it, too, didn't want to be called upon. Picking up her bag, She headed straight for the door, making sure to avoid looking at her teacher, whose eyes she could feel on her back. She placed herself between two other students so their closeness would appear as if they were deep in conversation, and any interruption would go unnoticed. It was during this time between classes that she would finally see her friends. Although they saw each other every day, there never seemed to be enough time with Joy and Kuda. Aside from Mama, they knew her longer than anyone else and loved her just as deeply. All the things she couldn't tell her mother, they held on to.

When she was out in the hallway, her eyes searched for Joy, who usually came from the left side, and Kuda, whose teacher Mr. Robinson had foolishly made them work outside. The showers were now demanding, completely over their earlier reticence and slapping the ground with increased force as the children rushed inside shrieking, their surprise and excitement heightening the emotions of their classmates. Now everyone was restless, smelling the scent of wet earth and ready to skip over their seats. Only their uniforms kept them bound.

41

They couldn't get dirty. The teachers would be upset and their parents would be disappointed.

A single, high bun made its way through the bouncing ponytails, tight plaits and shaved heads. She waved and Joy raised her eyebrows.

"It's higher today," She said.

"Are you sure?" Joy asked, patting the bun lightly.

"It looks like it could touch the sky, and you look like you're flying."

"I think I might change the hair mixture and make it more water so that my hair doesn't feel so slippery between my fingers. I wiped off too much oil today. I don't think that's good."

She lightly pressed her palm on top of Joy's bun, then brought it back to her plaits, which Mama had redone the previous night. "Now my hair has some of that special mix."

Joy's laugh was that of someone who didn't do it much and needed another person's pleasure as permission. In Joy's mind, it felt greedy to claim a sound or let her body change as it made room for giggles; throwing her head back or stomping her feet was out of character. So she would lean into one of her two friends, link her arm into theirs and let the embrace allow her body some seconds of delight. She did that now while they waited for Kuda.

"Have you seen her today?" Joy asked as the groups of children dispersed.

"No, I didn't have time to wave at her this morning. I barely made it to the prayer before the bell rang."

"Maybe their class went on longer than expected."

"No, those boys are in it," She said, pointing to a group of stragglers rushing in with Mr. Robinson close behind, brushing his wet clothes.

"Do you think she's sick again?" Joy asked, her mouth tightening and her brow creasing.

They looked at each other with apprehension, considering the

THE ONES WE LOVED

reasons their friend would miss school and trying not to think of the most obvious cause.

"Do you think her grandmother came back?" Joy asked anxiously, looking at She.

Kuda's grandmother didn't go to church like the rest of the women in town who had children. Her granddaughter had not known the old woman to cook food for the family, and never for Kuda to take to school. Their friend roused herself in the morning, learned the lessons of women's bodies on her own, tended to her aches and knew of a mother's love by the ways her friends moved with their own. Joy's mother was attentive, also generous. And She's was quiet, always fair. Both so different but evenly measured in how they dressed themselves to care for their girls. Kuda had once thought her grandmother acted out of sorts because there had never been anyone to help. But She's mother had no help and still loved her daughter.

All the work Kuda's grandmother did was outside of Waterfall. No one knew what it was, but the way people looked at her made Kuda know it wasn't cleaning, as her friends' mothers did. It was this mysterious work that had taken her away the last time, though the woman never needed a reason to leave.

They waited for a few more seconds, urging the doors to burst wide open and for Kuda to come in, uniform a little askew, skirt backwards or shirt collar not lying flat, before walking in step to their next class.

"We can go by her house after school," said She.

"We should take her some flowers. That will help cheer her up," Joy said, and She nodded her head in agreement. "I saw a few good ones on my way here today that we can go and pick up."

Everyone was already seated when they walked into God Studies and Reverend Mr. Shoko cleared his throat loudly as they settled into their chairs. The girls looked at each other and smiled. He had been at the school since its opening, and the girls' best shared joke

43

concerned the Reverend and his speech. Once, while the trio were resting by the small stream near Kuda's house, She had realized that were he not reciting bible verses or sharing parables, Reverend Mr. Shoko would have nothing to say. And if he did say something without a bible verse, it was an *um*, an *ah* or a *mhmm*. The bible was his word, and he would tell anyone who listened that all of life's questions could only be truly answered in the book, from the inquiry he most expected, "Will I pass the class, Reverend Mr. Shoko?" to the bizarre, "Can the doctor give me new skin like a new suit, Reverend Mr. Shoko?" Even the most pitiful, "Will my mother stop being sad, Reverend Mr. Shoko?" and the most fearful, "If the landowners happen to kill me for nothing, will my anger stop me from going to heaven?" All these were answered in verses, and the children nodded, they shrugged, and they waited.

After the bible, it was Social Studies, with lessons on living good in a place that looked healthy but seemed unwell. Then a half-hour break was given so students could expel the energy built up during the morning classes. Science class was right after, a wise choice because the students were alert if not enthused. It wasn't that there was no interest; a lot of them just knew they would have no use for these formulas. The lessons from Social Studies drew out their boundaries, and they knew what they would be allowed to do.

"There are now many scientists who started off from where you all are now," Professor Miles always told them. "And they are doing their own experiments and making discoveries." He insisted that all his students call him professor so they could get used to the idea that someone who lived like them could have such a title. There were different kinds of sciences, She knew, but Professor Miles never told them which one it was that he had studied. Sometimes it sounded like he was teaching something he had heard in passing. She'd told Joy and Kuda about her suspicions, but neither one of

THE ONES WE LOVED

them cared enough to hold it against him. She didn't either. It only made her feel bad.

In the afternoon, Sewing and Carpentry separated the boys and the girls until their final subject. Geography. It's the one that made She grateful to be in school, and Joy and Kuda had never agreed on why their friend liked it so much. None of them had been anywhere but Waterfall, and there was nothing especially thrilling about the land that surrounded them. The flowers weren't that striking or ugly and the river, which was the best part, was simply terrifying in its strength. It had come for the town some years ago, when the three girls were not of remembering age. The stories about that fortnight of pounding rain had been told and heard so often that all three felt as though they had seen the water rushing through the windows, breaking down the doors and shattering the roofs. Their best thing also made it difficult to be here.

Miss Bride, their teacher, had been one of the first people to arrive in the town and make her home after everyone chose to start over. "No husband or children, but a name like Bride," She heard the women saying in a judgment winnowed by curiosity and church. "What is she pledged to, then?" They hadn't sent their husbands to help build her home like they had done for Mama. Miss Bride built it herself, two large rooms made of wood. That house added a different geography to their town, She had thought, after walking by with Kuda and Joy. A perfect place for the woman whose lessons dealt with the shifts in the world's formations: why the trees grew as they did, why droplets of water formed on the morning ground and why the soil was the color of blood.

"Everything around you is your geography," Miss Bride had said on her first day. "It decides who you become."

"Does that mean people are geography too?" one of the students had asked.

45

"Yes. Yes, I think it does."

"What about houses?" asked Joy.

"Yes, they are also a type of geography," answered Miss Bride, smiling.

"And stores?" piped Kuda.

"Yes!"

"What about the people who left?" asked She. "Do they belong to my geography, or the one they ended up in?"

Clasping her hands behind her back, Miss Bride tilted her head to the side before answering, like someone trying to hear a thought that was much lower on the ground.

"I think they belong wherever they are loved."

7.

BLINK AND MISS called it "The Spill," a toss-away name that told more than intended. Unlike the people in Waterfall, who spread their lives between church and school, in Spilling River, they worked to never scatter too far. They had been uprooted once, so they moved tentatively, not making too much noise. This weightlessness of feet didn't stop the landowners from treating the alley separating The Spill from Eastern Farms like a latrine, covering the ground with shit and urine. It was their only road home, so the townspeople were careful not to step fast or hard as they lined up outside the shacks on either side. Stout and low with space for one body, the single rooms were built from leftover metal scraps too small to cover a roof but substantial enough to be wasteful if discarded. The townspeople would pass the farming tools they were prohibited from keeping, handing them off from person to person to person to person until they reached the one in the shed, who would pile them high, holding his breath and working fast so his neighbors wouldn't have to stand outside too long, breathing in spurts.

These slipshod sheds next to the reeking alley also stored the bags of seeds brought in from other towns past the end of the river. The landowners rode out on their horses twice a year, returning with what was needed. In the past the townspeople had walked the distance, setting off when the bags were half finished and returning just as they were being turned upside down and shaken. When they tried to find something good about the ways their lives had changed, they held on to the fact that now it was the landowners who did the traveling for seeds. Even if it was the horses that did the work of running and carrying.

In Spilling River, they were allowed to grow their own food from the bags inside the shed next to the shit and urine. But the townspeople knew their seeds were clean because after the landowners doled out parcels to each family at the beginning of a season, they would take them to their homes, place them in a pot and cloak the parcels with spirals of smoke from lit bunches of green grass, dried purple flowers and a spindly black weed pulled from the anthills. The seeds needed smoke to be cleaned, and the smell the townspeople could not identify with their noses showed them that the bunches were doing what was needed: cleaning the seeds of urine and shit so that when they were planted, they fed their bodies well. It was a ritual that had lasted long enough to be respected, and was still young enough to raise tempers because the children hated the smoke's smell. But they tolerated it and would never plant the seeds until they had been smoked. It's what was done.

When the people of Spilling River were uprooted, they were given tracts of land, a generosity that lessened when they saw the sizes—as long as the arm of the tallest person in a family and as wide as the children standing hip to hip—and understood the divisions of labor that would need to be made for them to work for the landowners and also feed themselves. Children would work on the family plots while parents worked on the larger estates. As long as the landowners were filled and appeased, the townspeople could live with a few seasons of

THE ONES WE LOVED

poor harvests while their children learned to till and listen. Parents would teach them at home, sharing guidance about the placement of the sun, the driftings of the wind, the types of birds that circled overhead and how the children would need to work different because of it. They called out directions as they watched from the fields, paying attention both to the rows they planted and to those made by their youngest just a little way farther.

Some of the men from Waterfall had tried to clean up the alley, an action meant as a sort of penance and which had been silently appreciated, until the landowners stopped one of the oldest men of Spilling River and forced him to eat a bag of shit after a day spent hunched over under the sun. He had never walked outside again, and the townspeople in Spilling River stepped out of their skin that day, learned to take it off before going to the farms every morning so that if they were made to feel unlike people with legs and arms and hearts that suffered from loss and joy, they would remember their skins were at home, safe inside. And so no one could make them feel less because their skins were somewhere else.

For He's grandmother and grandfather, Spilling River was their home. Among the rocky gardens sprouting vegetables, surrounded by anthills and slanted pathways, they were able to raise their daughter, He's mother, without any queries. She had been one of the first born after the move, a time of celebration and confusion because, while she was born of them, the young girl looked like nobody in her family, living or past. She was what most people would later call bent, after they had reached a place of comfort in her presence and learned to accept her difference within their town. Someone who lived her life a little off balance because of her skin that cracked and bled under the sun. She needed ointments, thick pastes that calmed the burning when she worked outside too long, for which the other children taunted her when they were far from their parents.

49

The landowners found her amusing; in particular, the one with the red hat. It probably saved her life, their amusement. It brought them glee to see evidence of the town's wrongness, and they left her alone so daily sightings of her could be taken as proof that Spilling River was fated to be pained. Her parents placed their hands against their hearts, which had been sore since leaving Waterfall and which now could rest because their daughter would be allowed to live. She was safe in Spilling River, and she later found the heart of a boy who wanted to be part of her bent life.

"We are all bent," He's father had told her, setting aside the disapproval of his family. They wanted him with someone whose burden equaled his own, and He's mother had understood. Everyone lived at the whims of the landowners, and what parent would want their child to choose a life with more misfortune? He's mother had seen her life as one where she would only be a daughter, learning what she could, helping where it is needed, and caring for her parents when they became less capable. A love that bloomed out of want, not responsibility, made her life seem bigger, and Spilling River became too small. Being bent was no longer a purpose, just a piece she could hold and take with her, and perhaps elsewhere, it would be a piece she could let go.

The two pledged themselves to each other and made it known to their parents that they planned to build in a foreign place.

"Where will you go?" He's grandmother had asked her daughter.

"We don't know yet," she had said, "we'll just keep walking until we find a place that calls to us."

"Who will take care of you?" He's grandfather had asked his son.

"We will take care of each other," He's father said, certain that they could start a family and it would all be right.

He's parents had been called to a town without landowners, where

THE ONES WE LOVED

the soil was rich and the people loveless. They were a kind-shame people: those whose speaking began with words that sounded like love, but then were traded for shame in the moment before you accepted and could reciprocate. You felt shame for wanting kindness, and shame for failing to receive it. As though something about how you heard what was said made it so people treated you kindly, and with shame. It was a barren way of living.

In this town, his mother and her skin were granted no solace. It bled and bled like before, and now it was parents with children who taunted. Her eyes suffered and only her hair seemed to wish her well. The children who were sent to touch her thick long hair while she sat in her doorway weaving said it felt just like their own. Yet she had a child whose skin looked like the ones who taunted. And who had her face. You saw her when you looked at him.

After the first season that the town's crops had failed to grow higher than a man's head, they had looked at his mother and her skin that bled. She had kept her face turned away from the sun and the accusations that her bent life was causing bad harvests. When the rain fell like stones that dented roofs, they pointed again at her skin with the blood that had dried under the ointments. His mother died soon after the second season, perhaps from the changed geography or the suspicion of her neighbors. How could a body live well when no one wished for it to be so? His father didn't know how to heal without the love of a girl who had given him a son. So he walked into the river and never came out. It wasn't a death, he had promised as he waded in. Only a leaving.

The people who had jeered shrouded his mother's head with fallen branches. Her face looked too much like the boy who looked just like their little ones. He was put on a bus by a repentant stranger who worried because someone so young had been made an orphan.

51

His mother's parents ran to meet him at the bus stop after their neighbors told them that a child who looked like their daughter had arrived and was sitting alone. After his return, and time had turned the loss into a new life, He wondered if his parents would have been better here, if he would have known them as people who loved instead of those who died. And had the chance to know the people who had called his father a son. The neighbors of Spilling River were reserved, yet good, and accepted silence as a response to any question. It meant an end and also left room for whatever would be said when the found words were necessary. They had smiled when He started leaving for the fields with his grandparents, passing him a shorter hoe when he was unsure what to do with the large one his grandfather offered. Only two had asked about his life before, and they became his friends.

The nightmares had begun after he finished planting his first row of maize, a sign that some satisfactions were undeserving of even brief admiration. It was around this time that his grandmother started waking him while the sky was still dark, bundling him between her legs so his feet could only move if her own did. Together they would weave, the student and his teacher, wrapping their grief as tautly as the reeds. While his grandfather snored haltingly in the corner, his grandmother taught him to make baskets, shoes to wear inside, tiny cups to serve peanuts, large and small mats to sit and rest their heads on. The same way she had taught her daughter when she was still a girl. For ten seasons, longer than his parents spent together and with their son, his grandmother eased him into a life of slow smiles, tender looks, ready hugs and tiny reflections of his parents so he'd never forget. This brought his grandfather closer, who found it difficult to look at the boy whose way of sleeping, waking and talking too closely resembled the daughter he mourned. Sometimes He wanted to look less like his mother, even asking the sky for a different face. Later he cherished looking into a pool of water and seeing her first before seeing himself. As though she watched him while he worked.

It was a month after his grandmother died when He realized that she woke him so early so he wouldn't be trapped in the dreams that stalked him. Dreams that would come during that hour when the darkness was at its most blue and his mind was fragile to the ghosts that demanded visits. Grandmother would wake herself and He so the dreams would pass on by and find no pain inside the mind of a lively boy weaving with the mother of his mother. Only after she died, and grandfather followed, did He realize those dark nights into mornings were the only time he could talk to her before her mind was weighed down with thoughts of the land, rains and her daughter, before she spent the later part of the morning hunched over while cleaning their home with the sweeping stick, then hunched over at the fields working with the soil.

Now, He thought of his parents as he and the boys sped through the alley holding their breath, and when they reached Spilling River, the rain straggled for a moment. Of their daily conduct and habits that his grandparents had shared with him, and the parts that he added and supposed because there were some questions he never thought to ask and plenty he knew would cause too much pain. His parents had been real. He knew that from the stories and the caresses he still recalled. But it also felt as though they had lived too big of a life, one that was only possible in a story that became a lesson. As he got older, the memories grew dimmer and the stories larger, until they became what was told to him around a fire and before bed when the mind was open and accepting, and in times of quiet when memories fill the spaces where life has slowed.

But when He looked at his friends, he saw his parents in these younger two who had chosen each other. In the way Blink and Miss followed Kind Eyes, and Kind Eyes called for Blink and Miss. He imagined them meeting Blink and Miss and Kind Eyes and loving his two friends like their son.

We are all bent.

That is what He heard his father saying.

And this is what he also said from his lips that sat on his mother's face.

8.

THE PASSENGERS HEARD a long squeal as the bus drew to a stop. They knew it was the last one on the route because the driver clapped his hands, leaned back into his seat and, from the droop of his head, immediately fell asleep. It was night, and the only light shining through the bus's back window was a lantern placed on the low branch of what looked to be a pine tree.

The boy heard feet shuffling and tried to make his own do the same, but they remained set in the position they were placed when the bus departed his home. He tried to open his arms, which were folded against his chest, and was only able to make them rest limply over his stomach. He could feel his hunger. His stomach felt hollowed out, and as he wrapped his arms around his body, the boy wondered how much strength it would take to squeeze out this life that had been shadowing him since he was a child—delivering imitations of what joy could be into his hands but never letting him grab hold. He had tried holding on less possessively, treating the joys like flowers. "You can't break what is soft," the boy's grandfather once said, after seeing his grandson's despair when the flowers he had picked for his grandmother and put in his pocket crumpled when he pulled them

55

out. They were still worthy, his grandfather told him, because what is soft could never be crushed. So the boy tried to live softly, too, not gripping what he loved, treating what mattered like the flowers he picked—carrying them close and leaving them gently. He should have been harder, he thought. Grabbed everything and never let go.

He wanted his body to stay in this seat, and for him to go somewhere far from it, no longer a part of its shuffling and breaking. He turned his head to look out the window but couldn't see this new land. Already he knew there was nothing it could promise, and he had nothing to give except his weak heart and lesser mind. It was another town. It could easily be the same. His body braced and withdrew as he remembered. What if there was another alley?

"I'm sorry," said a voice behind him.

The boy didn't know where the apology was directed and waited for more words to follow, or if meant for him, a nudge to draw his attention.

"I didn't think we were ever going to stop," it continued. "I heard that this trip would be about two days, so I readied my mind for two days of sitting with a few stops in between. But we've been on the road so long I thought I was going to chew my way out of this bus. And I'm so tired! Isn't that strange? I wonder what that is—to sit for hours and feel as if your body has been worked to the bone. Isn't sitting also some kind of rest? So then what do you really need after you've been on a bus for more than two days and feel like chewing your way out?"

The voice chuckled on its own, leaving gaps inside the amusement for someone to join in and agree. No one did. The boy knew what he really needed. In this hour, it was something to eat. He looked up to see if all the passengers in front of him had descended and saw that several were still seated, like him, slowly deciding how to unwrap the limbs they had tightly packed so they could sit and sleep with some measure of ease.

THE ONES WE LOVED

From where the girl was lying down, the lantern in the tree looked like a strange bird. During the drive, somewhere after the third stop and her gradually numbing buttocks, She had curled herself in half and closed her eyes for sleep. The seats were close enough together that when the bus jostled its passengers after driving over a pothole or the smallest pebble, her head and folded knees bounced against the seat in front of her instead of sliding onto the ground. Carefully placing her legs on the floor, she rose and heard a crack in one knee. There were people getting off the bus, some heading in the direction of the lantern, others towards the darkness on the opposite side. Leaning on the backrest, she felt something pull on the ends of her plaits and shook her head.

"I'm sorry," said the voice.

The girl turned her head slightly to nod, accepting the apology. But that gesture opened a doorway for someone who'd wanted to tell the stories that had been rising as the journey grew longer and longer. She heard only parts and bits: *Two days. Chewing. Resting body.* Laughter and then silence. She had to decide when to leave the bus, and whether she would go towards the lantern, or follow those who seemed to know that there was something in the opposite direction. There were now only a few people still inside. Did they also not have a place to go?

The hand had whispered in her ear before telling her to never come back, but She wasn't quite sure that her body could make it out the door. It felt out of the ordinary to disembark and touch this new soil like a visitor arriving for a new life. Her old one was still twitching in her pores, asking her to return to the place where her walking was a regularly timed thing that happened on its own, and not something she needed to remember, as she'd had to do the second her feet boarded the bus.

"Where do they put it all?" She asked.

57

"What?" said the voice that was now standing beside the girl, carrying two large sacks.

"Where do they put it?"

"Did you lose something?" the voice answered, a little bewildered.

"All of this pain. Where does it go? Will someone carry it? Is it supposed to be me? I've always dropped everything. Even water in a bucket."

The girl raised her head and saw that the voice had walked ahead and was now next to the bus driver, where it briefly stopped to place one of the sacks on top of its head and hold the other close to the chest. Then it descended the three steps before going towards the lantern.

The boy saw a woman with two large sacks leaving and realized he had one bag. All of his life could not have fit inside the sacks that woman was carrying. He thought of the living he had done, and whether it was real because all of it could be left behind, and what stayed could fit in only a bag. How much of a few instants and objects could a single life embody before it just disappeared?

Maybe he could disappear here.

The boy lifted his bag.

The girl eyed the lantern tree.

9.

"Move slow with that," Kuda said, pointing to the stool that She had lifted. "I think the leg broke when she threw it."

The girl nodded and Joy's left temple throbbed, a vein visible. "You don't have to look so upset. Your grandmother's done this so many times because that woman is a horrible person. If she never wanted to raise a child, I don't know why she asked for you."

Kuda's parents had passed away when she was a baby during that fortnight of rains, when homes were washed away as people clawed out of their windows and doors. Many had been able to make their way out, but Kuda's parents went with the floating roofs and the bricks that smashed against the banks. Their neighbors found the child inside a box caught in tree branches that were too weak to hold two adults, but perfect and right enough for a child. After their deaths, the people in Waterfall had discussed who would raise the orphan, and the grandmother who had lost her own son had asked to be the one responsible.

"Joy, people are not horrible. They just do things that are hard to understand," She said.

"How long can we say that? Her grandmother has been doing this for years, leaving for days and coming back to destroy everything. It's never going to stop," Joy said loudly, her temper rising, before her tone curdled into something bitter. "That's probably why her son died."

"Joy! You can't say that!" said She in shock. "Never say it again! So you're saying people deserve to be punished with death when they make mistakes?"

"That's not what I meant," Joy said, looking at Kuda apologetically, her tone losing its rot but her words resolute. "I have only always prayed you had a different grandmother. One who didn't work so hard to make you feel out of your body. I am sorry." Kuda nodded, partially listening and massaging the muscles in her legs, which would contract whenever there was a confrontation. Her grandmother never hit her. In fact, hard as she tried, Kuda couldn't remember her ever placing a hand on any part of her body. The girl knew she must have been held when she was younger, but those memories refused to emerge from where they were stored.

The woman had first left Waterfall when Kuda started walking to school on her own. She remembered that morning, putting on her uniform and waving goodbye to her grandmother's turned back; it had been as it always was, until she returned home and found no sitting, pacing or dreaming body in any of the three rooms. The girl had waited inside so no one walking by could see that she was alone and hungry. When she returned to class the next day, head slumping from poor sleep and chin slipping from the ledge she made with her palm, Reverend Mr. Shoko had asked for her grandmother and discovered the absence. Kuda had stayed with She and her mother those few months, until her grandmother returned, went to the school, cut into the last class of the day and brought her back home.

After closing the door, the returning woman had started speaking to her granddaughter. Harsh sentences that felt like sharp pinches on the soft part under her arm. They were the first shared words after months of being in two separate times: one living as a woman who

THE ONES WE LOVED

didn't have anyone waiting, and the other a child who couldn't stop searching all the women's faces in Waterfall, trying to find a familiar look in all of the common stares. Kuda had thought the woman was upset because her granddaughter didn't stay home. So Kuda apologized. Agreed that she had acted out of nature by speaking of the goings-on in their house to neighbors. Nodded as her grandmother warned that a small mind on a quickly growing girl meant a carelessness that could not be fixed, a mind that couldn't understand simple things like a temporary absence, cook a meal alone without calling on the attention of teachers and friends' parents, or stand without appearing hungry for pity and care. Was she not cared for enough in this house with its open windows, large bed and clean water, all serving one child? Her grandmother spoke and she listened, letting the words spill out of a mouth that had left without a remark and returned carrying slights collected at different times that had been kept for this moment.

Kuda cleaned the house, which had been untouched, and did what she could to relax the hard lines on her grandmother's mouth. She made herself hardly present, moving mindfully without making too much of a disturbance or speaking and saying a wrong thing. A few months later, her grandmother left again. Instead of going to her friend's house, she waited. And she changed their home, picking up furniture left outside the shack at school and making a small horse from mud and water, which she dried outside under the sun. When her grandmother returned, the house would look different, with somewhere to rest her feet and something pretty to look at. If it was nothing like the house she left, Kuda thought, then she would stay.

"It's so beautiful," Joy had said then about the horse, touching it delicately so her hands wouldn't cause any damage.

"Your grandmother is going to call you a little builder," said She proudly, like her own hands had made it.

61

When Kuda's grandmother returned, she spoke first. About a house that was no longer right because of furniture that was badly chosen. And the mess that would be made if more mud animals were placed on the table, leaving dirt on the surface. Everything that was new, she took outside and pushed it further from their yard with her foot. And the horse was placed back in Kuda's hands after her grandmother held it carelessly and broke the middle, separating the back from the front.

"Why would she do that?" She had asked the next day when Kuda came to school, clutching her skirt in shock. She'd quickly let go after remembering that their uniforms kept a record of each rough hold. She didn't want to look unkempt.

"That is so cruel," Joy had said.

Kuda could only guess, with each leaving and coming, that her grandmother did not know how to be in the house once her granddaughter learned to walk and became more like the child she lost. So she came home and wrecked it.

Joy and She had finished sweeping and straightening what had been upended and left askew. They all sat together on Kuda's mattress, contemplating each other's faces and tensions, trying to find a way back to their banter and easy contempt for somewhere so dull, yet so hard to leave behind. Those who did go came back soon enough. Like Kuda's grandmother. Those who were dying went slowly, almost like they didn't want to pass on. The girls would never quite admit to this, but being here made it easier to vent about the things that angered them, but that they were powerless to change. Those things gave them a way to see themselves, knowing exactly what it was they disliked and why they felt so strongly about it. Perhaps that was why Kuda's grandmother returned. To be reminded of her frustrations, spill out her disdain and leave emptied. Waterfall could take the overflow of emotion.

Sometimes Joy would think about what her life would look like if Waterfall had not been the place that taught her to hate the sunrise—when the rays meant another day spent trying to belong inside the outline both her parents had made for the daughter they prayed for and imagined. For her to fit, she needed to be someone whose nature was as glad and giving as her mother, as cheerful and open as her father. Since her fifth birthday, when all the other children were squealing and dodging as her father chased them around their yard, Joy had known her heart was made with heavier blood or whatever it was that kept it pumping and feeling. It wasn't anything her mind could explain, except that her emotions didn't come and go easy. They clung to her like a wet shirt and made her feel cold through and through her bones. Her mother had been anxious when it seemed like her daughter could not be pleased beyond a smile, and so Joy had learned to hide the stones weight of the wet shirt. At one time, her mind had been convinced that Waterfall was the root of the problem, before realizing it was the place that gave her a reason to pretend, and persons to consider. Leaving would make her responsible to no one, and so for as long as Joy lived in the town, shrugging off the wet clothes was the thing that kept her parents happy. And they deserved that joy.

It was Waterfall that made She realize that new beginnings were a charming curse. In Reverend Mr. Shoko's class, she had learned that it was a God who made it possible to start again, and with Miss Bride, she understood that beginnings were about choices as much as they were the result of luck and fortune. She knew no other place except for here, yet somehow she was sure this was not where she belonged. She knew of Mama only as the woman in Waterfall, but she wanted so much to know her as the person who had left the place her husband remained. Starting over had taken away a life She knew should have been hers. One where she had more family, more stories of her father and more of Mama. In Waterfall, Mama became someone who loved a

God loudly and her daughter forcefully. Leaving would mean making this town a part of her beginning story, but She didn't want to claim Waterfall. There were too many questions. So she would stay until she knew more.

Looking at Kuda, She wondered what it was like to know exactly how your past had unfolded, even when all her friend now had was a grandmother who came and went like a summoned memory.

"You really think her grandmother enjoys doing things that make her sad?" She asked Joy tentatively, weighing every possible answer that could be given, and if it would be worth the question.

"Why do something so much unless you get something from it?"

"Because you don't know how to do anything else," She answered pointedly.

Joy's tensed shoulders fell as she looked at her friend. "You can't really believe that."

"No one would fight all the time unless they always needed to do it," She responded. "Maybe her grandmother can't help how her feelings come out."

"That sounds like something Reverend Mr. Shoko would pull from his bible," Joy said with frustration.

"Reverend Mr. Shoko has never been sad enough to fight anything," She shot back.

"She could have killed me, my grandmother," Kuda shared, breaking through the crackling fires that risked erupting when her two friends talked about the woman who raised her. She, always looking for a reason. Joy, too angry to find one.

"When I was a child, and the top of my head was still moving, she could have broken me," Kuda continued. "I know there's ways to do it, I've heard the stories."

"How do you know she didn't try?" asked Joy, who'd pushed aside any pretense of being tender.

64

THE ONES WE LOVED

"I would have remembered," said Kuda, sinking deeper into her mattress and remembering the time when her grandmother's eyes spoke of her granddaughter's missed death, a passing that would have been swift and loving. Kuda would have never known this way of being, and her grandmother could have been a woman who moved alone. But it was this life that the woman had chosen, while knowing that it would push against the peace she craved. Kuda felt her anger, breathed it in when no one was around and felt the choice her grandmother made. It was only in Waterfall that she could come and be the woman who moved according to her own impulses. Her grandmother could be the one who was broken here, and Kuda could be the child who survived.

The two girls sitting on opposite edges of the mattress looked at each other, while glancing at their friend's quiet form. The silence stretched on, like a thin blanket pulled beyond its capacity to give warmth to everyone. Kuda snuggled into the bed, brought her legs up to her chest and made herself small enough to miss. Joy exhaled loudly, rubbing her face with her hand and using the other to fiddle with a loose thread poking out of her school shirt.

Clenching her hands, She felt her nails dig into the soft cushions of her palms. The girl would have squeezed deeper but feared breaking one, a loss after months spent not biting them. She'd stopped when they'd shown themselves to be a convenient type of weapon, something realized after an accidental scratch a few weeks ago drew a thin line of blood on one arm. These nails were teaching her how to move with greater control, when reaching for things she needed, the people close by.

Inside the house, the silence stayed. It yawned and crawled around the rigidness in Joy's posture, next to the now calm heart moving under Kuda's chest and inside the bruised palms of She who just kept squeezing.

65

10.

THE RESTAURANT WAS busy tonight. There had been a rush of customers, all of whom had found it necessary to enter the slender doorway with the grace of a cow herd. Gogo J. was elated, but She was tired
and rattled. Every sound, from the cooking sticks clanging against pot
rims, forks scratching up nearly done plates and greedy throats slurp-
ing down thickened soup, was obtrusive. The last few days she'd taken
her time going from the kitchen to the dining area, but today, the
nose-scrunching, head-swiveling gas that filled the room of so many
men eating double fried beans made her want to rush through the
service.

Even those passing by knew it was a frenzied night at Gogo J.'s and
so they circled back, eager to see and meet whoever had arrived and
was contemplating setting a more willful claim on a plot of land, or
just inside the room by pulling up a chair at a table, tilting under the
weight of dialogue and food. This was the town She had been led to,
but it was this place that coaxed her to stay, more than the directions
given or the invitation of its owner. The floors were thoroughly swept,
and the smells inside reminded her of a sweetness that she had left
behind.

The restaurant had been empty when she wandered in that night off the bus, ragged and off balance. The old lady hadn't asked any questions, simply gestured towards a seat with her finger, passed her a glass of water, then a bitter and spicy root to chew. That first taste of something more than her tongue after the journey had livened up her senses and warmed her stomach. When She had started rocking in her chair, bouncing as though she were still on a ride, fingers squishing and flattening the food Gogo J. placed on the table, the old lady closed the restaurant door and sat down, looking her over. The chair creaked from She's moving, the plate scratched the wood and a voice, her voice, started to make a sound. Like a moan. The old lady started tapping the table with a fork, making the bangles on her arms rattle. The girl met her eyes with what she hoped was thankfulness. It hadn't been quiet since she held the gun. She couldn't have it be quiet.

"You can stay. Upstairs. There's a room there, big enough for a tiny bird like you," Gogo J. said, saving She from unbraiding the words that had tangled up in her mouth. After some moments, she began.

"I don't have any money."

"Well, we can find some way to fix that," Gogo J. had answered.

Scrutinizing the merriment gathered around the packed tables, She wondered who in this crowd would decide to stay here because they had come by the restaurant first. Kuda would have loved this place, even if it meant being far from home. Joy would never have left once she saw how freely the girls moved. Mama would have pretended not to like it, until she tried Gogo J.'s food, and then the old woman would likely have been the only one lucky enough to hear the mixed spices that Mama used to make She's favorite dish. Brushing the faces out of her eyes, she hurried over to the counter in front of the kitchen, where Gogo J. placed the hot plates that were ready to go. Balancing four along her arms like Gogo J. taught her, She walked over to one of the tables. The men were slapping each other on the back, drunk on

68

THE ONES WE LOVED

company and the dreams that looked more enticing in the nighttime. They whistled in appreciation and their eyes grew several sizes as they prepared themselves for second servings.

"There we go!" said one who began digging in before She'd properly set the plate down. She bit back a smile and quickly drew her hands before the man confused them for food.

"I think we are going to need more of this," said another, shaking the empty bottle of tangy sauce, which had been full when her shift started.

"I'll see if I can find some more," she said before making her way around the room.

When She had first started working at the restaurant, she found herself trapped between the furniture during busy days. After watching her ask the diners to move themselves so she could pass, Gogo J. had pulled her to the side and told her never to interrupt anyone who was enjoying their food, just so she could do what she needed to do.

"Figure it out or stay where you are until they leave," the old lady had said decisively.

Now, with plates piled high, She made sure to always know her placement when the bodies increased. Among the chairs that leaned back on two swinging legs and the drink cups placed on the floor so elbows and hands could easily rest over the tables, She knew where to turn, the spot to twist and stop and how she would come out. All she needed was to follow the laughter and go between the silences.

The girl never suggested doing anything more than serving. Gogo J. cooked in the manner her life was set up—on her own and with little regard for what was usual. Did it make sense that she stewed the rabbit in a pot filled with pine cones, placed on top of another topped with various flowers? Yet the old lady insisted it gave the meat an aroma that tickled your nose and sank into your tongue. It was unlike anything the girl had seen but she believed. That stewed rabbit

69

with thick gravy, hunks of bread baked inside a wood oven and fried beans topped with slices of ripe lemons is what had brought the customers rushing in. Standing by the counter, refilling the sauce from the pot Gogo J. kept hidden, She saw him next to the window. Squeezed in tight behind a group of six, he was alone. The boy with the dark eyes and the changing face. Blinking fast, then opening her eyes wide, and blinking again, she tried to clear her sight. She stared harder. It was the same person. She had seen him on the bus, before the hand spoke. His face had looked like a hundred different people lived inside his body.

"What is he doing here?" She whispered.

"Girl, quick stepping with that sauce!" yelled Gogo J. from the kitchen. "If these people see you stand there too long, they might realize where I keep the extra and ravage all of it."

"Sorry, Gogo J.," She said and filled up the bottle before returning to the men who greeted her as though she was returning from a long trip. While collecting plates left clean by the trio beside them, she looked back at the boy from the bus. His rolled-up shirt was wrinkled and dirty. No one seemed to know him, or if they did, didn't care to bring him into their circles. His pants were frayed at the knees as if he had spent a long time crouching, but the bottoms were well cut and hung in the right place above his ankles.

"Gogo J., do you know him?" asked She, nodding in his direction.

"Who?" asked the old lady as she waddled out of the kitchen, adjusting her dress and placing her hands on top of the counter, letting the sweat run down her forehead.

"That boy over by the corner," said She.

"The one looking all serious and bothered?"

The girl nodded her head.

"This is my first time seeing him," answered the old lady.

"I think I know him," said She.

"How come?"

70

THE ONES WE LOVED

"He was on the bus I came on."

"Are you sure?"

"Yes."

Gogo J. waited for her to continue. The girl looked at the boy as if to call out to him.

"Is there something you need?" asked the old lady, pointedly.

"What?"

"You're looking his way as if he owes you a debt. So what do you need from him?"

"Nothing. All I was wondering was if you knew him."

She started wiping the counter and searched the room for empty plates. As hours passed and the sounds of congealed duck fat popping and sizzling joined the diners sharing stories of near accidents in the fields, he remained the same. He moved only to melt further into the corner, his attention outside.

"Don't spend too much time thinking about him," Gogo J. said, when the quiet began to last for long periods. "There's nothing about that boy that you need to be worrying about. He came here on his own, you came here on your own, and that's the story. No need to lose yourself in a mystery that needs no solving." Stepping away from the stove, Gogo J. raised her arms over her head, stretching and straightening, her back seeming to break and mend at once.

Looking at the old lady, She furrowed her brow in confusion.

"I thought you said you didn't know him," said She.

"I don't," answered the old woman, hands on her hips while making small circles with her waist.

"Then how do you know that he came here alone? Maybe he has family here."

"That boy is as alone as the sky is wide, and both have been that way since the beginning," said Gogo J. knowingly. "Looking the way he is, I don't doubt he ran from something as bad as you did."

71

While Gogo J. spoke, She's mind wandered.

"So don't go looking at him like you are hoping to find something. Because he'll never let you have it," Gogo J. finished, ending her brief exercise at the same time. But the girl was no longer listening. While She kept looking at the boy who joined a group of men leaving, the old lady glanced at her one more time, before returning to her pots and pans. It only took one table signaling they were ready to leave, and everyone would start to follow, slapping their money down and calling out declarations of love to Gogo J. and the girl who had served them. The old woman started to suck on a sugar cube, something she always did after a long service.

"Don't forget to clean up the tables with that soap I made this morning. We are going to need it to remove all the oil stains."

"I won't forget," said She.

11.

KUDA'S GRANDMOTHER SAT in front of the church door, her body still, except for the sound of cracking knuckles. Placing her thumb against the curved bone of her index finger, she added greater force, pushing the single digit into the skin on her left hand until a sound snapped through the midday solitude. Whenever she stressed her fingers, she felt fearful, curious, relieved. Could something permanently pop out of place? How would she live with an out of place finger? The force was never strong enough to cause pain or damage, but she always waited to be surprised.

Every time she stepped off the bus, Kuda's grandmother was always ready to say something kind that would describe the longing in her heart while she was away. Quickly walking from the bus stop, her feet would head in the direction her eyes no longer had to search out, while her mouth practiced the right words. Arms would be spread a little further apart, leaving enough space between her hips for Kuda to wrap her in a hug. When she got to the door, letting herself into the house that changed a little with every return, the words that had been turning in her mind and that only needed to be properly strung in order of most relevant fell out of her mouth with none of their softness. Somehow from the time she got off the bus to the instant after she closed the door behind her and accepted a greeting, the words became the backhand of the palm she wanted to gently rest against Kuda's cheek. And the woman couldn't make them mean something different. Make them feel as light as the best memories that happened before they were a family, when Kuda was not yet born, the church was not on top of this red earth and Waterfall was a home that did not know pain.

On this return her granddaughter didn't say a greeting. The words still came out. And there was no greeting.

The voices of her neighbors harmonizing and weeping floated to her ears, and the woman moved from the entrance to the left side of the building. The church stood next to the piercing-spirit tree, a fitting name because of the thick, needlelike thorns that grew on its branches. If Kuda's grandmother allowed her spirit to feel what was shrunken by grief, she would pull threads of shame from the rope that seemed to drag her to this church whenever she failed Kuda. This breaking down was lonely. She didn't go to the places from her girlhood: the river, up the hill or that towering tree where she would sit on the branches and look out at the land that spread so far it turned into bright slits. It was from that tree that she'd first seen them coming—a small group with a man in front whose body worked to look weary, but whose strength she saw in his footprints, which stayed long after others had stepped over them. Even the horses had appeared to twitch away from him, not seeking any assurance in his touch or presence. And she no longer went to that tree, because it had stopped making her feel as strong as its weakest root. Going to the river brought her near the waterfall, whose water she could no longer enter. Once she'd thought of going close to the edge to feel the cascading droplets landing on her skin. And if the landowners saw her, she would receive her punishment right there, near the place that had cleansed her people.

THE ONES WE LOVED

But she had thought of Kuda and faltered, of the blood flowing into what was supposed to remain clean, and let go of the idea.

The places she knew no longer promised comfort or safety, so Kuda's grandmother came to the one that she did not know and listened to familiar people singing to a distant presence. She knew most; several were a false mystery; and one she had grown to know as well as the soft part on Kuda's head that she watched closely when she was a baby. Sometimes when she watched her granddaughter sleep, the woman thought she still saw it move.

Kuda's grandmother leaned into the church, pushing her back against the building as if to fall, and slid her heels into the red earth, the striking swathes and swathes of soil that shimmered in the sun and drew hungry hands. Sometimes she thought if the town had been covered by weeds, it would have been left alone. But who would have known to plant an ugly covering to protect the fabric underneath? When she came to the church, she asked for the same thing and talked to whoever was still listening to her. While a service was delivered behind the oak doors, she lulled her mind with her own sermon that helped her remember Waterfall as a town that was still her home.

"Look what they've done," she began, sinking her heels deeper into the soil.

"Look what they've done. Look what they've done. Look what they've done. They've . . ." Kuda's grandmother stopped and felt her mouth slacken, her tongue useless. What did you call something that was bigger than your words, that couldn't fit around your teeth or rise from your throat? Is that why nothing changed? Because she couldn't explain all that her eyes saw and cried over?

Her body swayed and her eyes traveled past the farms, past the school, past the river, past and past and past. "This is my home. Why would you bring them to my home?" She brought her hands to her

75

chest, pounding and pounding fiercely, matching the rhythm of her heart. "They have to leave. They have to suffer."

Placing her head between her knees, she moaned. "This can't be the end. This can't be a life."

She listened.

"What do you need us to be, so we can be free from this life?"

Waterfall seemed to shiver. The question was a cold sweep.

"Do you want us to be like them? People who speak of peace and also draw blood?"

Waterfall seemed to harden.

"Who am I to take a life?" Kuda's grandmother grunted. "No. Who are they to take ours?"

Her question hobbled, then became a rising accusation. One that grew because the hurting did too. Because where there is grief, there is trust, and where there's trust, faith would always remain. The wind that lifted. The one that remembered.

"My parents lived for me. Their parents lived for mine. My life is their life. Their lives are my bounty. So why would you let someone come who believes they can take my life, those of my parents and their parents? Too many people have lived for me. So tell me why you would send someone to kill a good harvest? To ransack the bounty?"

The waterfall hesitated, and she didn't see it. It almost forgot how to crush down. And she didn't see it.

"I should have sent her to you. Away from this place. Away from me. She needs to be loved, I need to be free and you won't let us have both."

Kuda's grandmother smiled regretfully, then cracked her knuckles again and waited for a feeling of pain. Every time she saw her granddaughter, she needed to hear her body. Push it until it gave any response. Then she would know that something could momentarily make her feel a more immediate pain, beyond this constant aching that

THE ONES WE LOVED

now bored her. It left the woman exhausted. She stayed for a minute, collecting her past and placing it back inside the secret that kept her coming back to the building. As the cries in the church shifted from one leading voice to a chorus of blessings shared and received, Kuda's grandmother knew it was time for her to rise.

When the first neighbors reached for the wooden knobs and opened the church doors, they saw her and raised their hands, curtly nodding their heads. Those who had lived in Waterfall as long as she had found it draining to look at her face, more so than their work on the farms or the straining in their necks while trying to see their waterfall through the landowners' homes. Those who had come when the old life in Waterfall had grown distant looked at Kuda's grandmother and glimpsed a reminder of all that could go wrong if they happened to look askance at the world they fervently celebrated in their prayers. Everyone took a lesson when they looked at her face, and all made an internal promise to reject the spirit that made her live as she did. They saw their paranoias and ruins. They never saw what she had learned, and only one approached her as though she were good.

Kuda's grandmother saw someone coming out of the church and shaking the hands of those who openly sought her palms, someone who understood how to make grief a part of living. Her own had taken over her life, and she did not know how to make the hurt wrap around the moments that gave her joy, so that her laughter could still sound free, a fleeting truce that did not feel unearned.

"Were you waiting long?" She's mother asked, taking the extended arm and walking next to Kuda's grandmother. Nodding at the congregants they passed, Mama missed the questioning eyes of those who did not understand this friendship.

"I never notice the time," Kuda's grandmother answered, remembering why people chose to touch those they care for—with their

77

arms linked, she felt assembled, sturdy. "I could have been sitting for a day or a week. It would be the same for me."

"That is your best and worst thing," She's mother answered, her voice knowing. "You do not feel time, so patience is no burden, but the past is a constant entryway. A path that never recedes and remains exactly as you lived it."

"Is that something you heard today?" Kuda's grandmother asked, seeking to be unaffected by the insight but only hinting at a fresh wound.

"It could have been. You should have come in."

"You know I never enter," said Kuda's grandmother, her voice sounding far, and Mama hoped the invitation had landed as gently as it was intended.

"How is Kuda?" she asked, pivoting their meeting in a different direction.

"Don't you already know?" came the response, an abrupt indication that the change had not been well received.

"I have been here most of the week cleaning, and when She is home, we talk about school." She's mother paused and glanced at her friend. Though their arms were still intertwined, she'd grown tense. "What happened?"

"I don't know." The voice was clear. "I failed, and I think she now knows when I'm failing and showing her much less than she deserves." She spoke it as a statement, without fear of condemnation.

"What makes you think she knows this?" She's mother deftly prodded.

Shaking her head, Kuda's grandmother pulled her mouth into a tight line, because Mama's simple question had tugged at the casual discontent she always laid over her face. They were now farther from the church, walking towards Samson's Cross.

"Because she looks at me as if everything I do no longer surprises or saddens." It was an honest answer. "Before, when I would lose myself,

THE ONES WE LOVED

there was always something on her face that told me to stop. I would see the hurt and pull back. Kuda would say something with her eyes, and every flinch was a response I knew how to read."

"So now you can't read her eyes?"

"I can't read her because she shows me nothing anymore. Today I came back, and it happened as it does. I reached the door and forgot how to talk to her with care." Mama listened as the reason for the church visit was revealed. Her friend never came to her home, only here. "I yelled at her," she continued, "even when I was trying to simply talk. Her face didn't move, her eyes didn't twitch and her mouth didn't change shape. She stood there, and I stood too."

"What did you say?"

Kuda's grandmother wavered. Her friend would not damn her or lend pity, but she struggled to form the words when there was nowhere for them to land. Without Kuda in front of her eyes, the words undressed and stood as they were.

"I told her that she needed parents."

She's mother was quiet.

"I said they were the only ones who could show her love because they were supposed to. That if it was a matter of choice, no one would choose to love someone who spends their time just waiting and watching. She's so odd. Always watching as if she wants to say something. Eyes always following like an animal, just watching and watching. Her eyes always search me. What does she look for? Searching my body, and never looking away. I told her that my body couldn't rest when I was close to her, and that when she moved, my skin seemed to open like a million tiny holes were sucking in air."

"Why did you stop?"

"Because I had nothing left to say." Kuda's grandmother looked at her friend, grateful that she loved her enough to interrupt so her teeth wouldn't bite off her tongue.

79

They continued in silence and their feet rustled through the grass and announced their presence, joining the dozens of others who had cleared a path. Kuda's grandmother pulled her arm out of the link and clasped her hands behind her back. She's mother let her own hang on either side in case they were needed. Nearing the turn that led to the school, they went right towards Mama's home where She had spent the day after refusing to attend church. This left Mama fearful but she didn't share her turmoil. Her friend had a greater need for comfort.

"It's so much taller now than when I was a child," said Kuda's grandmother, looking back in the direction of Samson's Cross, her voice heavy and thick with longing.

"What is taller?" asked She's mother, concerned she'd missed a reflection while thinking about her daughter.

"The tree close to the school, by the road, right before the hill."

"I've never seen a tall tree," she answered, looking back.

Kuda's grandmother stopped, still looking back at the school. "You did something good here," she said, her eyes shining. "When the children are there, they can forget and become more than what we are."

Mama followed her friend's gaze. "I didn't do anything on my own," she said softly. A slight pain started to build across her chest, but she ignored it. "Why do you do it?" she asked, even softer.

Kuda's grandmother started crying. Her shoulders began to shake, and she bit her lips so no sound could come out, breathing through her nose, hands still clasped behind her back.

"She hates me now. She has to. She must."

"It could help to speak to the Reverend," She's mother said, not sure whether to go on. If he could soothe the landowners, something could also be done for Kuda's grandmother. When Mama had first suggested building a church and for him to be the leader, Reverend Mr. Shoko had laughed. Who could he lead? He had left Waterfall

THE ONES WE LOVED

when he was a boy, and only just returned. But Mama insisted, and remained steadfast in her belief that it was only him who could convince the landowners to lend bricks for more than houses.

"The landowners will not listen to me. They will kill me," Reverend Mr. Shoko said, day after day, and with each ask, Mama grew more persistent, bolder. When he realized she wouldn't stop, he asked her to come and see the landowners with him. If he died, she could bring his body back, and if they succeeded, then she could be the witness to recount everything that had happened, because his mind would not believe enough to share.

What had she known that he had not? How could she see the town of his birth in a way that he never did?

"It needed to be you," Mama later told him, after the landowners agreed to the church. And agreed for him to be the leader.

"Why?" he had asked her.

"If they feel safe, we will be safe," she said.

His body still grew stiff from time to time, and some days sharp stabs would remind him of an old accident while in the fields. But when he first stepped on the pulpit and became the leader, the pain ceased. When he looked over the heads of the people searching for a message, he was the Reverend.

"You should know better than to ask that of me." Kuda's grandmother looked at her, saying a peculiar thing with her eyes and wiping her tears.

"I didn't mean any harm."

"I know you don't. Have you ever hurt anyone? Have you hated how you live bad enough to want someone else in that pit with you?"

"Forget what I told you. I wasn't thinking," Mama said, feeling faint.

"You know I won't," said Kuda's grandmother. "I can't." It was the saddest she'd ever sounded. Looking back at the school, her eyes narrowed as if seeing it through a veil.

81

"Your daughter knows that you did something to soften her life. So her hands and mind can do more than struggle to hold on to what used to be so clear. When you look at her face, she shows you what your hands have given." Turning to look at her friend, Kuda's grandmother grabbed her hands and pulled them up to her chest. "You did something good here," she repeated, this time stronger.

Mama felt her friend's heartbeat through her fingers. She tried to smile and could only shake her head. She closed her eyes and let her mind return towards the road they had walked, towards the church, after the river and beyond Waterfall. To a place that had a different school where her child could not have walked through the gates. And a town where her person remained. The one who had wanted a school. The one who never let go of her hand. The one who did something good here.

12.

KUDA LISTENED WHILE Reverend Mr. Shoko talked to the class about starting and finishing. There would be love in his lesson. There was always faith, and before class was over, there would be gratitude. Reverend Mr. Shoko was grateful for everything. But he had so little. Is that why it was easy for him to be thankful? When all you possess can be counted on two hands, even if the other is lame, what is there to be but happy? When blessings became too much, began to overflow, that was the moment gratitude turned to hunger.

Looking at her classmates, at Joy and She sitting beside her, and the students around and behind the classroom doors, Kuda knew they were all grateful for the same blessings. This school they went to, the homes they lived in, the food they had, the town that was still their own in ways they couldn't describe but that kept them here. That should have been enough to make her feel the same as the others. But then Kuda saw how she was raised and understood that something was different, because among the blessings given to her classmates, there was one she lacked.

"Did God want me to raise myself?" she had asked Reverend Mr. Shoko four summers ago. Kuda had thought God was teaching her how to take care of herself so when all the adults were taken during the Rusher or Wretcher—the moment when the faithful would be taken to heaven while the godless remain on earth to suffer through chaos—she would be the one to teach the children left behind how to live on their own. How to boil their water for bathing, cut their own vegetables for stews, clean the house and yard, and wake up at the same time every day so they wouldn't be late for school. When that time came, she could scold the children on behalf of their parents, speaking to them over her shoulder as she rushed around taking care of those who did not learn how to properly raise themselves.

My grandmother made sure I always knew how to do things on my own, she would tell the taken parents. She knew they would be able to hear because if God could listen in, so could they, no matter where their new lives continued and how their bodies re-formed again. Kuda would tell them every day how their children were doing and remind them that her grandmother had left her prepared.

See, I can stir the ground maize properly, she would tell them, *with the right amount of water so the porridge is not thick. And I'm going to keep stirring so it comes out without any bumps. My hand doesn't get tired, see?*

Kuda had been ready for the Rusher so she could finally say her grandmother had been doing something right with her leaving. And tell everyone they had been too eager and indulgent in their stares of pity, and her teachers too quick with the long sighs when she came in late because she had only noticed the yellow stains on her shirt from the pollen after it was dry on the clothesline, and there wasn't enough time to clean and dry again, so she tried to dab with a cloth and only made it worse, which is why she was late. But Reverend Mr. Shoko told her that everyone chosen would go during the Rusher, not simply the adults.

"Was I meant to be a child who is also an adult?" Kuda later asked. Reverend Mr. Shoko hadn't answered, but he wrote something on a letter, which he then told her to give to her grandmother. Kuda had raced home so her hands wouldn't follow their own impulse, open the paper's neat folds and bring the letter to her face so her eyes could quickly read the words. She had been anxious but impatient when she handed the letter to her grandmother, who looked at Kuda and then back at the paper written for her and passed on by the girl who now waited for something to happen that would be unlike the other moments of unease. On that day, Kuda's grandmother left and didn't come back until the end of the year. It used to take her weeks to return to herself after her grandmother wandered back, and now it took a little less time. It was Joy's idea to stand still. Her grandmother had returned and Kuda did as Joy had taught. "If you quietly stand and move your mouth only to count the seconds until the talking stops, people will think of, ask and answer the questions you didn't know you had. They will give you responses that would never have come from using your tongue."

Her grandmother arrived at the door, and while she talked, the girl stood still and only counted.

"People will tell you the truth while you're still," her friend said. "In the beginning it will take more seconds, until it doesn't, and after, you will only need to look and see everything." It had been different, and it felt wrong, but Kuda complied. Now she was alone and back in her solitude.

The counting was the act that made her feel cold. As if the words from her grandmother were reduced to intervals of sixty seconds broken into five-second increments. One, two, three, four, five, breathe, continue. In five seconds, there was no greeting. After ten, there was the misplaced anger, which Kuda knew was caused by someone she couldn't see. It was never this outpouring of emotion that made the girl ache, but the purpose behind the rantings. Why did they only settle on the surface of her grandmother's face in Kuda's presence? She heard her

85

speak to the neighbors, giving a simple "good morning" or a "be well," and her voice was not quite as jagged. After twenty seconds, Kuda had forgotten the fact that her grandmother had not pointed a question about her well-being in her direction. And in thirty seconds, she had an answer. "You don't know what I have to do to feel untethered from this town. To be freed from it, for just a while. None of you do."

Then, Kuda knew there were others her grandmother spoke of who also felt the sadness wound up in her fists. Others who caused her to leave. People who made her feel less than free. After a minute, Kuda had more questions, but equally as many answers. If the granddaughter was silent when her grandmother came home, not shooting questions about the trips taken, the people met or the objects brought back, what else would break through? Maybe she would speak the truth. Finally say why she left and whom she had loved while she was away.

Maybe even more, the woman would speak of whom she loved when she was in Waterfall. And say if that loving also felt like work. Like the worst subject in school, God Studies, where the love in the parables always made Kuda feel like the people were being forced to love or perish. *How can you not choose love if the other choice is to die,* she always asked, speaking to no one and trying to remake the parables according to her life, so they could make sense. Kuda didn't want to feel like she was failing when the moment came that she could no longer love her grandmother. And she didn't want to die because she stopped doing the hardest job.

If she stood still, would God do more than tell stories? Kuda now thought, watching Reverend Mr. Shoko closing his eyes as he often did when the lessons spoke to him deepest. Could there come answers about the parents she no longer had and the adult who didn't want her to be a child? Would God finally tell why she was born to work and not to be cared for?

THE ONES WE LOVED

Fiddling with a notebook page that did not flatten against the rest and instead made a little curl at its lower left corner, Kuda decided she would ask God when the Rusher finally happened. Whether her grandmother would be chosen, too, was something she couldn't answer. She would be chosen because she was faithful, and in front of other parents, Kuda would ask God why her life had to be the chaos he took others out of.

13.

IT HAD BEEN days since the heaviness lifted, and while Joy's body felt weary, being close to friends lessened the discomfort. The wet shirt was falling on her shoulders more regularly, and this time it had also started to cave in to her chest, restricting whatever breath Joy tried to exhale and inhale as a tiny reminder that this was something in her control. It arrived on a Friday and didn't fall off until the third school day. Her mother had thought it was a fever, and Joy was relieved that at least her body was showing how painful her mind felt. Usually, her outer layer looked as it always did, unblemished and healthy, making the sickness inside feel like something only her dreams understood. On the fourth day, Joy's feet took her to the washing room, and on the fifth, her fingers laced up her shoes and left the house with a plan.

School was over and they were going to sit behind a large tree stump a few meters from the entrance, with a good view of the hill, which the girls agreed looked like a place where animals would have gatherings. Their parents knew about this after-school ritual so it was never a worry that they were up to mischief. They were walking towards the trunk when Joy stopped and looked at her friends with a determined expression on her face.

"What's wrong?" asked She.

"Let's do it," Joy said quickly.

"What are you talking about?" answered Kuda.

"Let's go to Spilling River," Joy said, already backing towards the road while daring her friends. "Miss Bride said to write about our favorite part of the town. Why can't that be the one?"

"It's not even in Waterfall!" Kuda fired back.

"They are two towns in the same place," Joy answered casually, feeling the shirt shift on her skin and hoping to shrug it off with an unexpected adventure.

None of them had been to Spilling River, and except for the men in Waterfall who went and did the counting, no one knew how it looked. Only that the people were like them, but without any school for the children or a place to pray. That they, too, had once lived in the red-brick houses of their town, shared food door to door and bounded over the fences until broken hearts had taken them to Spilling River. And those who knew why never spoke. It was a town of chance and compromise, snatched by the people who needed new homes and granted by the landowners burying resentment.

"Do you think everyone who lives there hates everyone in Waterfall?" asked She, linking her arm through Kuda's and pulling her friend along.

"That's what Reverend Mr. Shoko was yelling in church last Sunday," Kuda said. "That it was hate in their hearts that brought them where they are."

"It was the landowners," answered She, unable to rein in the disgust in her voice. "Everything changed when they arrived."

"My mother told me there was nothing here until the landowners came," said Joy cautiously, like someone speaking what they are still struggling to understand. "Just people trying not to go hungry."

"How would she know that?" asked Kuda, raising her brows and

THE ONES WE LOVED

skeptical. "She was younger than we are now when they arrived. Only a child, no? It would be hard to remember anything."

"Mama told me that Reverend Mr. Shoko talked to the landowners so the people in Waterfall would be left alone," said She.

"What do you think he told them?" asked Kuda.

Walking on the road towards Eastern Farms, the greenscape began to change. In Waterfall, any plant that carried leaves seemed to always be in bloom. The vegetables, the trees, the scrubs and the weeds. But after passing the hill that welcomed people into the town, life in the opposite direction grew harder to see. There were fewer bird sounds and plenty of anthills, many as tall as a tree. It was an eerie thing because there was not one anthill in Waterfall, yet on the road to Spilling River, you could not miss them. When you inched closer, planting your feet in the gaps where no trails of ants were leading in or out of the tiny entrances, it was bits of green that were visible. As if the ants had been daily taking every small plant down to their home and rebuilding a green town below.

"Do you know what he said?" Kuda repeated, looking at her friend, whose eyes were trained ahead. Clouds were forming and the girls barely noticed.

"Something biblical and weak," answered She, after some time. "Don't you hear it in the sermons?"

"Hear what?" asked Joy.

"The story of Spilling River. It's in all the sermons about destruction and wrath."

They looked at her expectantly, and so She thought about what to say. The words needed to be selected, not scattered to be picked up and arranged in any order. The beginning mattered. It always did. She was telling a story that changed some lives, and which, if she thought hard enough, had made Waterfall the place Mama found to be safe. She had to be right. Clearing her throat, she laid the first brick. "It started with a gun . . ."

"Reverend Mr. Shoko has never started any sermon with a sentence about a gun," Kuda, the constant church attendant among them, berated lightly. She's mother didn't like to press too much, and Joy was left to do as she pleased.

"Can you let me tell the story?" She responded, feigning annoyance and patting the perfectly lined pleats on her skirt.

"What if Kuda speaks like Reverend Mr. Shoko, and you speak like everyone else?" suggested Joy.

Both nodded in agreement and the girls took on their roles. The clouds drew closer.

"**First there was Waterfall,**" began Kuda, deepening her voice and imitating the absurdly somber intonation that Reverend Mr. Shoko lent to every phrase.

"With children and wives, and husbands and parents, and parents of parents," added She, her voice leveling from its generally higher pitch to a monotone delivery. A bit like an elder passing on a long-ago experience that was still being lived.

"**It was a place that was rich and good, with animals and families.**"

"These were families of the soil rooted so deeply in Waterfall that the lines of the town roads were embedded on their bare feet, and its trees grew according to how the people moved from place to place. They created shade where some were known to stop and rest and bore fruit close to the ground so the children could reach."

"**Five new families came with their belongings in their arms and on the beasts that had carried them, asking for shelter from the people of Waterfall.**"

"They arrived with guns that had been for protection during the journey made for better soil. Guns that would not be used now that they were safe."

"**Their neighbors helped the five families build homes, for each**

THE ONES WE LOVED

of them to live well. They shared the food they grew, the meat from the animals they raised, and the land that had served them well."

"It was a gun that changed everything."

The girls had started doing a type of dance as they walked and talked towards Spilling River. Kuda, as Reverend Mr. Shoko, moved in the middle of the road, right hand clutched against her chest holding an imagined bible, as he did every Sunday, pacing in front of the cross. Circling Kuda was She, who was not looking at the road ahead, but directly at Reverend Mr. Shoko, ready to pounce on each line he said with words about the people. And Joy watched them, her eyes moving from the friend who knew of Spilling River through the church, to the friend who had looked at the geography and seen something different. Anyone who walked past would have thought they were practicing a new game and deciding the rules.

"There was peace in the town," said Kuda. "And everyone was pleased."

"Until one of the children of the five families saw another child walking along the road, balancing sticks on his head with two hands," said She.

"That child was afraid," continued Kuda, thinking back to a sermon from a previous year.

"The child belonging to one of the five families wanted to see if the other could still carry the sticks with only one hand," added She, remembering the bits of a story that had risen to her spot in the tree, on a day when the men heading to the farms had walked by. "So he ran into his house and picked up a gun."

"Wait," said Joy, slowing down, her eyes on the ground as if seeing the child. "What happened?" she asked, wanting the truth without ceremony.

"Someone was shot."

Kuda shook her head and stopped walking, the clasped hand still close to her heart. "I've never heard that story."

"How would the Reverend tell it?" asked She. "That the people who brought the guns used them on the people who took them in?" Squatting low, she drew two lines in the dirt road and waited for her friends to lean closer.

"I didn't know," answered Kuda. "Reverend Mr. Shoko has never said anything about that."

"They broke a promise, and they should have been made to leave," She continued. "Except the people of Waterfall disagreed and split in two." Pointing at one line, the girl carried on. "Some stayed in the town they'd been in for years." Then she pointed at the other. "And the rest moved away that night. They collected their homes, placed them in bags and in their free hands."

Joy traced above the lines She had put in the ground before asking quietly, "What happened to the child who was shot?"

Looking towards Spilling River, She shrugged her shoulders. "I don't know. Ask God."

"And the guns?" asked Kuda. "What happened to the guns?"

Chewing her tongue, She finished the story she'd heard from those passing, while she watched from above. "The guns came everywhere after the first shooting. When the five families took more land, it was the guns that stopped our neighbors from refusing. When they sent children away from the school that had been in Waterfall before they arrived, it was guns that kept those children from entering through the door. They should have prayed for God to kill them all and not for the strength to live among them." This last part was a silent logic that circled her mind. She wasn't sure how her friends would react to that kind of imagined violence.

"There was a school before Samson's Cross?" Kuda asked in disbelief.

THE ONES WE LOVED

She let out a hard laugh. "The one in the train station. Why did you ever think they built it? They didn't even build their own homes."

"So people had lived together until the landowners came, and then they separated," said Kuda, a question and a realization. "But they were all neighbors and friends. They should have stayed."

"Or everyone should have left," added She.

"Why didn't the children from Spilling River come back to Samson's Cross?" said Joy.

"Would you return to the place that betrayed you?" asked She, drawing a cross in the dirt, before rising and rubbing her hands clean. "They were one town, and they should have acted as neighbors do when they watch each other's children, because all the young belong to one and everybody. So your mother is my mother, and someone's daughter is her daughter."

"You do not want to call on my grandmother," said Kuda, attempting to make a light moment for herself and the children from Waterfall who were now in Spilling River.

"And if I can't call on your grandmother, someone else will come for me," answered She. "They will make sure I am protected." This is why Waterfall couldn't ever be her beginning. The town had chosen to end on its back instead of starting over on two feet. If Mama had been able to start again, a town could do the same.

"So the landowners have all their gardens, and their guns, and Eastern Farms too," Joy said, looking at her friends.

"I've never seen a gun before," mulled Kuda.

The girls walked along the road observing the land that ran farther than they could glimpse, resting their eyes on the people they saw spread across. Three here, two elsewhere, a small family there. None of those working looked up, and if you had asked them, after the sun set, if they had seen three girls in uniform walking by, they would not remember.

95

"What do you think Reverend Mr. Shoko told the landowners?" asked Joy.

"That we would do nothing but pray and pray," said She with resignation.

"My mother told me that the people in Spilling River do not have God," said Joy, "but their praying is older than ours."

"What does that mean?" asked Kuda.

"I think it has something to do with what they believe in. They don't have a church, so what they believe must be older, and also too big to come inside."

It was like a broken telephone, She would later decide that night, while sitting at home waiting for Mama, who had gone to church. Their life here. Not because the telephones didn't work and the parts that make up the machines were all flung into the room behind Samson's Cross: the wires shaped like tightly written S's, dozens of them, the numbers that no longer receded when pressed into the grimy dial pads and the cracked handsets. But broken in that they were all spread apart. And so a story would be told, hidden, and then shared once someone came close enough to receive it. Then they would also keep it hidden, until they passed it on. And the message would be shared as it was first told, changing only slightly depending on the feelings of the messengers. It was a broken telephone but slowly working. Like everything else in Waterfall. The glowing embers that flickered when a curious gust blew by and shook out the ashes left behind.

Before the girls could decide to keep moving forward or return where they had started, a streak of lightning flashed ahead. Overcome by their discoveries, they didn't see that the fields had cleared and the people who had been working were now running, hoes under their arms.

"We should go back," said She, just as large drops of rain began smacking against the road. All three turned back, walking fast and

THE ONES WE LOVED

thinking about what they would tell their parents if the rain got worse and they arrived home dripping. As if it was paying close attention to their brooding, the rainfall increased, and the girls quickened their pace, now running. When the sky opened up moments later, they were sprinting, their hands pumping against the building wind, unaware of how their uniforms looked or if they appeared unkempt moving so fast. They rarely saw the world like this, rushing past and blurred.

For no reason at all, She started to laugh, rain pelting her face and her bag hanging limp on her back. Her shirtsleeves were blowing in the wind, and her socks were sliding into her shoes. Kuda looked over, wanting to ask for the joke, when a leaf smacked against her cheek. Joy stumbled over a rock while trying to use her bag as an umbrella. While the rainstorm lasted, the students from Samson's Cross acted like children. The hurt and confusion that descended when She passed on the tragedy of Spilling River had burrowed into the corners of their mouths, which were now lifted to tell the story of the day they got drenched while running back home.

So caught up were the girls in their tight freedom and fast-buried grief, they almost ran over three boys lying in the road. Their bodies looked like puddles, opening up their own freedoms a little more.

14.

"I WANT TO live with He and Kind Eyes," Blink and Miss told his father.

They were sitting at the table that had felt small when his mother was alive and she heaped steaming pots of food across its entirety. Pumpkin porridge, spinach with meat slices cut thin so they lasted longer and absorbed more of their stewed flavor, ground maize, sweet potatoes just like everyone else and sugar water sweetened a little further with the sap she'd find hardened on the trees surrounding the farms. There was a time that Blink and Miss will never forget when his mother had eyed the table at dinner and, seeing an empty space among the dishes, went outside and returned with a handful of what appeared to be a flowering grass. She had then ground the plant using two strangely shaped rocks she turned into a mortar and pestle, added enough water to fit in her palm and a little of the stewed sauce. She had placed the mix in the empty space that could barely fit one adult fist, before sitting down.

"So there's enough of everything," she had said, although her husband didn't ask, and her son was wondering how she knew that flowering grass was edible.

"I saw the ants taking them," his mother said, looking at him and answering his wordless curiosity. "I trust the ants."

Now it was just the two of them and the table felt so much bigger without his mother's invisible hands serving food, encouraging appetites and taking the instincts of insects as truth. Too big for his hands to make enough food so his father didn't leave hungry. That was not the reason Blink and Miss wanted to live with his friends. He didn't think so.

His father kept eating, savoring each bite of the food his son had made that reminded him of the way his wife had cooked.

"Did you use the same pumpkins from the patch that your mother started?" he asked.

Blink and Miss nodded his head and allowed his mouth to make a half smile. "That's the only place I get them. I don't know what's different about that part of the fields, but everything grown there is better."

"This is good," his father said. "It's very good."

Blink and Miss felt an aching. He loved his father but knew the life he now wanted could only start in a different home. His father reached for the pot in front of him and spooned more ground maize onto his plate. Kind Eyes had also caught a rabbit when they were returning from the fields and given the largest cuts to Blink and Miss because, he said, "Your father eats enough for three drunk men." Blink and Miss had roasted the meat and then brushed it with a powder that his mother had made, which she'd never taught him how to make on his own. Her only son had been using it sparingly, trying to save it until he had figured out the ingredients and knew how to make more than what remained in the bottle. His father had reached for the rabbit immediately and kept looking up at the pot to see if there was still more. His son did not eat as much but the old man kept an eye out.

"He's like a meerkat looking around to see what's happening," Blink and Miss had told his friends during one of their days in the fields.

THE ONES WE LOVED

"It's probably something from his younger days, when food was scant for him and his family because the landowners took more than they do now," he added, finding the humor first before landing on the reality. Blink and Miss was not yet born then, but those stories were a part of Spilling River. His mother used to say the date of his birth was the day everything changed for the town. One day the landowners had been everywhere, always, barreling into their homes, riding through the small streets on their horses and swinging guns from arm to arm. Then the townspeople blinked and they were gone, so quick you wouldn't have believed they had once entered into the townspeople's homes as easily as their own. Now Blink and Miss only saw them and their guns when they sometimes came to the fields. It's why the time felt right to leave his father, without worrying about him facing the landowners alone.

Blink and Miss looked up again and cleared his throat, but before he could speak, his father leaned back and looked at him.

"Did you already find a place to build your home?"

"We will be living on the first street with He. In his grandparents' house. Kind Eyes has already moved. And there is enough room there for all of us."

His father was silent, still looking at him. He moved forward about to speak, before leaning back again.

"I will still come and see you. I can stay with you some days, too, if you would like. And I will come by to cook for you."

"I can cook on my own, son," his father said.

Blink and Miss gave him a disbelieving look, and his father came as close as he'd ever been to smiling. "Who do you think made the food for you after your mother died? You weren't cooking then."

Blink and Miss tried to remember those early days but only saw his mother's face and heard his father's loud voice.

"Don't worry about what I'll be eating," his father said. "I'll be fine." Rubbing his hands together, he looked down, a sign there was

101

something that needed to be said with care. "Have you told anyone else about this?"

Blink and Miss shook his head. "There is no need to say anything. We are just living together."

"Is there anything else that will be different?" his father asked.

"What do you mean?"

"When you live together," he started, "will there be anything different about the home?"

"It's just going to be me, He, and Kind Eyes," Blink and Miss responded, trying to answer the question his father wanted to ask. "We will act the same way in the house as we do when we are outside."

Nothing that happened in Spilling River stayed secret. While He's presence in the house would mean things were the same in one way, the boy knew that living with Kind Eyes would also mean something had changed.

"Life here is not like it was when I was a boy," his father said, pulling him out of his thoughts. "Then, we could walk with our heads up and move our feet as fast or as slowly as we wanted. We could take our time with our crops, hunt beyond the trees and rest when our bodies needed." His father was playing with his hands, telling the story with each finger, drawing out the times he remembered bit by bit. "We were not afraid, and because we weren't afraid, the choices we made were our own. So our fields could be what we chose, our houses could look how we wanted, and our families would be those we loved. When the landowners came, our choices shattered."

His father took a sip of the sugar water in front of him and put the cup down before picking it back up and finishing. He went on.

"There are things we lost when the landowners came. We fought to build this and some will say we succeeded. But we did not stay as the people we were. The fighting, the humiliations, the deaths, the loss, all of it changed us."

THE ONES WE LOVED

This was the truth of the town that Blink and Miss had felt, but that no one would speak out. It's what he needed to hear and what kept him awake as he worried about how he was seen by his neighbors and the landowners. So why did it all seem too much for a boy who just wanted a home with those he loved? His father felt the storm roiling in his son but continued on because what was started had to be said completely. If not now, there would only be mistakes and remorse.

Blink and Miss's father had said little about the conflicts in Spilling River, yet his son had stubbornly envisioned how his father could have once lived as a boy. It broke his heart to think of him young and reckless, then contained and disturbed, every move furtive and with nothing done out of pointless boredom. His father never laughed and so, in his daydreams, Blink and Miss would place different types of laughs over his face, testing each one to see if it could sound like something made by a man who had once moved without eyes pressing against the base of his skull.

"But the children didn't change," Blink and Miss said, when his father left an opening in the story while reaching for the right expressions.

His father stopped to look at him.

"The children who came after fighting the landowners were just like the people you lost," Blink and Miss explained. "They weren't born from the fighting. They came because of the past."

They were silent for a minute, one with the questions, and the other who already knew the land and the world that surrounded it. Who knew that the fighting had been twofold and it was the first battle that brought them to a crawl.

"There is no honoring the past, Blink," his father said. That is what his mother had called him. "Only mourning." It seemed now that was how his father was saying farewell.

"Do you think I should go?"

103

His father got up and started to put away the pots still full of rabbit and ground maize. He hadn't finished the food, and Blink and Miss rummaged through the day's events, looking for an observation that would bring him back to the table to finish all the plates.

"I think you shouldn't be afraid to live with the family you love."

"No. Should I leave Spilling River?" Blink and Miss asked, turning to look at the face that never laughed and whose hands didn't quite know what to do with the pots they had lifted.

"You will find landowners everywhere, son," he said.

That night Blink and Miss commanded his mind to only remember with imagination. He thought of how he felt when he was with Kind Eyes. Remembered how it was when He joined their family and how easy life felt when the three were together. They were a family. They were a family. They were a family.

15.

WHEN KIND EYES was not with his friends, he went home. Not the one he shared, but the one where he was born. Sometimes he would meet his father out in the farms, where his eyes would cast around for the tall, fast-moving form that always threw seeds from the left. His mother, who started her days sitting on the porch peeling maize or nuts and ended it sweeping fallen leaves in front of the house, was watchful and spoke little.

An accident with a landowner's machete when Kind Eyes was still a child had left one of her legs longer than the other, and she couldn't stand for hours without feeling a pain she tried to lessen with lullabies and rubbing ointments. Kind Eyes remembers the days after the accident when his mother would say nothing about her injury as he asked and asked, in the way children tend to do when they feel something change around them. The twins, a sister and brother, who weren't really such but followed after each other like a pair of pigeons, were even younger when the accident happened and so only knew their mother as someone who could not quite stand upright.

Although the true events were hidden from him, Kind Eyes knew that his mother had deserved none of the pain she had endured. So he started going to the farms long before his father asked him to join. Part of him hoped to meet the landowner who had hurt his mother. His father thought his son was keen to help and so showed him how to till, how to plant and when best to harvest. Kind Eyes listened, and while his mind learned all the ways to hear the soil, his anger crouched between his eyes, waiting to spring after it recognized the machete-carrying man who had hurt his mother.

"You are like your father," his mother had told him one day after he'd returned from the fields. By then he had been going for almost five years. His hands were pulling life from the land, and his rage was still waiting.

Smiling, while sitting next to her on the porch, Kind Eyes had expected to hear about his father as a child, and how he, his own son, resembled the man in the story.

"How are we the same?" Kind Eyes asked.

"You hold on to my suffering as your sole purpose, when it's the part of me I think so little about."

Kind Eyes had looked at her face, wanting to glimpse a sign of sacrifice or deep regret, and was met only with calm.

"I don't know what you mean," he answered.

His mother had narrowed her eyes, and her lips tightened, making him think there were words she was holding back to avoid making her son more of a liar. It was the conversation he thought of most when he came home.

The twins joined him and his father when they were old enough to walk long distances without needing to be carried on already tired shoulders, and though they liked the work, they relished skipping over planted rows with others their age. The men who counted had been a bother until the twins realized they were only there to watch and could be easily forgotten the more time they spent in the fields. Now

THE ONES WE LOVED

when they played, they almost ran through them, dipping between their legs and using their arms as covering from the sun.

"Do you think they'll be fine with this life?" Kind Eyes had asked his father, the first year the twins lifted a bag of smoked seeds and sprinted to the tiny family plot that their brother had cleared the night before, leaving only a few weeds so the twins would feel like they had accomplished much on their first dig. Kind Eyes joined his father in the landowners' estates, now also watching from afar as the younger children sorted the plots that would feed their families.

"They will have to be," his father answered, dropping seeds into the ground and covering them with the heel of his foot. "This is all there is for them."

"They asked me about school several nights ago," shared Kind Eyes, revisiting that afternoon when the twins wondered out loud—talking to each other first but still expecting him to respond—if sitting down in the morning, sitting down at the sun's peak, and only getting up when their shadows were behind them was a way of living only meant for children who went to bed without needing to clean the soil from under their fingernails. The twins didn't know yet how to talk about something simply, so they did it beautifully, like children do when they pick up on words quicker than they do their meaning. They were curious about this thing that was so important it took people away from the fields for a full day, and then again the next day and the day after that.

"School?" His father had stopped to look at his son, surprised by the reveal. "Who told them about school?"

"I don't know. They just asked me if that was something everyone did," Kind Eyes responded.

"And what did you tell them?"

"That I don't know."

"You should have said more," his father had said, before returning to his seeds.

107

"Well, you can talk to them too."

His father shook his head.

"The moment has passed now."

Father and son worked quietly, side by side, trying not to think about Spilling River and whether it would be sufficient for the people they loved. Around them, their neighbors were hunched over, others rushed through the field while standing straight like his father, and some sat down to hear the birdsong.

"Would you have wanted to go to school?" his father asked him after dropping a dozen seeds, stealing a glance at his face.

"There is no school here," Kind Eyes replied, careful not to give an answer that would have condemned the choices his parents made.

"What if we had moved?" his father continued. "Gone somewhere else. Maybe Waterfall. There is a school there."

"How would that have helped us? What could school have given us that we don't know?"

"Something more than farming," his father replied. "You could have been thinking about things that I don't even know to imagine because no one has ever asked me. You would just know how to think about more than this world."

"I know what I need to."

"You know what I have told you, and maybe that is not enough."

Kind Eyes stopped himself. His father was angling to be proven right. To be told that school was good, and he had failed by keeping his children away. Sometimes the man would do this. Return to his past to dig up the choices he made, which looked different when held up next to the lives of those who lived close. If he stayed silent, his father would usually talk himself back to the truth.

"We wanted to be different from them when we came here," his father started, under his breath.

"Why different?" asked Kind Eyes, moving closer. He didn't have

THE ONES WE LOVED

to think about which group his father returned to when seeking to be found wanting. He never held up the landowners as people to covet. Always those in Waterfall.

"Because we would have died if we stayed the same. Same people. Same place. Same work, on the same days. Same memories. Same children," his father said. His words grew strained, falling from gritted teeth. He was now remembering what he had distilled for his children in two statements, in an order that changed each time it was repeated.

"They live there. We live here."

"We live here. They live there."

"Something about us had to change. All that pain for us to break away and just turn out as they have?" he asked, shaking his head, his voice sounding like the remnants of bitterness. *What would that be called? Would school have taught him?* Kind Eyes wondered guiltily.

"We needed to be unrecognizable, in a consequential way," his father finished.

"Our lives are different," Kind Eyes said, emphasizing the right word. "They live there, and we live here."

His father nodded, but it was as if he was talking to someone else, listening to another story.

"We used to have a school. We had the train stop. Turned it into a place for learning."

"Who were the teachers?" Kind Eyes asked, his curiosity overpowering his reluctance to interrupt.

"Anyone who knew more. Often, the eldest of us. My father was one of the teachers. He taught me, your mother and your quiet friend's father. I think if she'd had the chance, your mother could have been a teacher too."

"What would she have taught?" Kind Eyes had never heard about this loss from his parents' childhood. He knew about the move. They all did. It's what was left behind that no one talked about.

109

"Whatever was needed. Anything she wanted to. How to listen to the wind, watch the skies and bring more ants to heal the soil." His voice grew low, like he was losing breath. It sounded like he was running, but they were still in the fields, moving slow, almost coming to a stop. "We taught them too. And then they killed us. Now we learn nothing."

Kind Eyes listened, his heart beating faster as he accepted every memory being set in his hands. He held them delicately. It was like his father was digging up an anthill, and each past moment was a line of red ants that could bite when roused from their monotony. Fearful of carrying wrong all that he was being trusted to hold, he placed them in the same holes he dropped the seeds they were still planting. So they'd return to the soil and grow inside the stalks of what fed those who had taken from them. He would never be able to hurt the man who harmed his mother. But perhaps Kind Eyes could take his breath, cover the pipes that brought the landowner air with the lines of disturbed ants linking the memories his father passed on. For his parents. For the twins. And his friends.

"There's still a school in Waterfall," he said, without any real faith.

"And what is it they learn now?" his father answered sharply. "What they are told? What they promised? They don't even work the land as we do. They come to lull and disappear, and leave without listening to the soil." The man saw his way back to their truth. School would have been good. But it was better to be without one than to be told what to learn.

Kind Eyes nodded and looked up at his father, whose eyes met his own. There was fury. There was also love. And something that seemed to be more than sadness, but not quite regret. Could school have taught him to see and understand the harder parts of his father's mind?

"Spilling River is our home," the son said. "All we know is here. What we love is in this land. Grandmother and Grandfather are close and sometimes I can hear them if I listen. This is where we belong."

THE ONES WE LOVED

"This is our home," his father repeated. A fact. A choice.

When the light started to fade, Kind Eyes looked up and told his father to go home. "I can finish the last few rows. You can join the others in the alley."

His father had looked towards the trees and beyond them, before turning back to his son.

"No, I will finish. Take your brother and sister and tell your mother I am behind you."

Kind Eyes would have insisted, but his father had moved on from the conversation, never having stopped working.

"Do you want me to come back and walk with you?" he said instead. His father chuckled.

"I will find my way home just fine, my boy. I won't get lost."

Kind Eyes smiled sheepishly. When he was younger, he had been afraid to walk home alone, worried that he would get lost, even though there was only one way back. As he headed towards the twins, who had buried their feet into the ground and were now covering them with clumps of soil, he called out to his father.

"My favorite teacher told me that planting at night was a dance with the spirits."

His father laughed and spoke the rest of the warning. "Spirits who use the darkness to collect the fears tossed in the daytime. So we can return and not grab what we discarded."

The twins pulled at their older brother's hands.

"I am right behind you," their father said.

When Kind Eyes wasn't home, this is where he was. Where the land always remembered its people's fears.

111

16.

"Mama, I don't know why I have to go with you every Sunday," She said in exasperation. Her resolve, which last night had been strengthened by irritation, teetered, as Mama narrowed her eyes, reminding them both that rejection was an act of disrespect. But She imagined looking up at Reverend Mr. Shoko for most of the morning, felt the rough wood of the pews scratching against the backs of her folded knees and swallowed her apprehension. "My spirit will not be condemned if I miss a few days."

"How do you know? You never come to church," Mama answered gravely, looking for her purse.

Her eyes swiftly moved between reading her daughter's face and looking at the open areas in the sitting room, which made her seem indecisive, less in control, probably because She had never watched her mother moving as someone who did not know where her feet would land next, always confidently reaching for things with hands that never let anything drop. When She was younger, this had seemed like a daunting achievement but something she, too, could do if her feet landed in the exact places that Mama's quickly passed through and her hands reached for the same living and still objects of her

life, like large pots, sunflowers, schoolbag, mhiripiri, school uniform, the sweeping stick. She had thought if Mama's shadow were
her own daughter, She would easily understand the woman who
raised her to pray, work and believe. But the closer She stood and
tightly grasped Mama's hands while Reverend Mr. Shoko delivered
his sermons, the harder it was to believe that God loved her more
than this woman.

Mama pushed the sofa to the side, praying the purse was trapped
against the wall. Flanked by two wooden chairs and big enough to
seat four people, it was the largest thing in the room, but not the
most used. That was the small stool. Mama had found it outside
the church one night after evening service. In her mind, it was a
gift from a God because she'd been muttering about how good it
would be if they had a small stool to rest her feet after a long day.
One Sunday later, there it was, waiting for her to pick it up. For all
the good things they had and all the good that stayed, Mama always
gave thanks to a God.

"Where could it be? I put it on the table every time I come back.
Are you sure you haven't seen it?"

"No, Mama. I haven't."

"Help me move the table."

They slid the wooden piece to the left of the room so she could see
if her slim, leather purse had found its way underneath. Mama always
placed things where they belonged. That she hadn't yet realized how
out of character it was for her to misplace a well-used item meant her
mind was distracted by something more.

"Mama, is something wrong?"

"Of course something is wrong, I cannot find my purse. And if it's
not in here, I don't know where it could be, which means I am going
to be late for church."

"Is it just the purse you're worried about?"

114

"What else is there?"

She started to chew her tongue and went into the bedroom, groping behind the metal bed frame where she had squeezed the purse last night and dusting it off, even though there was no dirt on it. Mama, who'd followed, said nothing as she retrieved it from her daughter, who was scrutinizing her face anxiously.

"Thank you," Mama said and walked towards the sitting room, where she picked up her hat from the sofa, adjusted her skirt and delicately brushed her blouse with her fingertips. Her rushing had slowed. Turning to face her daughter, who had followed out of their bedroom, Mama waited, not wanting to leave and also wondering what to say. Eying her daughter's face, she tried to find something recognizable, beyond the face that looked like the man she had loved and something more like the faith she had found that needed to be passed on because it was not people who stayed.

"Mama, I'm sorry."

"I know."

"I just really don't want to go."

"I know."

"Can I stay home?"

At that, Mama sat down heavily, her body suddenly realizing it needed to rest for a moment. Kneading the purse's leather corners, the woman wondered how this lone thing had upended what was meant to be a serene and easy Sunday morning. "You can stay."

"Mama, don't be upset."

"I am not. I am confused."

"About what?"

"Why do you not like going to church? What is it that you hate so much?"

"Mama, I don't hate church."

"You never want to go."

"I've go—"

"And when you're there, you make it very clear that you want to be somewhere else," Mama continued, cutting her off before she could respond. "You don't listen to the service. You spend your time looking at the ceiling, humming something I don't know or pressing your fingernails into your palm so hard you leave marks."

Of course her mother noticed all the things She did to make the time her own—so that the preaching continued, but where she sat, it was little tunes and tracing the grooves in the wood above Reverend Mr. Shoko's head.

"It is our home in this town," Mama finished, holding the sentence lightly, with care.

"This is our home," She responded, as her heart hastened and the tips of her toes grew cold.

"No, this is where we live. Church is where we belong."

"Mama . . ." She started, stopping short to build her resolve, before looking directly at the woman who knew her the best but still didn't understand.

"Why can't you talk to me the way you talk to a God?"

The question screamed and writhed on the floor, waiting for someone to breathe life into its form and make it whole. To give it an answer and a reason to exist.

"I don't understand what you are asking," Mama replied, clutching her purse harder. She, who sighed and sat on the sofa, left room between them for two people.

"There's so much you don't say, Mama. You talk to me, but it's a God you trust. And I wish you trusted me with our life. Your life, your story. It's also mine, and I don't know it. I don't know who else you have loved away from a God. And did they love me too? I don't know if you've had friends, as I have Kuda and Joy. If you've doubted something, and needed to be convinced. I don't know your favorite

THE ONES WE LOVED

memory, or if you spent time in the fields alone or with someone who taught you how to know it as well as you do. I don't know why you never went to school and what you did with your time then." She was begging now, and it made Mama squeeze her hands into fists.

He had left. She's the one who stayed.

"There's just so much you have never told me," She whispered. "I want to know who you were before you were my mother. I want to know if you were like me."

"What don't you like about our church?"

"Mama?" the girl asked, barely able to utter the word. Her mind had prepared to receive answers, and it took her a split breath to realize that from what she took out of her heart and placed in Mama's hands, all that was drawn was a question.

"What don't you like about our church?" Mama repeated, her face unchanged, except for a slight twitch above her eye. There would be no answers. The girl leaned farther from her mother, pressed her legs into the sofa and started fiddling with her fingers.

"Mama, whenever I've thought about church, I've never felt the way you do. That safety I know you feel, I don't feel it."

"Then tell me what you feel."

"I don't think we have time now."

"No, you can tell me."

She wouldn't get the responses she needed. So the girl gave those that had been requested.

"It feels like fear. Like death lying in wait. As though I am only safe until the moment God chooses to glance away, and then the doors will burst open and we will be in danger. It feels like we are only safe for as long as heavenly eyes stay on us. But they can't just look at us. And the danger is patient. It knows all it has to do is wait for God to look away only for a second, and it can have its way. I don't trust that we're safe there. I can't lean on it, and I don't believe it."

117

She had spoken quickly to run over any interruption and because the questions that had gone unheard were still bundled on her tongue, searching for more breath and more time.

Mama clasped her hands together, pressed them into her lap momentarily, then stood up.

"I am going out now."

"Oh. All right." She watched her adjust her clothes, again, even though nothing was out of place. Mama had three suits for church—white, yellow, green—and they all looked the same: knee-length skirts and stiff blazers that never went unbuttoned. Mama always wore brown stockings that had been gently dyed in a pot of boiling water filled with seeds from the spirit-piercing tree next to the church. All three suits were worn in rotation with the same two additions, her long floral scarf that could be tossed over her shoulders or placed as a mat on the ground to avoid sitting on the grass, and the purse.

"I'll be gone most of the day."

Nodding her head, She looked up at the ceiling. "I'll see you when you come back."

When Mama reached the door, the girl unraveled her body and walked over to give her a kiss on the cheek. "Are you still going to pray for me?"

"I always do."

Mama opened the door and walked out. Her daughter watched her step out into the yard, her white heeled shoes polished to a considerable shine crunching on the stones that ran from their door to the gate some three meters away. Her mother swung open the gate and turned around to give a small smile and wave. She was going home. And her daughter went back into the house. The purse was still on the sofa.

17.

"Do you think it's a man?" asked Kuda surprisingly loud, as though this option had shocked as soon as it came out of her mouth. She sat cross-legged and on the floor, her eyes closely watching the liquid she was pouring into a small plastic jar in front of her. The mix needed to reach about halfway before she added the paste that Joy had made, then let it sit for as long as it took to harden.

"No, I don't think your grandmother would leave as much because of a man," Joy answered, her voice low because her chin was pressed against her chest so She could easily oil the base of her scalp. "What do you think?" Joy asked her friend.

"I think if there was a man, he would have visited Waterfall at some point to see her, and to make sure that there was no other man here waiting for her to come back," She answered.

"Not a man here, only a child," Kuda said dryly, adding the paste, putting the lid on the tub and shaking it side to side.

"Be careful," Joy warned, raising her eyes. "You don't want the lid coming loose and the whole mix splattering on the floor."

They were sitting in She's house, the best place to be when there was no school and when they were far from their tree trunk. Joy preferred it

119

because unlike her parents, who came into her room every few minutes when her friends were around to see if she was feeling well, She's mother only asked about school and if they had enjoyed the last service. Kuda loved coming because She's mother always sent her home with jars of food good enough to bring words to a mute. Today she had been on her way to church when Kuda and Joy arrived, but there was still food.

"Have you ever asked your grandmother to take you?" She asked, fidgeting a little on her mother's stool and trying to find the most comfortable position. Now that Joy's hair was ready, she was parting it into sections so she could start to braid. Joy's mother sometimes did it, but her plaits quickly came undone because she didn't want to pull the hair tightly and hurt her daughter.

"That's all she worries about, hurting me," Joy had told She.

Kuda was quiet as she thought about the question. "I don't remember. Perhaps when I was younger, I asked. But I think I always knew that her trips could never include me."

"There's probably no landowners where she goes. That's why she loves it," said Joy, holding on to a box of pins that she would raise towards She whenever her hand tapped her shoulder. She would grab about three: one would pin the hair back, and the other two, she would grip between her lips until the next braid. The more pins she used, the more complicated the style would be.

"If there's no landowners, then why does she come back?" Kuda asked, tentatively.

"Because of you," She said reproachfully. It was the obvious answer and Kuda was a fool for not knowing.

"It's not me she returns to."

"But what else is here?" Joy asked, wondering if her parents could ever leave her for any longer than a school day.

"I don't know. But whatever it is, it's not enough to keep her in Waterfall, but it also won't let her stay wherever she goes."

THE ONES WE LOVED

"What if she never came back?" asked Joy, unable to see Kuda's eyes but feeling She's hands pull her strands a little harder than usual as a means to silence her. She had to keep going. "Would you be happy?"

Kuda eyed the jar she had been steadily shaking, switching hands to rest the arm that was starting to burn. "I don't think I'm supposed to be happy. Being alive is goodness enough." Their friend's response was cursory and dry, and it could have been an answer offered in class to pass the time and dutifully participate.

"So you're just supposed to be sad?" She asked, wanting to embrace her friend, but not knowing how to hold her.

"I think I'm meant to be how I am now," Kuda replied.

"Aren't you happy?" Joy asked, her head jolting up before She gently pushed it down. "Even now?"

Kuda shrugged her shoulders. Halfway through the braid, She reluctantly loosened her grip so Joy could lift her head. Kuda saw the concern in her friend's eyes and met it with relief, before placing the jar on the ground.

"Who do we know who is happy?" Kuda asked.

Now it was their turn to shrug their shoulders, the rise and slump filled with anticipation and uncertainty.

"Miss Bride."

"We don't know her."

"Your mother."

"She's not happy, she's busy."

"What about your mother?"

"She's grateful and she cares a lot."

They thought of more names. "My father. I think he is happy. But sometimes I think it's because that is easier than being himself," Joy said.

"But don't you see," Kuda told them, leaning into the circle that had grown smaller and smaller as they scoured for happiness, clinging to

121

those they believed had it, whose unseen bodies now sat among them. "Happiness is just happiness."

"So, does it become something different because of who we are?" asked Joy, who could never be as she was called.

"I think so," She began, playing with the edges of Joy's hair, which bristled in her hands. "It's like those shivers we feel all over our body when it gets cold quickly or when it's hot. We don't know when they'll happen, but when they come, we just feel them. I think happiness is like that. It settles on a person and then they feel it. But for us, we don't do anything for no reason. Everything needs to have purpose. So we don't let happiness settle. It comes for us, perhaps we feel it, but then it goes. So we don't know if we were happy, or just shivering for no reason."

"Would you want to be happy? Here?" Kuda asked. "Where the school built for us teaches nothing about our lives, and the people who raise us imagine themselves in their past instead of seeing us in their futures?"

"Mama never thinks about her past. I'm the only one who does," She said wistfully.

"Why?"

She thought. "I think she was happy. Then."

"But you weren't a part of it," Kuda mulled softly, "so if she was happy then, without you, what is she now with you?"

She shrugged. This is probably why Reverend Mr. Shoko used the bible for all that children needed to know. A person never had to shrug if all they had to do was grab a book, turn a page, pick a verse and speak words written by someone who had believed them enough to write them for people who would be in need later. Whether their lives were the same or different. The words possessed a certain security, no eraser marks from an unsteady pencil or crossed out words from an overly eager pen.

THE ONES WE LOVED

"So you're saving up your happiness until you get to someplace better?" Joy asked.

"I just think there's more that we should have. More that we need," Kuda replied, releasing a long breath and returning to the jar of oil that had started to form a shiny mark on the floor.

Stretching her left leg, She placed her foot over the slick, using it as a cloth. Joy scrunched her nose. "You could have used something else."

"If I get up, I'm going to leave you with a half-finished head," She warned. Joy swallowed a chuckle and rested her head on her friend's lap.

"Would you leave with her if she asked you to?" She asked, from one side of her mouth so as not to drop the pins she was using to style Joy's hair. They had already talked about the heavy things, so it felt safe to remain.

"Life would have become something different if she ever asked me to join her," Kuda said.

"What do you mean?" asked She.

Kuda was about to answer, then started laughing because of how strangely She's face moved as she talked, the pins peeking through her lips. When she raised her eyebrows, her face looked like a puppy scared out of deep sleep by a noise.

"Why are you laughing?" She asked, confused by Kuda's growing fit.

"Your face is just . . ." began Kuda, who pulled her mouth and eyes into an expression that resembled her friend's face. Joy, who was glancing from the corner of her eye, chuckled, and with her neck set stiff to not disturb the braiding fingers, looked even more ridiculous. The two girls were now competing to see who could make the most comical face. With a half-done head and comb tucked in her hair, Joy was an obvious victor.

"If you don't stop laughing, I won't be able to finish both of your heads," She finally said, silencing her giggles with a long exhale. "And I want to finish today. I'm not doing more tomorrow."

123

"Fine," answered Joy and Kuda in unison.

"If it's easier for you, you don't have to do this style," Kuda proposed, pointing to the drawing she had done that looked like the anthills they had seen on their way to Spilling River. "You can do something else."

"No it's all right, I can do it. Just stop making us laugh," She said, throwing her a warning look.

"So let's just return to my sad life."

"Yes, it is sad that you only have two friends," Joy said.

Kuda grabbed Joy's toes, and Joy shrieked as her friend tickled the soles of her feet, and She raised herself from the stool, lifting her hands in surrender.

18.

It had been some time since She soaked her full body in warm water. Her room right above the restaurant barely had enough space for the four-legged chair next to her bed, let alone a round metallic tub. So, standing in a shallow blue bucket, she squeezed her washcloth and let the water run down her back, splashing onto the floor as she wiped away the oils from last night's dinner service. It was just after sunrise that she would climb the stairs up to her room and step into the small bucket, hardly awake, before falling onto the bed, barely dry. She would never have crumpled underneath the quilt without letting some water onto her skin, but it took all her will not to fall asleep on her feet.

Six hours later She would wake up and put on a shirt and skirt. In the reflection of a small window that showed more of the sky than anything else, She would check the corners of her eyes for sleep crust, the edges of her mouth for any dryness, her hair for loose braids, and then grab an apron from the chair and head down to the restaurant. The first one there after the break splitting lunch from the dinner preparation, She would once again wipe down the furniture; there were a dozen tables and plenty more chairs squeezed in a room that was only meant to hold half that many. When it got too full, people would sit in any place where there was space, including the window-sills. Gogo J. would amble in an hour after She, having gone to her bungalow next door for a nap and change of clothes. Gogo J. only had two outfits. The plain black she wore during the lunch hour and the fancier one for nighttime, also black. The glamor lay in the lack of sleeves, so everyone could see Gogo J.'s smooth arms, piled with bracelets from her wrists to the tops of her elbows. With every move, they would catch the light from the naked bulbs hanging low and shimmer like slivers of sun. On days the night service was good and loud, Gogo J. would turn the bracelets into instruments, shaking them while she sang.

When She had first met her that night she stumbled into the restaurant, she had thought the jewelry was something all the women wore in this town, but after observing different arms, she realized Gogo J. was the only one. She was also the only woman who owned a restaurant.

Sitting down on the tall stool behind the counter, She saw that deer was on today's menu, which changed depending on what was in the pantry and cooler. Everything in the pantry came from the garden, and all the meat in the cooler was delivered by young men who went hunting every week, fished regularly and trapped enough to sell and feed their families. Rabbit was always on hand, small fish, deer on good trips, and then quail and something She thought looked like a mouse but was much bigger and more ferocious even when lying on top of the slab in the kitchen where Gogo J. skinned, cut and por-tioned. The young men offered to do it, but that would mean paying them more money, so the old lady did it alone.

Everything here was as different as the way She now walked. The food was not the same. There was no school close by, so the children spent their days running in and out of their houses, shooting down

THE ONES WE LOVED

birds with their pebbles and rubber bands and stealing strips of dried meat from Gogo J.'s porch. They thought they were moving stealthily, toeing the brink of insolence with their theft, but what the children didn't know was that Gogo J. purposefully left out the strips for them to enjoy. "Let them think they're stealing it," the old lady told her once. "Give them a little excitement to make the days pass faster." The girls in this place moved with large splotches of sweat on their clothes and no one said anything. No one noticed. When she'd see the women by the river washing clothes and bedding, some would be bent over, others squatting and some sitting on the ground with their legs wide apart and their dresses or skirts pushed high up, draped over their thighs. No one minded.

It was by the river that She liked spending her time on the days Gogo J. didn't need her at the restaurant. If she went there in the afternoon, when the sun was its highest, she would find the children splashing along the bank, some diving to the bottom and others bravely feeling their way over the slippery rocks and looking for a place to begin their entry. The squeals traveled back to the town, and every now and then, a parent would walk over just to make sure it was the sounds of glee not fear rocking the windows.

She didn't know how much time had passed, but the pleats on her skirt were no longer visible and the carefully kept school uniform had become the clothes she wore before she got on her knees and scrubbed the stairs leading to her room. Her life was now lived across two levels—the downstairs restaurant and her upstairs room. So much work, every day, no rest, no time to be late. There was no one in this town who cared what She had left behind and she was just the girl who served the food. If her hands stopped moving while she was awake, she knew they would do too much harm. So she kept going until she could barely raise them past her waist. And right when they seemed ready to fall out of her body, she would go outside and find the alarmingly red

127

fruit. She'd seen them outside on her second day in Gogo J.'s house and her heart jolted. When she touched them, she didn't know how to feel: relief for finding something she already knew or shame because she left Waterfall like a criminal? Next to this same bush with red fruit, She had gasped and shuddered and relaxed and stiffened, feeling somewhere on her body an itch that couldn't be scratched and a blooming of heat in places under her skin. She had almost laughed. It was like all the years of clamping down the excess emotions and physical responses had reached a peak, and all she could do was feel everything at once. In a moment when she only wanted to feel one thing.

What she remembered clearly, through the blur of sweat and tears that mixed to become blood, was a small hand roughly taking her wrist and pulling her out of the crowd.

"Let's go," it had said.

She had followed, not knowing who it belonged to or where it was going. As the hand had insisted and led, She realized she had never been that close to that face before.

"I've killed us all," She had cried, an emptiness filling her chest. "They are going to kill everyone. I am so sorry." Between sobs, that was all she could say. Over and over again.

The hand had knelt and held her close, tears running from its own eyes. "You did what should have been done to right the world. Thank you."

"I have killed everyone," She had said.

"Listen to me," the hand had started, pinching She's wrists. "You did what I should have. You fed the fire I muffled when I failed to shoot the boy who shot my son. I did nothing when the bullet mangled his hand, and instead of fighting back, I stayed and worked for them. I sent him away when he was older because I didn't want him living in a place that had hurt him, and with the person who had failed to protect him. But it was too late because when he came back, he was

THE ONES WE LOVED

not my son. I can never leave him, but he is no longer my son. Every time I hear about him preaching in that church, I know he is not the boy he was before they shot him."

Putting its arms around She's waist, the hand had pulled her up and placed her on its back and carried her to the bus stop. The hand said to her, "You are going to go somewhere far."

"Where will I go?" She had asked. The hand whispered in her ear.

"You can't ever come back, all right. Stay far and gone," her friend's grandmother begged.

She now struggled to remember each part of the face that had nakedly shown the pain of several hurts. Had Kuda's grandmother always worn that grief? She wanted to tell Kuda because who else would tell her? But the girl couldn't go back.

What a strange place to land after leaving the one that was never home. This was where Kuda's grandmother had come whenever she left Waterfall, She realized. And the woman always returned to her home.

Waterfall, for She, had become the town halfway between a blasting engine and a resting stop. A lay-back station where she'd lived through Mama's journey. She would have stayed until Mama was done with it, until she'd walked enough times from the church to their house to the sunflowers and back to herself that they could find their way home. To where Mama had started and her own mother had taught her to cook with red fruit.

If the bus had kept going, that would have been fine, too, but this is where Kuda's grandmother told her to stop. So she waited for the moment someone would tell her to go. Then she would know if this was the place to live or the lay-back town to put a hand on while shaking the stones out of her shoe.

129

19.

THE HANDS ON the clock moved patiently on Fridays, like rock formations, She thought, but with none of the beauty that comes when the rock has been reshaped by all it has weathered. It was almost disappointing, both hands plotting to make them stay in school much longer than necessary. She took another glance and saw that the big hand had barely moved between 12 and 3, where it had been since she had last looked. To her left, Joy was drawing in a notebook. Next to her, Kuda had cupped her chin in her hand and was looking at the chalkboard. While it might have seemed like her friend was intently listening, the shaking pencils on her table meant her knees were bouncing impatiently underneath. Miss Bride had not come in, and so instead of Geography, the last class of the day was God Studies, and Reverend Mr. Shoko was taking them through a parable.

As always, they began with a prayer different from the daily benediction, then Reverend Mr. Shoko would recite the books of the bible, first to last. And repeat them again while replacing his students' impassive stares with an admiration that he imagined. Sometimes he would mention a prophet, and if his mood was high, talk about them like they also lived in Waterfall and went to his church, were personal friends who enjoyed his sermons and needed his advice. He walked over to the board, writing the lesson in big letters in the center before picking up his bible and reading. *It always looks new*, She thought offhandedly.

"Before leaving on a journey that would take him far from home for many days, a man brought eight bags of maize seeds to his servants." Reverend Mr. Shoko paused and looked at the class, eying them from above the rim of his glasses before continuing. "After dividing the seeds according to the competency of each servant, five bags to one, two bags to another, and one bag to the last, the man departed."

"So the first one was given the most seeds?" asked Dumisani, one of the students who regularly participated in this class.

"Yes, Dumi, he was," answered Reverend Mr. Shoko. "And when he received his bags, he quickly invested them."

"What is *invested?*" asked Dumisani.

"Ahhh, good question." Reverend Mr. Shoko put his bible down for a minute, adjusted his glasses and looked at all of them directly before continuing. "To invest means to take something valuable and put it somewhere where it will make more money."

"Somewhere like where?" asked Dumi.

"Well, a place like a bank, where you can put all your important things. And the longer it stays there, the more time you have to build interest."

"What is *int . . . ?*"

Reverend Mr. Shoko raised his hand to signal to Dumi that he was already going to answer that question.

"Interest is a certain amount that grows over time, depending on what it is that you have of value. The people who work in the bank know just how much interest different things can grow. And it all depends on how long it's been in the bank."

"And can anyone have important things in the bank?" asked Dumisani.

"Of course. I can, you can and anyone else who wants to," said

THE ONES WE LOVED

Reverend Mr. Shoko, moving his hands in little circles like he did when he got especially excited.

"Do I need to have lots of things to go to the bank and get interest?" asked Dumisani.

"No. Whatever you have is fine."

"Then how come I don't know anyone who has anything in the bank getting interest?" asked Dumisani.

Reverend Mr. Shoko looked at the boy and furrowed his brow. "What do you mean?"

"No one I know has ever gone to the bank and no one has interest. My mother keeps all of our valuable things in the house because it's safer there."

The rest of the class was now paying attention and looking at their classmate who was dutifully trying to understand what it was that he was missing, from a process that sounded so simple; She looked at Joy, who'd put her notebook away, and at Kuda, who was no longer slumped on the desk.

"Well, sometimes the people at the bank decide who has enough to keep in a bank. And sometimes there are people who just don't have enough."

He looked at Dumisani, who opened his mouth then quickly closed it. Reverend Mr. Shoko waited for a minute before picking up his bible and continuing with the story of the three servants and their bags of maize seeds.

"After a long time, the man returned from his journey and he called his three servants so they could tell him what they had done with the bags he gave them. The servant who had been given five bags of seeds had planted each one, and now had ten bags turned to maize. The servant told the man, 'You gave me five bags to invest and I was able to earn ten more.' The man was very happy and said, 'Well done, my good and faithful servant. You have been wise in dealing with the amount I bestowed,

133

and so now I will give you more to do. Let us celebrate together.' The servant who had been given two bags came forward with two more and said, 'You gave me two bags to invest and I earned two more.' The man was again pleased and said, 'Well done, my good and faithful servant. You have been wise in dealing with the amount I bestowed, and so now I will give you more to do. Let us celebrate together.' Finally the third servant who had been given one bag came and said, 'I knew you were a harsh man, harvesting and selling crops you didn't cultivate. I was afraid I would lose your bag, so I kept it safe in my home. Now I am giving it back to you exactly as you gave it to me.'"

"But the man was angry and said to the servant, 'You are wicked and lazy! Why didn't you do something more? I gave you a gift. You could have sold it for more money.' The man ordered that the bag be taken from the servant. 'Take it and give it to the one with the ten bags of maize.'"

The students were loud with their surprise, forcing Reverend Mr. Shoko to raise his hand for quiet before continuing. "'When you take what you are blessed with and turn it into prosperity for those who trust you, so many more blessings will be added unto your hands, and you will find yourself, always, with more. But if you do not act, and fail to add abundance to the blessings given, then all you have will be taken, even what is little and few. Now take this servant away from the somber darkness of truth, and toss him into the light where all that is faithless and shameful is easily done and seen.'"

As the final words sat in the room, the class fell quiet. Reverend Mr. Shoko always closed the bible reverently, but today the pages sounded loud and disturbing as the halves met. He looked at the students, who were all chewing over what they'd heard and the feelings it raised inside them. No one fidgeted, cleared their throat or looked at the clock. No one wanted to open the silence, which right then felt like several palms trying to stop a flood of water from flowing through a hole in a leaking roof.

THE ONES WE LOVED

Reverend Mr. Shoko cleared his throat and took off his glasses. "Does anyone have any questions?"

Everyone looked around to see who'd free their palm. Reverend Mr. Shoko glanced over at Dumisani, who was staring at his desk.

"Dumisani, do you have something you want to say?"

Dumisani looked up and opened his mouth before closing it again, while She looked closely at his fingers, which were tightened around a pencil and then relaxed, testing to see how far he could grip it before it broke. Then, She looked at Kuda and Joy, who looked back at her and gave sad smiles. They also understood. It was probably the same thing that Dumisani was trying to say but couldn't quite figure out how to do it without making them all see their lives a little bit differently.

"So the man punished the servant who had been given the least amount?" Dumisani asked.

"It wasn't a punishment. Not quite," answered Reverend Mr. Shoko. "The man was upset that the servant had not done anything to increase the amount that he had been given."

"But the servant told him why," replied She, who had not meant to speak. Out of her mouth had come the words that made Dumisani keep tightening and relaxing his fingers around an object that could break with the right pressure.

"He didn't want to make the man angry by making little, because he had been given little," She continued. "Why did the man punish him for that?"

"Because he was lazy," answered Reverend Mr. Shoko with a hard note in his voice. "The servant was given something to show how well he could do on his own, but he did not use it," he said, glancing at each student. "He took the bag and hid it. He did nothing with the gift he was given."

"But if it was a gift, isn't it up to him to decide what he wants to do with it?" asked Dumisani, his face wrinkled in confusion. He was now looking at She because her question let him know that both their

135

minds were wrestling with the same problems. There were ruptures in the parable where all the needles that pierced their lives fell through, making even small movements uncomfortable.

"I think the man is cruel," Kuda said.

"I think so too," said Joy.

"He punished his servant for making the only decision he could, based on who he knew the man to be," said Kuda.

"You don't think his laziness is something to be ashamed of?" asked Reverend Mr. Shoko.

"No," Joy replied.

Reverend Mr. Shoko waited for her to say more. Straightening her shoulders, Joy looked directly at the person who taught them how to look at God.

"He wasn't lazy. He was afraid. Fear keeps people safe. It's what lets us know when we are moving in the wrong direction. It keeps us from jumping into the river during a storm or hiding inside a bush with thorns. Our fears are our shields. You always tell us to fear God because that protects us from feeling his anger if we disappoint him. The servant feared the man, and he did not want to disappoint him, so he kept the bag hidden and gave it back like it was. How could that be wrong?"

"It's wrong because the man was giving his servant an opportunity," said Reverend Mr. Shoko, his voice rising, resistant to this moment of mutiny from his class. "He wanted him to do something with the maize seeds given to him, and he believed that he could."

"Was the maize a gift?" repeated Dumisani.

"What do you mean?"

"If they were gifts, then what they did with them was their decision," answered the boy.

"He's right," said Joy, nodding her head. "You cannot control what someone chooses to do with something that belongs to them."

"When the man punished him and rewarded the others, the man

was telling them that there is nothing they control," added Dumisani. "Even the gifts they received are meant to be given back to him in some way," said Dumisani.

"That is cruel," repeated Kuda.

"You are all choosing to focus on the punishment," said Reverend Mr. Shoko. "Remember, the servants were workers paid to work for the man and do what he requested. When he gave them the bags, he was giving them the opportunity to do something without needing to ask. He wanted to see what they could do on their own."

"And those who did something were rewarded?" asked Dumisani.

"That they were!" answered Reverend Mr. Shoko, clapping his hands together. The triumph of the motion failed to match the hollowness they all felt.

"But shouldn't we also think about why the servant was so scared of him?" said Kuda. "The man did not do his own work and he was harsh. So why should we try to blame the servant for doing nothing when the man did nothing too?"

"And he was still rich," echoed Joy, who was now sitting on the edge of her seat. "This story makes it seem like if you have less, you have to always please those with more, even when they don't do work for themselves."

"And then when you fail to do something for them, you're wicked and lazy," finished Dumisani.

"It's like they are controlling your life and deciding who is the person who deserves good things," said Joy.

"Like the landowners," said Dumisani.

"What?" said Reverend Mr. Shoko, arms folded and his brows rising ridiculously close to his hairline.

"The landowners. They want to control what we do with the land and who is rewarded for it," said Dumisani.

"And if we don't do what they want, they will treat us like the people in Spilling River," Joy said quickly.

137

"They will," Dumisani declared with a heaviness in his voice.

"If someone looks at them wrong, they can be punished," said She, remembering the time Miss Bride had passed one of the landowners' wives without a greeting and found herself pushed to the ground by a man who couldn't have been the husband and had to be the son. So much younger than Miss Bride and pushing her down with his hand. Miss Bride hadn't seen She, up in the old tree no one looked at, and She never told anyone what had happened.

"Now, that's not true," said Reverend Mr. Shoko, but no one heard, and all the students were listening to each other, sharing things that had been previously clenched and unexamined, now released after hearing about a man and the servant he punished. Reverend Mr. Shoko watched them, swallowing his tongue so he wouldn't tell them the things that had happened so that they could be sitting in this classroom, weighing their choices in hands that had never held heavy loads. They were focusing too much on the cruelty, Reverend Mr. Shoko wanted to yell—this piece of the story that merited the least attention. He knew the wealthy man was terrible, and he cast that aside because it was futile. Cruelty could only devour, and always quickly. Slower than death, but never lasting as long as hope. He wanted these children to focus on the relentlessness of hope. How hard it was to have so much, and also how necessary. Such a feeling was so audacious. Like tending to soil you could not claim, but whose yellow flowers only recognized your hands. Or turning bags of maize into wealth you could not call your own, but whose growth was still your victory. And delivering Sunday sermons to the person who didn't come to church but who Reverend Mr. Shoko knew was always listening to his voice because she had heard it before he first came into the world, so it lived in her skin and followed her feet. Hope was a miracle not even God could perform. God knew the power of sacrifice and of being the supreme creator, but nothing of

THE ONES WE LOVED

how to trust while blind and hold on to mercy in the absence of justice. He wanted the children to see hope, and maybe become it.

"So, are we the servants?" Dumisani asked, looking around.

"No," said She. "We are not the servants. We are the bags of maize seeds."

Reverend Mr. Shoko looked at her.

"We are the things used by people who want to get interest from how we work."

"Is that good or bad?" said Joy. "Because if there are no bags, then no one has anything to take."

"Do you feel good being a bag of maize?" asked Dumisani.

Reverend Mr. Shoko clenched his jaw, and two claps rang out across the room, interrupting nothing but the layer of chalk dust covering his hands. "This has been a very interesting conversation," he began, "but I don't think you all understood what the story was saying."

"What did we not understand?" Dumisani asked.

Reverend Mr. Shoko looked at him closely, running his eyes across his face, hoping to catch some sign of insincerity that he could berate. But there was none. "Good work will always take you the right way. Even if you think no one is watching."

"Then I think you didn't understand what we were saying," said She.

"And what would that be?" asked Reverend Mr. Shoko, growing increasingly agitated. He was always composed, but in this hour, as the children toppled each pillar that held his conviction, he started to feel carved out. Like a bed without a river.

"We don't have a problem with work. We all work. Our parents work," She said. "But that's all we are expected to do. The story didn't say the servant slept the whole time the man was away. He was still a servant, and even though he wasn't doing work to make more, he was still doing something that made him a servant."

"And that still was not good enough," continued Joy.

139

"The man called him lazy," added Kuda.

"The same man who didn't grow his own crops," finished Dumisani.

None of them had come in hoping to be particularly involved, and yet the class had drawn something out of each one, forcing them to face what they never dared to unravel. They felt their parents in the classroom, not as hovering adults, but people who didn't deserve how they lived.

"My parents are not lazy," said Dumisani. "But I don't think they will ever be rewarded."

"That is a different situation," said Reverend Mr. Shoko. "The landowners have their own rules. But we can also make our own rules." He lingered on that last phrase, hoping that it would creep into the minds of the somber, young faces in front of him. There were choices, still. Not good, but choices.

"They have a church. We have a church. Their children go to school. We go to school. What does a God tell them that we do not hear?" asked She.

"Why would God make us live in a place where other people have rules that we are forced to follow?" asked Joy.

"Why wouldn't he give us our own world?" said Kuda.

"But he has!" answered Reverend Mr. Shoko triumphantly. "He has! A world that has no rules except that we love and pray. That's what heaven is. A place where hope arrives and never leaves."

"But we can only see this world when we die. So what do we do until then?" said Dumisani, more to himself than anyone else.

The questions had tumbled fast, and Reverend Mr. Shoko was unprepared. "I see everyone has a lot on their mind today, so here's somewhere to put your thoughts," he started. "I want you all to find a verse in the bible that makes you understand what it's like to work for something you love. Then tell me after church on Sunday."

It was quiet when the bell rang.

No one rushed out. It had been a difficult class.

20.

SHE DIDN'T KNOW how to swim. Had never desired to learn or wondered what else lived under the rippling surface. But for the first time, She could hear the voices between each fold. They sounded like her neighbors, yet this river was not in Waterfall. If she could gather it in her arms and hold it close to her heart, perhaps it would start to breathe as she did. And after its first breath, the weeping would wash away. What holds the water when it cries out? Not the land that keeps it closed or the rocks that whittle down, smaller and smaller, with each lapping touch, eaten away by the swells.

She walked towards the riverbank and stretched her arms.

He watched, idling close to the rocks where most of the town's children would take turns sitting when the sun was blistering, competing to see who could last longest while the heat warmed its way into their clothes before becoming a fire against the skin, forcing them to cry out. She moved with purpose, as though his presence was one she had anticipated and was now doing what was needed because He was watching.

When she felt the water between her toes, She knelt and scooped some into her hands, brought it up and let it fall down her face.

Someone was close. She felt it like she had when Mama would stand by the door and wait until she passed the gate, passed the house with the frozen ice and the one with the grasshoppers (or did the grasshopper house come first?), and then passed the sunflowers, until She was too far away for the color on her skirt to look anything other than dark. But Mama had kept watching and the girl felt it. She knew it now but didn't turn around.

Instead, she walked ahead, and when the water touched her knees, She kept going deeper. Back in Waterfall, she would have stopped, but that river knew how to take care of itself, how to return to the place it once called home. And sometimes it retreated with more than it needed. The one here followed the path it flowed within, and even when it lingered or chased the feet of the children running along the bank, its arrival, however playful, was jittery. It needed to be held.

He waited for her body to relax and for the swimming to become pleasant, but She waded in like someone moving towards a sound that could only be heard by the person searching. Was this water her sky? The boy began to walk forward. He had meant to return to the town, but his feet led him towards the girl who was talking to the water. He wanted to stop her. Tell this girl from the restaurant that this water should not be listened to. That if it talked to her like the sky had done to him, then something terrible would happen, and if the water failed her, after she'd trusted it the way he'd trusted the sky, the world would change too much and her life would be like his, with nothing to look at and nothing to trust. And where do you look if you can't turn to the sky or the water?

As her feet lost the ground beneath and she started to fall, She kept pulling the water close, her arms like a butterfly's wings, opening and closing. Her eyes, which had been shut when she entered, adjusted to the darkness with a little help from the thin glimmers of light coming in from the moon. She was sinking. Falling under the surface, with

THE ONES WE LOVED

no fight, and no panic. Her eyes recognized life in this new environment: a pair of shorts floating, a large pot lying on the bottom farther down, a blunt knife, a tossed bottle. This town was also here. Had the water taken the shorts off a careless swimmer? More likely one of the women lost the pair while she washed. Letting her mind flow to Waterfall, She wondered what parts of the town also moved below the surface. There could be tools used on the farms. Leftover bricks from a house. A uniform with a leaf on the pocket. A bullet. She knew there were at least three of those, and before she could think of more, She saw a hand.

Her own were still moving, bringing the water into her chest. Who owned that other hand? Her heart was beating, slower than before, and tiny bubbles were coming out of her mouth. The hand drew near, and she stayed because she didn't want to lose all that she had collected against her chest. Then She saw the face of the boy from the bus. The one who came into the restaurant every day since she arrived, and sat quiet. The one she would see walking alone in the morning, and alone again in the evenings.

The girl wondered if the boy had heard the water crying out and left the bank to join her in this town with the shorts floating by, the pot at the bottom and the bottle. He could swim. She saw it in the way his feet pumped up and down like a strange walk, and how he spun his body so that instead of sinking upright, as she was, he was now on his back, almost as if he was resting. He let his arms fall open, and She wanted to reach out, but the weeping water was still pressed tightly into her chest. He turned his head to look at her, and when she opened her mouth to speak and ask what he was doing in this town, he quickly twisted his body and drew close.

She didn't scream when the water entered her mouth and her chest started to tighten. Her neck seemed to grow smaller, and the light started to disappear around the things her eyes could see. Just as she

143

closed her lips, he moved directly in front of her sight and pulled her into his arms. She felt his heartbeat slowing, and his hands on her back were soft, sturdy.

The water can't take her, he told himself. Too much had already gone, and though he didn't know her deep enough to grieve, and neither did they have weeks and months of shared experiences that would leave him regretful, the boy had already done a thing that was too deliberate to be treated lightly—he had seen the girl. So he would recognize the missing space. He would look at the town—the restaurant she served at, the street she walked down and back at that seat on the bus they had taken together—and know that she would not take another bus ride back or away from any place. And he would have something else to miss that had been taken because he had known a thing about its life. Known that she went into the water, arms open and closing, simply known, and hadn't lent a hand. One person had enough hands to do what a town was too busy moving to do. A place distracted by responsibilities that are passed from farm to farm, that are slid under doors and mumbled, spoken but unheard, so someone can say they told but no one can be blamed for not listening. Too busy working, sitting, thinking—a town couldn't look and lend a hand.

He was holding her up, lifting them both, his feet separating water. As they floated to the surface, She saw just how far her body had traveled. Who would have come to find her except for Gogo J.? And the old lady did not know how much she liked to visit the river. No one would come. Would he stay even if they never spoke a word? She wondered if people stayed and loved easier without words, letting their memories mold their actions. So that even if there was no talk of love, a meal shared meant love was felt and held. A chosen tree meant a home was built and love was held. A crowd of people giving food and an escape showed love was known and cherished.

This was the first time they touched. The first time He noticed her

THE ONES WE LOVED

as though he had been looking to find her face. When She looked at him now, under the folds and insides of the weeping water, he didn't turn away like he had when he came into the restaurant or when their eyes crossed in town. It was in the water that the boy from the bus came and introduced himself.

If somehow they rose to the surface—She without ever taking her hands off her chest where the water lay, and He without loosening his hold—then he would hear the words she spoke that were swallowed by the water. Those that got stuck in the bubbles coming out of her mouth and which felt like the words of someone who had left Waterfall without a beginning but thought about making one here.

21.

His friends were sitting closely when He arrived, heads bowed, ankles and thighs tangled. Kind Eyes whispered something to Blink and Miss and both laughed, leaning into each other.

"How long have you two been sitting here on the first good planting day we have had in weeks?" He scolded playfully, throwing himself next to them.

"It's not raining!" shouted Kind Eyes.

"The sky is clear blue and there are no clouds for kilometers!" added Blink and Miss, his eyes moving slowly while reviving and slapping his limbs into action.

The boys spoke quickly and nervously, almost bashful as they tended to do when He found them talking closely.

"I know all these things already. I was out in the farms doing what you both wasted away the day not doing." Secretly, He was always happy when he saw his two friends together.

Even though they never told him, He knew they had something that he didn't share with either of them. When he came to live with his grandparents, it was these two boys, always walking barely one foot ahead of the other, who had come by his house and asked if he

147

wanted to go play by the river. It had been the three of them after that. But always the two of them since before him.

"Did everyone leave at the same time today?" asked Blink and Miss.

"No one wanted to leave early. We don't know when we are going to have such a day again."

He reached for a few strands of tall grass and started weaving. One at the top, another at the bottom and twisting them at the ends.

"So people probably noticed that we were not there," Blink and Miss said, looking at Kind Eyes.

"I would think they had their eyes on tilling the ground and not searching for two layabouts," Kind Eyes answered, smiling at Blink and Miss. "No one even thought of us."

They stayed quiet, each thinking of the same thing in a different way. He had lived here long enough and his two friends all their lives, so they all knew what the people were like. None had ever violently scorned He's two friends, and their neighbors treated them as if the two boys were older and needed to be shown the type of respect worthy of elders. His mother had also been different, and while she had been met with hesitation, Blink and Miss and Kind Eyes were greeted with care. Like something delicate that could be broken without gentle handling. An ant's mud home climbing up a tree, fragile.

Yet it was not quite enough for the two boys to move with the same freedom of others who knew love, especially for Blink and Miss. People accepted them from boyhood, and still Blink and Miss was mistrusting.

Kind Eyes, the older of the boys by a few months, didn't think badly of the townspeople. For him, it was a blessing living in a place where his face was not stamped into the ground, because he had realized quite early that, although his neighbors understood him, there were other towns where the two of them would be broken—he could

148

THE ONES WE LOVED

tell that from the way the landowners looked when they came to the farms and saw him talking to Blink and Miss.

"We are safe here," Kind Eyes would tell Blink and Miss, who, once in a while, would bring up the possibility of leaving. "They know us. They care about us."

"They treat us like we are not like them," Blink and Miss once said.

"We are not," Kind Eyes answered, and Blink and Miss had shaken his head.

"If they do not see us as being like them, they will not protect us like family," Blink and Miss said, his eyes begging Kind Eyes to understand. "They will cry for us, even feel our fear, but they will not balance their lives next to ours when the time comes."

"They care for us," Kind Eyes had repeated.

"They will not protect us," Blink and Miss answered again.

Their friend didn't know how much they wrestled with the idea of leaving, and neither of them thought to ask him what he knew of the towns on the other side of their home.

"How many rows did you finish?" asked Kind Eyes, breaking the silence and taking his hand from Blink and Miss's arm, which he had been gently cradling.

"Enough for all three of us to not go hungry!" said He with a big smile breaking open his ordinarily reserved face, while also holding out a tiny box he had made from the grass.

"At least tell me you planted more than potatoes to put in that little box?" asked Blink and Miss.

"We cannot just live on those alone," Kind Eyes added, looking at He from the corner of his eyes and waiting for the inevitable defense.

"I do not understand you two!" shouted He as he leaned in to make a point. "Potatoes are the most perfect food anyone can eat!"

"Perfect . . . ?" asked Kind Eyes dubiously.

"They can be toasted over the fire, baked slowly over hot coals

149

underground, added to stews and maybe, even though I haven't tried it yet, eaten without cooking them at all," He said, adding a hand-clapping finish to his feverish defense.

"Without cooking?!" responded his two friends in unison before folding in half. Their laughs could be heard moving through the breeze, it, too, eavesdropping on this moment of leisure. Something in the day seemed to exhale gratefully, better off now that the three were together.

"Well. Why haven't you tried eating them just like that, then?" said Kind Eyes.

"I have. With butter."

"No, you strange boy, he means not cooked," said Blink and Miss, still chuckling and wiping tears from his eyes.

He pondered for a beat before barreling on. "I have been too busy planting because my friends always let me do all the work!"

At that, the laughter that had slowly subsided erupted, and it was a good while before any of them could speak without cracking up at the sight of someone else's scrunched up face.

"When you really think about it," He said after collecting himself, "potatoes are the only things you can smother in soup and they will not become too wet, or difficult to eat. They would be perfect."

"You are going to go to your grave believing this, aren't you?" said Blink and Miss.

"Until you prove me wrong," said He with the confidence of a reverend.

"I cannot wait to hear you tell the woman you love that all you eat is potatoes," said Kind Eyes, his eyes twinkling at the thought.

"Not all I eat. It's the best thing that I eat," said He, laying proper emphasis where necessary. He lifted himself up to see if there were reeds in front of him that he could take home and use to make a mat for their entryway. It was dampening easily when it rained, and he needed something to take some of the water.

THE ONES WE LOVED

"We will come with you tomorrow," said Blink and Miss, "to stop you from filling our section with just potatoes. We also need vegetables."

"We can take some from Godknows's mother," He said. "Her harvests are always strong."

"It's because her side of the farms has better soil," said Blink and Miss enviously. "The trees for shade but not too much, and enough room among the leaves for the sun to come through and lightly touch the roots." His voice had mellowed, which it did when talking about farms and plant life. His friends shared a look and wriggled their brows.

"Do you think she minds that we take her vegetables sometimes?" asked Kind Eyes nervously. "She knows it's us because you're always looking at her harvest like you're in love," he said to Blink and Miss playfully.

"I don't know how she gets them so big!" said Blink and Miss, his voice dancing with appreciation. "After this season ends, I'm certain one of her leaves will be large enough to fit the hands of two men."

"Maybe the sky talks to her and no one else," He said with longing, looking at his friends, who waited for a beat. He fidgeted with the woven grass in his hand.

"It finally stopped raining," said Kind Eyes helpfully, squeezing He's shoulder. "I think your voice in the sky is listening."

Blink and Miss nodded while He let his eyes wander to a cloud in the sky that looked like an upside-down gourd.

"It did stop," He answered in agreement, taking the words one by one, and letting them become part of his day.

"Did you thank the sky?" asked Blink and Miss, who took his friend's beliefs in parts, but held on to the pieces strongly. Blink and Miss didn't talk to the sky, but his heart was grateful whenever the land and the skies softened for the town.

151

"I'll do that now," answered He, moved by his friends and how they listened. A part of him also worried because he had not seen the absence of rain as an ask fulfilled. He hadn't noticed what his friends understood so effortlessly, and he felt strange because of it. He always thought he wasn't hearing the sky, but could it be that he wasn't looking correctly? His mind tried to grab hold of this unexpected thought, but it slipped away.

I won't forget to thank you, He promised to himself.

As the sun sank behind them and the night's sounds closed in on the boys, they nestled into the dark, safe and not ready to break the spell that had given them an easy kind of afternoon. When light crept back around tomorrow, it would find them as they had been the day before: one dreaming alone and two whispering words unheard but whose bits carried through the still air as hushed promises, quieted fears and stolen kisses.

22.

Joy woke up and immediately knew. Her body wasn't ready and her head was being pulled down by something far more leaden than sleep and bad dreams. She should have stayed in bed, but her legs were used to this routine of walking forward, while her mind wanted to recede further into her head and become less. So, like she had done before, as her mind shut off the morning—the smell of her mother's porridge, the sound of her father's shoes hitting the floor as he pulled them from the ledge where they hung, the acrid taste of last night's dinner in her mouth, which she hadn't cleaned with water and her chewing stick—her body reached for everything she would need for the day.

She knew not to bathe because tears would start to run once her body was submerged in the tub. Nothing had happened. Nothing terrible ever happened, and yet when she woke feeling as she did, Joy couldn't help but think that something had been done to her, and she just didn't remember. She reached for her shirt and pulled her arms through the sleeves, shivering when it brushed against her chest. The previous night her mother's church friends had made a joke about how well she'd be able to feed her own children because her chest was growing to be just as big as her mother's. While the women laughed,

153

and her mother shot her several glances in quick succession with a nervous smile on her face, Joy had felt her mind start to deaden. Like it was moving further into its shell for protection, a snail or a tortoise sensing danger and looking for comfort.

The church women meant to praise, and yet Joy always found herself feeling watched and studied. Pulling her skirt over her legs and feeling it brush against her hips, closer than it had last year and the year before, she felt her chest contract. She had tried to eat less so she could be smaller. When her clothes started to hang off her body like pieces of fabric tossed on thin branches, Joy had thought people would stop talking and forget she was there. But they spoke and advised her to eat more because a woman needed to have enough of a body to properly carry a child and balance a pot on their head. Joy didn't want a body that changed so it could do what women were supposed to. She just wanted one that she could understand.

"Joy, are you awake?" she heard her mother call out.

She clenched her jaw and let out a dry breath. The first sound was low and felt like the beginning of a tearful response, and so she paused, gathered her voice and tried again.

"Yes. I'm awake."

She hoped her mother hadn't noticed anything different in her tone.

"Come and eat before your porridge gets cold."

Joy looked at her bed, where the wrinkled blankets were piled to one side. She wondered if that was the cause of her heavy mind. Could it be that as she slept, something would creep inside, first on the top blanket, which was thick and red, then make its way under to the second, which was thinner and light blue, into her clothes and stick to her brain? She began to talk, asking and answering questions like there were several people in the room and each one was telling her something funny or bringing back a memory sweetened by age.

THE ONES WE LOVED

Do you remember that time we laughed so much we almost choked?

I think I started crying because my ribs were in so much pain.

We should tell Reverend Mr. Shoko our idea for a new lesson.

The one where we just tell stories about our families?

Yes. I think we all know each other, but there's also so much from our homes that we don't bring to class.

You can wear your jersey over the shirt if you don't want to close all the buttons.

Just close those at the top.

You should try wearing pants.

Only the boys are allowed.

How many chicken wings did you eat three days ago?

Mrs. Maynard was looking at you oddly. She probably knows something that the others haven't seen.

No, she doesn't, she looks at everyone that way. As though she's never seen anything stranger than the thing in front of her face.

Someone is watching you.

Where?

Behind the wall.

The conversations circled different days and years, and the people Joy talked to were those she knew, and many she did not. Sometimes she felt guilty for creating newer faces and closer relationships with people who didn't exist. It made her feel ungrateful for the life she had and undeserving of the friendships that sustained her body. She made an effort to talk to these imagined voices less and less, but when her mind felt as it did today, Joy leaned on them, hoping that if she pushed hard enough, her thoughts would take her to that place behind the wall so she could become like the voices, only coming when called on, and never return to Waterfall. Praying had not made any change. Neither had talking. Her mother once told her that when she was a baby, she could speak words sooner than

155

any other child her age in the town. It was as if she couldn't wait to be heard.

All that rushing, and Joy didn't know how to be understood. *What a loss*, she thought ruefully, looking down at her uniform that stretched and bulged in all the wrong parts. Her stomach began to turn, so she sat down, crossing her legs into a half-formed figure eight and laying her forehead on the cool floor. The skirt would wrinkle and the shirt buttons would come undone where her chest squeezed through. Her brain pushed against her skull, clogged up like a too-small rag cleaning up a too-large mess. There were many things to keep contained, and one would have to be left unattended. Would it be her body or her mind?

With her forehead pressed against the floor, Joy felt her mother's footsteps through the wood. There would be fear and questions if she found her in this state. She was going to be late for school. Something had to be left unattended.

Her mind or her body?

23.

"I would have brought some food to your house," She said, putting a plate in front of him and wiping his forehead, which was speckled with dust and wood chips.

"I was already on my way here," He said between mouthfuls of rabbit. The first bites were fast; he shoved the food in his mouth like he did every time he came, eating as though someone was behind him, ready to pick up what he could not finish. She shook her head, astonished that he never choked. When the first pangs of hunger had been dealt with, he looked up and smiled. "I also wanted to see you."

"You're lucky it was slow today and it was only me working."

He knew what she meant.

"I wouldn't have been able to see you if it had been busy," She said.

"And the old lady wouldn't have let you give me any food," He added.

She sat down on the floor next to him. They were sitting in her upstairs room, close together beside the bed and blue bucket. Their legs were bent at the knees so they could both fit, and she leaned forward so she could look into his face.

"Gogo J. wouldn't have been happy about it, but she would have passed me a plate for you eventually."

"No, she wouldn't," he replied. "That woman hates me and I have no idea why. It's as if she has already made up her mind about who I am even though we have never talked or had time for any disagreement to start between us."

She started chewing her tongue and looked away. Gogo J. didn't like him, and He was right, there was no reason for it. Since the day he had come into the restaurant, he'd always stayed to himself and made no trouble. That first time she caught sight of him, he later told her, had been his third time at that table. Yet she had not noticed, and neither had Gogo J., who never missed anything. That's how little he let his presence be known and how easily he could hide in the open. The fifth time he came, she walked over and asked if he wanted anything. He had said no, but his cracked lips and the loose pants that hung off his body told her that he was starving. And so she had wrapped up a plate, and before he left, pressed it into his hands.

"Make sure you bring it back cleaned," she had said as she walked away.

After that day under the water, when they became closer than passersby but were still timid like children, He had asked her why she talked to him, wanted to know what made her do the thing he'd been wanting to do the four times he had come into Gogo J.'s.

"The food is great, but I kept coming in so I could talk to you," he had told her.

"You were looking out the window," she answered, confused.

"Yes, because I was trying to think about what I could say, but the hunger kept distracting me."

The honesty had made her laugh. "Well then it's good for your stomach that I approached you."

"Yes, it is. I probably would have fainted from not eating and then never got the chance to hear your voice." She had laughed again.

"I think you should talk to Gogo J. more," She told him now. "Let her see you, and don't skulk in the corner waiting for me."

"I don't have to prove anything to her," He said defensively.

"What do you mean *prove*? This is not an examination. You're just letting her know who you are. It's not as if she will hurt you."

He kept eating and said nothing, and she knew he was retreating into the place she had felt him returning to a few times.

"What do you think of the rabbit?" she asked, pulling him back.

"It's really good. Might even be better than Gogo J.'s," he said, taking a piece from his plate and putting it in her mouth.

"Don't say that!" she said and looked around quickly to make sure no one had heard. "Gogo J. makes the best food in this whole town. That is the only thing you are ever allowed to say," she added playfully.

When he was finished, she took his plate downstairs and he cleaned everything she had used to cook so the old lady wouldn't know that someone had been walking around her special place.

"Do you want to go down to the river?" he asked her.

"Yes!" she answered excitedly. "I was on my way there before you came by."

She looked around and made sure everything was properly put away before closing the restaurant door behind her and dropping the key in a wooden block under the veranda. She had started her work in the afternoon as usual, but it had been slow, and when Gogo J. set out for home, she told She to close up in an hour if more people didn't come. He had walked in right after.

"What exactly is someone going to steal if they break into the restaurant?" He asked curiously, grabbing her hand as they walked in the middle of the street.

"The hot sauce," She replied without hesitation, her laugh starting before the sentence was out of her mouth and drawing one out of him as well—his reserved and more noticeable from the creases around

159

his eyes; hers unrestrained and full, tears shining in the corners of her faint-red eyes.

It was night but not too late that everyone was inside. Some were sitting next to their homes playing a game of chance and money, a few called out to each from their windows, holding entire conversations this way. And some were on their way home after a day out hunting or farming. In this town, the boys and men hunted and the women went to the fields. The tillers came back earlier to set up the dinner meals, so when the hunters returned, the food was prepared and space was ready in their kitchen for whatever catches fell in their traps. Because He went to the fields, he always came back early with the women.

He had been able to find somewhere to sleep, a room smaller than She's in a house belonging to one of the hunters. It was in the back, next to where they kept all the dried meat, so he went to sleep with delicious smells in his nose and woke up to the sounds of the hunter's three children screeching through the house, while their mother tried to get them ready for the day. In exchange for the room, He took to fixing the family's roof, which had small holes that let in too much wind—often the youngest child would wake his mother at night because the oldest had rolled up the blanket in his fists and under his body to trap the warmth, while unwittingly keeping the same from his brothers. She had come by several times and thought the family was good for him.

"I like that you're with people," She had said. "This way you have to talk to them."

As they headed for the river, he saw some of the men looking at her before turning their attention away. She had changed since she first arrived. That look from the bus was still in her eyes, but the winds that announced her arrival in any room or past a street were no longer frantic. Her body had concealed what ailed, and the people around

THE ONES WE LOVED

her were no longer inclined to sidestep out of her way because she wouldn't change course and instead chose to run into people rather than make her feet pivot. She met eyes now, paid attention to bodies and once again mirrored behaviors as people in a community were raised to do, returning smiles when offered, receiving greetings and understanding that streets were used by others and were not simply where she walked alone with her winds and stuck feet.

She knew the men were looking at her differently, but what she really cared to notice was how the women looked at He. As they had left the restaurant, she saw them fixing up their dresses before he walked by and changing the tone of their voices so that when they called out from the windows, their voices didn't sound shrill and intrusive but had the timbre of good virtue. Calling out in voices that knew what they wanted, how to claim it by name and what to do once it was in hand. Looking at him when he reached for her arm, She knew the boy had grown less restrained since she first saw him looking through the window at Gogo J.'s. The girl momentarily sifted through her words because something didn't feel right, and she wanted to be precise when thinking about him. You couldn't grow while still being less, she thought, so what was the difference in him? She decided that He had become someone that could be reached. A person who could hold a word and keep a trust. Who now moved like someone you wanted to walk alongside and listen to. Even while his face could change from all the lives of the people who lived in him.

A stranger seeing them walk together would have thought they had known each other from their youngest years, not pulled each other from drowning.

"I still don't understand how it is that you can't swim," he said to her after they reached the river. She flopped onto the ground, and he took off his shirt before joining her, sitting face-to-face. They were silent for a short time, She watching the moonlight make little windows on

161

the water that tilted and curved as the current hurried on, He looking at the black dot on her cheek and wondering if there were more anywhere else on her skin. He was trying to know her and remember her at the same time.

"There was just never an opportunity for me to learn," she said, gently resting her hand on his chest and feeling his heartbeat through her fingers. It had filled out since she first saw him hungry, and with working in the fields, his body had sculpted itself into one that she nervously longed to touch. She was careful when she held him, not wanting to reach too far that he would shrink from her hands. And still remembering the lessons from a past when her body was meant to show nothing of the world's effects. No sweating, no pain, no rage. And nothing like this feeling pounding in her fingertips and the bottom of her stomach.

He saw her eyes move over him and felt his breath quicken while his heart slowed. She seemed to be looking beyond the face he was wearing to one he didn't quite know how to put on without being embarrassed. He wanted to touch not just her hands and face, but everywhere that would make her keep looking at him as she was.

"But I thought you said you grew up around lots of green? So there had to have been a river nearby."

She winced when he brought up her home and tried to think of what she had said in that weak moment she had described Waterfall.

"There was a river, but it wasn't one you could swim in. It thought too much of itself."

"In what way?"

"Sometimes it would be really calm and you could almost fall asleep just looking at it. Then other times it just turned into a storm on the ground, breaking everything that came close. So it wasn't something to know well. You saw it and then turned to admire something else because it could change and become something hard to deal with.

THE ONES WE LOVED

And it was too big to not know how to deal with, so I just stopped seeing it. It was there and so was I, and that was fine."

"What did you spend your time doing if you weren't looking at your biggest thing?" he asked, letting his hand rest on her shoulder, careful not to grasp as he waited for this answer. He needed to know what else she looked to.

"Not that much. The same as you," she said evasively and hoped her smile would hide the fact that she didn't want to keep answering questions about home.

"So you also spent your time in the fields," He said with amusement.

"No, no, not the fields. I walked around. I went to see my neighbors and that was really all we spent most of our time doing."

"Who else were you with?"

"What?"

"You said, we."

"Oh." She was silent for a second. "My friends. There were two of them."

"Are they still there?"

"Yes, they are."

"When you left them behind, did they forgive you?"

She looked him directly in the eyes because that was such a strange question, and she wanted to know which face he was wearing when he had asked.

"What do you mean?"

"I mean were they fine with you leaving," he said, looking away and removing his hand from her shoulder.

He was retreating again.

"Yes, they understood," she said, her nails leaving tiny scythe-like prints on her wrist.

"Good."

They were sitting closely enough to feel the other's breath on an

163

arm, but something had forced its way between them, and now they were mute, half-formed sentences fading around and between the new and old lives they were trying to make. She felt her eyes start to itch and immediately raised her open hands up to her face. It was a familiar pose that she'd often done to appear prayerful whenever Reverend Mr. Shoko had told them to bow their heads. At this moment, she thought only of the red flashes in Gogo J.'s garden.

"Do you want me to teach you how to swim?"

She shut her eyes tight, imagining the stinging, and shivered, her body expelling something from her bones.

"It won't be hard, you'll be safe." He didn't think she'd heard him.

"Teach me!" she said suddenly, leaping up.

"Are you sure?"

"Yes! Will I just sink?" There seemed to be a wish in her voice as she asked, recalling her last time underwater.

"No, if you're calm, your body will naturally keep you up."

She stripped down, removing her skirt and blouse and leaving the thin slip she had on underneath.

"Come!" she said and ran to the water. Not looking back, She felt her feet slide over the stones, before the ground disappeared and the sky started to ripple. She waited to feel his arms pulling her up, while hoping something stronger would drag her down. She didn't want to bring any ghosts back to Gogo J.'s. They yanked at her hair, her legs, her dress, her feet. She needed to leave them behind, and if they took her, too, then there would be no need for all this cleansing. This life would be off her body, and she could step into another one with more happiness and more chances.

As he followed, he realized this was the first time he had ever really seen her body, without having to feel it through her clothes like he did when they held each other on her bed. What an odd moment to feel so close, surrounded by water that kept them apart, pushing him into

THE ONES WE LOVED

the current and her towards the bank. The water was cold on his skin as it clung to the pants he kept on. Her braided hair floated on the surface. She wasn't too far down. He grabbed her outstretched hands and watched as she rose and took in air, slowly opening her eyes.

"Put your arms around me and hold on," he instructed after she'd caught her breath. "Make sure to kick your legs so that if I let go, you will keep moving."

"Don't. Don't let go," she whispered, pulling his face close.

"I won't let go. Today we will just float," he said, smiling while kissing her forehead.

"Don't ever let go." He gently kissed her lips and breathed her in.

"I won't."

"Do you swear?"

"I swear."

24.

She heard him while He moved. It was not yet early enough for the town's children to be screaming their greetings and racing to the river, and the only other person awake would be Gogo J. He stepped around the room slowly, believing her to be asleep. He'd whispered her name when he awoke, and she'd felt his head rise from its place next to her own and look at her face where her eyelids stayed closed. Yet she'd been awake for almost two hours.

While He slept, She removed her arm from the place it had rested on his chest and let it float above his face, grazing the cheeks that made him look so young when he laughed because they turned round and bright. She put to memory the shape of his lips that turned into an easy curve when he happened to look her way. She studied his eyes that fluttered now and then. And the long nose that had a slight cut on the bridge, which she'd missed on those days they'd sat and talked and only saw for the first time when he'd bent his head to drop a kiss on her stomach.

The day before, She had been in her body. Last night was the first time she had been with someone who'd seen her naked, felt the hairs under her arms, on her nipples and between her legs. The room upstairs had been dark when they climbed into her bed. As their eyes adjusted to the low light, their touching felt secret and private, even to her feelings of doubt. What they had done was nothing she had learned in school, but it unexpectedly reminded her of moments from home. Of the hurried, whispered conversations among the church women that they addressed in head nods and quick glances. Whenever the women would come to the house for their weekly bible study, She learned not only about faith and Mary, or forgiveness and Job, but of the pain that came from having children. While they ate what Mama prepared, she learned not about a pain of the mind, but the body.

At these weekly meetings, she heard of the times when the women went to bed tired and woke up sore after the night, as if rest had not been enough for their needs. Some would suggest moving slower while in bed, and others recommended rubbing a warm cloth over the places that hurt. She had told Kuda and Joy about these discussions, and her friends had listened with fearful interest. What were the women doing in bed that had to be done slowly, and still caused pain? Now she wished she could tell them about what the women had talked around and over. There was no pain when he touched her breasts, kissed her neck, moved her thighs with his legs and gently held her arms over her head. She was happier than she could have imagined was possible after becoming a person without a home or a beginning. But a surge of embarrassment followed her ecstasy when she realized she would have to face him in the morning.

She had been listening to him pour some water into the bucket pushed in a corner. It was cold, and He let out a small gasp as he lowered his feet inside. He bathed quickly, and while his hands slapped against his skin, she stifled the urge to get up, grab them and pull them back into the bed that now smelled of him. From the small ledge, He took her soap, made by the women in this town, who would mix ground pine leaves and oil until hardened. In Waterfall the soap

168

had been black and made by Joy's mother, who never told the steps she took so the bars were ready every two weeks, wrapped in brown paper and smelling like rain. She rolled over, leaving the memory on the other side of her back.

He was now drying himself, and some of the water fell on the bed and dampened her toes under the thin blanket. She stayed still and listened while he opened the jar of oil that Gogo J. had given her and rubbed it on his body, moving from his legs, which he placed on the bed for balance, to his arms and then to his face. She smiled; he went from the bottom up, and she started the opposite way. He stood next to the bed before sitting down and running his fingers through her hair, where the thick braids had come undone. She held her breath and closed her eyes tighter. What would she say if she opened them? She knew she looked unkempt. And that her breath smelled like yesterday had rolled into the weekend. He leaned close and pressed his lips against her forehead. "I know you're awake," He whispered. "I'll see you in the evening." She tried to stamp it down but failed, and the laugh came out short and too loud in the room's quiet. She pulled the blanket over her head, and he pinched her legs, chuckling.

"How did you know?" She asked, her voice only slightly muffled.

"I know how you breathe now," he said, and the door closed just as she came out of hiding.

That was the change she couldn't explain. He knew how she sounded when she was filled with prickling energy, when she was struggling to keep her composure with each rising impulse and clenching her teeth so her voice wouldn't come out as a moan that shocked and thrilled her ears.

She pulled her knees against her chest and slid her hands under her feet, smiling as she remembered the night. He knew how she breathed.

25.

"WHERE DO YOU want me to put this shoe?" She asked, holding up a work boot that was coming undone at the bottom, held together by mounds of mud and a bit of the sole that hadn't weathered.

"Leave it by the window. Whoever needs it will walk by this way and see it waiting for him," said Gogo J. with the measured coolness of someone used to collecting belongings left in her restaurant that were personal and foreign—a pair of socks with fine threads on the heel spelling out the name of a child, a lover or a parent (who else would we want stitched to our everyday?), belts with man-made holes that signaled a changing body, a shirt with a faded bloodstain on the back (maybe left desperately or violently), a piece of paper with a scribbled message.

"How do you forget your shoe?" She asked incredulously. "I would think you would feel something missing as you walked out and one of your feet was touching the ground while the other was laced up."

"Girl, looking at those shoes, his feet were barely covered up. Probably thought it was just wearing even thinner than usual. He'll be back for it."

"Which one do you think it was?" she asked, leaning over a table and bringing her voice down so they could indulge in their favorite pastime: talking about the men who ate in the restaurant.

"It was definitely the one who passed me his handkerchief that he thought was a dollar bill."

They both laughed, remembering the particular guest who had come in several times before and whose name they never kept.

She and Gogo J. were cleaning up after another busy day, and tonight one of the guests had brought a new card game that none of the men had ever seen. He had spent the service teaching the others, probably cheating, too, while money changed hands and others resorted to betting their rabbit stews to win a hand. She was walking slower than usual, taking her time with each table and looking over at Gogo J., who was tallying the night's money. Every few minutes, the old woman would get up to move a chair, checking the tables She had just cleaned to make sure they suited her expectations.

"Does he live around here?" asked She.

"No. I do see him coming in and out of Mave's yard whenever he comes into town."

"So he helps her and her husband with work?"

"I don't think so."

"So what is he doing coming out of Mave's yard?" she asked, sure there was something left out of the story.

Gogo J. gave her a look that pitied her naivete and age, then moved her hands for emphasis. "Her yard is in the front of the house. Whenever I see him, he is arriving and leaving from the back." The old woman stared hard and waited.

It took She a breath to understand, and when the answer finally broke, Gogo J. rolled her eyes and giggled like a girl.

"Are you saying she is with him while her husband is out hunting?" asked She in disbelief.

THE ONES WE LOVED

"Absolutely. Although I don't understand her reasons. That man is as dull as tree bark is gray."

"Maybe they just sit and talk. Like friends. You can't know for sure what Mave is doing with him."

"Is that what you and that boy do every time you sneak off to the river? Sit and talk like friends?" Gogo J. asked pointedly, hand on her waist, another sitting in the air as if holding up the question for gaping ears.

She brought her eyes down and felt her face warming, sweat rapidly building at the edges of her hair. She looked closer at the table she was cleaning and rubbed at a stain that wasn't there.

"So, that's how I know they are not just friends," Gogo J. said, before turning her attention back to her money.

When He had brought up the idea of leaving while they slept in her room, She had immediately said yes, and while she didn't regret the choice, she did regret how she had so easily forgotten the presence of Gogo J. in her life. The one who had let her in when there was nowhere for her to go and who had made it easier for her to move.

Glancing in her direction, the girl knew she was going to miss this woman. During the early mornings as they made plans, She had told him there was nothing here to claim her attention, but looking at Gogo J., she knew how untrue that statement had been.

They would be leaving at the end of this season, and that was only three weeks close now. It was probably best that they do it silently. She wanted to savor these last days without worrying about what the woman thought of her decision and with no conflicts about his role in her life. Gogo J. still didn't like He, and although She had tried to force them both to talk, even took a long time cleaning just so they would have to be in the same place, it hadn't worked.

I wish I could understand what they didn't see in each other, she thought.

He always said he didn't know, and Gogo J. only shook her head and said he was no good for her life.

She knew he would stay if she told him that this town had become a root. But she wasn't sure that telling him would ever feel like anything more than a conversation that began with before and petered away with now—an unfinished thought trailing a split life. Somehow this town still seemed to be asking of her past: the children she saw plotting their hours in groups of six would become three in her mind, their unbuttoned clothes turning into uniforms if the wind happened to blow a certain way or if her eyes saw wrong and the light turned a hand-wrung blue shirt to black. Black like nighttime, but not the one that moved into tomorrow unguarded and generous. Each time the bus came, She worried that feet would disembark carrying a face she knew with news of a burning town and eyes that named her as the cause. Not of the town burning, but the feet landing here.

So when he asked, "Would you leave?" she said yes. Not knowing if he meant it with urgency or curiosity. Because he made her past yesterday and the day after, and also that day at the water. She understood her life in his eyes. Liked how it looked and appreciated that he remembered it. And it could have been the swiftness of her answer that made their leaving an action, not a moment in conversation.

"Where's your mind at?" asked Gogo J., looking at her thoughtfully.

"I am just thinking about what you said about the man, and the bark."

"And?"

"The tree bark isn't always that way, you know? When the tree grows in age, the colors underneath the bark shift. It goes from green to purple and sometimes even black. Over time, I think the changes in weather also affect how it looks."

"So are you saying that man is as color-filled as the tallest trees?"

"No." She laughed. "I think he might be dull, but he also could be a

THE ONES WE LOVED

lot of things that he can't show because the geography is not right for all his colors."

"What do you mean geography?" Gogo J. asked casually, although her brain was clamoring to know how the neighbors' wide bed had become a forest changing its appearance.

She's words stalled, then her will disappeared. "Nothing. I never make much sense this late in the night." She smiled weakly, resting her fingers against her eyes. The stinging and burning was not as painful. She would need to go back outside.

"What he is, is a man who spends time with a woman that placed her peace in the hands of another. There is nothing else to it except deceit and, very soon, disappointment."

She wanted to pull her tongue out of her body. This is why the girl couldn't have it be silent. When it was quiet, she spoke without care, crowding the space with phrases whose meaning revealed more than she wanted.

"I'm not saying Mave is right," the girl offered.

"And I'm not saying she's wrong. Not in the way that causes a scandal. But because she didn't find what she needed in one person, she went to someone else. And she'll keep doing it until she accepts that just because people are what we have, it doesn't mean they are what we need to understand how we live. Many times, all we need to do is to hear ourselves. Step out of our body and look at this thing we have taken with us to every place, pressed against other people and slapped awake. Really look and listen. For us to grow into peace, our bodies and our lives need a quiet mind, not another person."

"And what if the mind fails?" She asked. "People are there for when the mind fails." Her belief in that was unyielding. Like the tombstone she'd heaved from Waterfall, trapped between legs that now moved and eyes that wanted to see farther.

175

Gogo J. looked wary until she understood. Then she was angry, without any of the passion. "I told you to be careful. Now look."

The girl stiffened. The woman knew about the things she put on her hands.

"That boy is not the person for you. But here you are trying to bring him into your story."

The old lady didn't know. The girl relaxed but only for a moment, before standing upright to defend him.

"He is good and kind. Just like you."

"That boy is nothing like me," Gogo J. answered. "I have demanded nothing from you. He has."

"He hasn't asked me to do anything," She replied, her tone rising.

Gogo J. looked at her and waited. The girl was ready to speak but stopped.

She knows I am leaving.

The feeling in the room had changed and both glimpsed the afterlife of lessons learned through experience and forgetting. Only one had lived long enough for memory to become a teacher and not a pitfall. In Gogo J.'s mind, the lightness in She's steps had absolutely nothing to do with meeting He. It was from starting to face whatever it was that had brought her stumbling into her restaurant. And the girl was only just emerging. She needed more time.

"You are getting better," the woman started. "And you need to be here longer to do that. You need to be supported by someone reliable and not someone who is looking for the same thing you are trying to find. You need what I found here. That same freedom," she said under her breath, and She had to lean in to hear. "It's the only way you'll let the demons leave. They won't stay if you can look them in the face, but they will never leave if you move them to the side and place him in the middle."

There was so much about him that Gogo J. didn't understand, and she couldn't say she even tried to see the person that the girl had

THE ONES WE LOVED

fallen to love. Gogo J. saw them when they walked through the street together and knew when She had cooked for him, no matter how well She tried to clean up and make it seem like she hadn't been in the kitchen. She was growing closer and closer to the boy, and there was nothing to be gained.

"He is also a person of the fields," Gogo J. added, her tone turning gentle. "They never know peace. Always working against things larger than their hands and hopes."

"So you don't think he can bring me peace?" The question felt almost like an accusation.

Gogo J. steeled herself, looking at this reflection of her lesser years. The face didn't talk back, and it waited to see if there was more that needed to be uttered. These young lovers had been sitting on her heart, and there was no one else she could talk to. But the old lady knew about this type of love. Once, it had numbed her before she chose to leave it behind and begin again. In this town, Gogo J. was the woman with the restaurant who had somehow always been here, but for the few who could think back, the old lady was as much of a mystery when she arrived as she still was on this night.

"Who are you?" a traveler had asked long back, when the restaurant first opened.

"Have my food and you will know," she answered. The retort had stuck, and now whenever the neighbors talked about Gogo J. or were confused by who she was beyond the woman who cooked, they thought of her food and saw a woman who could make them all feel like someone was listening, knew them before chaos and saw exactly what they craved. The woman understood she could not question the curt answers that came from the boy every time she tried to talk to him. She knew the men also had no luck, because she had heard them talking about how different he was, refusing to hunt and not fully mixing with the others. She understood not wanting people to

177

know your life, but she opened herself up to the town with the ways she fed them. She made sure there was room for people to sit, that they left fuller than when they arrived and came back ready to see her and smell her food. Gogo J. gave something that they could rely on. Looking at that boy, as he was now, she knew there was nothing he could give the young girl that would feed her. Nothing that would be good enough to stay for.

"He needs too much," she said to her reflection. "And he takes from someone who already has too little."

Looking away, She touched her eyes and felt nothing.

Gogo J. let out a long sigh before putting her counted money into the strap of her dress and getting up to wipe the last of the tables. The girl said she saw him on the bus, *but I think he saw her*, the old lady thought to herself. And he followed her because that was what he needed.

"No, I can finish that," said She, after a while.

"I can do the rest. Go in the kitchen and make sure all the pots and pans are in the right place."

She got up and walked slowly to the counter, where she knew everything was as clean as anything that was well used and well kept. Gogo J. wanted to be alone, and as she turned around to tell her how much her time here had eased her life, she caught the woman dabbing her eyes. She looked away and headed to the kitchen.

I already told him yes, She thought. And still, she believed it was the right choice. She would ask him tomorrow if they could go sooner. Start their new life a bit faster.

Looking back at Gogo J., she collected the feelings that were starting to swell and placed them inside the bundled-up cleaning rag. After she built her life with him, she would come back and see her.

26.

"Look at you, peering over my shoulder like a little rabbit!" Mama said, lightly shoving She with her hips.

"I want to see." The girl laughed, dodging her mother, who was moving side to side and thrusting her hips wherever She tried to step and catch a glimpse of what was cooking on the stove. "How will I know what to do if you don't show me?" She whined.

"You are not ready yet," Mama answered, not taking her eyes from the pot.

"Not ready to hear about ingredients?" answered She, throwing her hands in the air dramatically.

Mama turned around and pulled her into a rare hug that lingered as a squeeze.

"You're too impatient, my girl. You need to slow down," Mama said while running a hand through her hair. "I need to redo these braids soon."

She smiled and wriggled out of the grasp, self-consciously patting the braids she had been careful with for a week past their due. They were making chicken feet. Joy's mother had given them to her daughter, who passed them on to She at school. "We have too many chickens now, so we are killing some and giving them away. You know we can't eat them by ourselves," Joy had told her.

Wanting to help, She had cleaned the feet well, peeling off the hard layer of skin that ran along the bone, scratching away the dirt from the fattened middle part with the most meat and plucking off the more resistant feathers missed by Joy's mother. It was a job she disliked, but she hoped that once Mama saw her help without being asked, she would finally teach her the secrets of how to cook different kinds of dishes with the same ingredients and still create flavors that were nothing alike. She knew that a delicious plate depended on the time a pot spent on the stove simmering and the amount of the spices used, whether a full hand or a toss that sent some floating into the air. The water too. A heavy pour would make a sauce that slid from one side of the plate to the other instead of coating the meat and vegetables. But She also needed real directions. The girl wanted to see the exact flip or swing of a wrist so she could make it just as Mama did, not just once, but all the time.

"Come over here," Mama said, pointing with her head to where She was supposed to stand.

Looking at her daughter and then turning back to her onions, Mama started. "It's about time. It's about patience," she said. "It's about trusting that you will never use more than you need and knowing when to give some away."

"Are we still talking about cooking?" She asked, teasing gently.

Mama laughed a little. "It's never just about cooking."

She moved closer and rested her head on Mama's shoulder.

"Did your mother teach you this too?" she asked carefully and held her breath.

"Yes, she did. And her mother taught her and her sisters," Mama answered fast as if her mouth had been waiting for a chance to tell.

She hadn't expected an answer and had readied herself for a diversion. It took her some time to come up with another question.

180

THE ONES WE LOVED

"Did your mother only teach you?" asked She.

Mama nodded. "I was her only daughter and in our family; what happens in the kitchen and what goes into the pots belongs to the women."

"So your father never cooked?" She asked, getting more confident.

Mama giggled like a child.

"My mother would have hidden his hoe somewhere he would never have found it if he ever moved her pots around."

Three things She had learned today. Mama was an only girl just like her. Her grandmother was funny and her grandfather worked in the fields. When she went back to Samson's Cross tomorrow, She would ask Reverend Mr. Shoko if there was something in the bible about chicken feet being blessed. She was about to ask another question, but Mama cut her off before she could continue.

"I think we need more mhiripiri. Can you run outside and pick three for me?"

The moment had passed.

She grabbed a cloth from the sink and stepped outside. It was almost dark, but the glaring red fruit was visible. The cloth was important because once, when she was young, she had touched the fruit to see if the red came off. Mama had then called her into the house for something she now couldn't recall, but She does remember rubbing her eyes and feeling an excruciating burn. She kept on touching them, thinking it was something inside her eyes that was attacking her body. From her screams and sobs, Mama was able to learn that she had touched the fruit and then touched her eyes. Since then, a cloth.

"You know they won't burn your eyes now," Mama told her when She returned. "You know to wash your hands immediately."

"I prefer having it. I am lucky I didn't go blind," She answered seriously, causing Mama to let out a laugh that sounded like a popping tire. Loud and quick.

"You wouldn't have become blind! We would wash your eyes with water like we did then."

"What if that hadn't worked? And there is no hospital near here, so it would have been a disaster," answered She.

"There is a lesson there if you look closely," Mama said.

"What lesson?"

"It wasn't just about the mhiripiri," Mama responded, while washing the fruit.

"That's the lesson?"

"Yes," her mother answered with resolve. "You didn't take the time to think about what would happen if you reached for something you didn't really know. You just touched, and you forgot, until you were in pain." Mama looked at her pointedly.

"I was a child," She answered.

"You weren't ready," Mama said and gave She a searching look.

"Well, now I use a cloth," she said.

"Because you're ready," Mama added.

Moving into the kitchen, She peered over her shoulders again.

"So when do you think I'll be ready to find out what else goes in the food?"

Mama shrugged her shoulders.

"Time will tell me."

"Thankfully, time doesn't have to tell you when to let me eat," She said, already tiptoeing away and ducking before the cloth Mama threw landed at her feet.

27.

He tossed his hoe into the shack and turned towards home. A day passed at the farms, and another day his friends had decided not to come. He thought of going by the water but instead walked towards home, stepping over the dark mounds on the ground. To forget the smell, he thought about the rains tempering their constancy, the thanks he'd given ever since his friends reminded him that the voice in the sky had listened and the food they would have this season. Some would have to be put into jars to stay fresh.

"Can you put potatoes in jars?" he asked the sky before chuckling quietly to himself. His friends would never cease to make fun if he tried. As he walked in the thickening darkness, his steps wavered first, then his mind. What they had done to that poor old man who had the misfortune of walking alone after the counting men tried to clean the alley and only flared up the animosity. Everyone had started walking in pairs and groups just to make it harder for them to be hurt. Walking faster, he kept his eyes alert, straining to see any movements ahead and carefully glancing back. When he arrived back at the house, he would tell his friends that whatever private time they needed to spend as two would have to come once they had been at the fields and returned with him. It scared him to walk alone, although as fearful as he was, He didn't want the remembering and dread to crawl out of his skin and be seen. If the landowners and their children were watching and waiting, He needed them to see him strong. His arms tensed and his feet were prepared to land hits on any place that was soft enough to be bruised and hard enough to make a crack that echoed before he broke into a run back to the farms. No matter what happened, He would never lead them home.

"I know they must be excited," he said, looking at the sky after leaving the alley and feeling his shoulders relax and the strain leave his coiled limbs. It would be a little while before he arrived in Spilling River. Once he was beyond the smell, however, the walk didn't feel treacherous.

"This is the first time they have a home where they can be alone," He continued. "And I know how good that is for them. It's very good."

His friends hadn't said much, but He knew they were worried about what the landowners would say if they saw them arriving and leaving from the same house every day without their parents. Even a house with their friend. But no one had asked. And no one in Spilling River had brought dishes of food for the new family in an old home, making young memories. *Giving food is for families who are arriving from somewhere else, have welcomed a new baby or have pledged themselves to each other*, He told himself. His friends' choices were met with silence not out of disregard but because it was an ordinary way of living. "Celebrating this move would be like noticing the five fingers on a hand."

The landowners rarely came into the town, choosing to make terror in the stretch he'd just exited, but somehow they always knew when things changed. After one of his neighbors died, they had told his family that the portion of land used for their own needs would have to be cut because there was now one less person to be fed. When

THE ONES WE LOVED

his grandparents had died, it was the same. The other day, one of the townspeople had gone to the place with the church and school. The landowners had come to the farms to ask what his business had been in the nearby town.

"I only wanted some seeds," the neighbor had said.

"There are seeds in your town," the landowners responded, while the townspeople stopped their farming and watched. The men from the other town kept counting.

"They have flowers there that we don't have," the neighbor answered, holding his hoe loose so it wouldn't seem to be dangerous, while the landowners swung their guns over their shoulders and between their legs. Seven of them had come to ask about his business. But only one ever spoke, always red-hatted.

"Why would you need flowers?"

The neighbor had waited a minute before answering.

"They were beautiful. The sunflowers. And I wanted to ask if the woman who took care of them would give some to us. They were just beautiful."

Everyone knew the flowers he was talking about. The rows of bright yellow some said could be seen blowing in the wind from seven kilometers away because they were so tall. The ones grown by the woman from elsewhere who knew how to talk to the land like the people in Spilling River.

"Those sunflowers do not belong to the woman. They belong to the landowner's wife," they had said.

The woman had given the man three sunflowers, and he had brought them back and planted them in a tiny clearing in Spilling River where once they grew, the townspeople would see them when coming and going. The landowners had pulled them out of the soil. Knelt in the dirt to take out a gift. And then cut in half the land portion that had taken care of the man, his wife and five children.

185

"This is not like the man who asked for the flowers," he said to the sky, nervously looking up. "There is nothing being done by Kind Eyes or Blink and Miss that is wrong."

With the open road and the birds relaxing into the dusk, it was a night his grandfather would have loved most. As the oldest man in Spilling River, it had been him who clearly remembered the days before the landowners came. Kind Eyes's parents rarely talked about that time, and Blink and Miss's father remembered, too, but he was much younger, and his memories were marked by the feelings of boyhood when everything shone without cause and was solely to be enjoyed. Only He's grandfather had spoken of the nights like this that felt like mornings, when his body would unswaddle and his mind would think of possibilities. Both grandfather and grandson felt awake in the night, and a stillness like this, that disappeared like lightning, was something to stroll into after a day spent shuffling.

When the old man's mind had started to leave, his grandson was relieved. The memories would no longer keep his grandfather company like an unwanted visitor, taking more than what was offered. The boy was also pained because there would be nothing holding his grandfather to this land where his daughter had been born. His grandfather forgot what they lost. And he also forgot whom he loved.

He had died before the attack on the old man in the alley, but he was alive when Kind Eyes and Blink and Miss would come by the home and eat with them. They had made his shoulders shake and the twin grooves in his cheeks deepen with their silly tales about animals whose body parts were those of others. Ants with bat wings. Birds with the legs of a dog. "They wouldn't mind us living in the house together," He said aloud, seeing his grandparents' faces. "All they wanted was for me to have a family. Kind Eyes and Blink and Miss are my family." Breathing deeply, he looked upwards.

"Do you think they are in danger?" He asked the sky.

THE ONES WE LOVED

Waiting for an answer, he saw the faint dot of lights coming from Spilling River.

"Do you think we should leave?" He asked the sky again.

He had been listening so hard, telling his heart to give gratitude while his lips sought guidance, that he missed the shadows on either side of the road. It was the sound of breaking twigs to his left that caused him to spin fast on his toes and see the figure rushing in his direction. He was about to swing a fist before he heard a loud yelp and Kind Eyes's familiar laugh.

"What are you doing here?" He said, almost screaming, his heart thudding against his chest.

His two friends had fallen to the ground, proud of themselves for causing the scare that had made him both deaf and unable to walk. Holding up their hands, they leaned on each other, laughing too much to stand up straight. Soon enough, He started laughing as well, grateful that he was not about to die and grudgingly impressed that his friends had been able to surprise him so easily.

After attempting to catch his breath and failing whenever he looked at his friend, Kind Eyes spoke first, wincing from the laughs that had started to hurt. The boy who had been afraid felt slightly better.

"We planned to meet you when you were returning from the farms," his friend said. "We wanted to say sorry for not coming with you today and also walk with you part of the way home."

Kind Eyes lifted himself from the ground and offered his hand to Blink and Miss, who took it.

"I wish you could see your face. I would stand next to a landowner if that meant you could see your face as we do," said Blink and Miss. "You looked like a monkey caught taking food from a house," his friend said, wheezing and wiping his eyes.

"You can both sleep on the porch tonight," He said, fighting back a smile and walking towards Spilling River.

"But we cooked!" his friends shouted, still laughing. Blink and Miss swung his arm over He's shoulders, and Kind Eyes grabbed the bag.

"You can eat from the porch," He answered, trying to be firm.

The boys walked towards the town, going back and forth about their days, which were not the same, even for the two who had spent it together. Blink and Miss would start, Kind Eyes would continue and add more than was necessary, and He would pull the real events from the two recollections.

"Did you know that Godknows is going to have a child?" Blink and Miss said, relishing the surprise he saw on He's face. This was his favorite leisure: sharing stories of Spilling River when they were still personal realizations, before they became the town's news. Because people always assumed he was sleeping or paying very little attention, they spoke without care around him, his presence never causing them to hesitate but oddly bringing a feeling of comfort. If he could look so serene, the news might not be so hard to tell or receive.

"With whom?" He asked.

Blink and Miss opened up his palms to show he knew nothing else, so Kind Eyes took his turn hopping into the jump rope, skipping between the interest swung by his friend and the revelation whipped up by Blink and Miss.

"I think it's someone from the other town."

"How could that happen? Where would they have met?"

"We live near," Kind Eyes said.

"But we're not close," He answered. "That would just be trouble. And trouble, and trouble and trouble."

Blink and Miss dropped the rope. "There is a baby coming, and I'm sure it's someone we know. We'll find out who it is when we go to the farms and see who is missing. Whoever it is will be home preparing for the child."

188

THE ONES WE LOVED

"Well that's good for Ma Godknows," He shared. "I think she wanted to have someone else to raise in her house."

"It's bad for us," said Kind Eyes seriously. His friends stopped to listen and lend support. Something had made him afraid. "This means she won't be so understanding when we take some vegetables from her side of the garden."

"Go back in the shadows," He replied, squelching a grin while Blink and Miss erupted into swells of chuckles that only grew as they walked. Kind Eyes eyed He slyly, happy to have teased his friend so unexpectedly in one night. Often far and wistful, it was a rare good when He could be made to stay in the present and simply enjoy their living.

"What are we eating tonight?" the boy asked excitedly.

"We made quail with vegetables," Blink and Miss said, with a note of mischief dangling just off the sentence.

"Is there not really any quail?" He asked.

"There is quail. Two actually," answered Kind Eyes.

"Did we borrow the vegetables from Ma Godknows?" He tried again.

"We did if she grows potatoes?" Kind Eyes responded and waited for the joy that would follow.

"We are having quail and potatoes," He said, almost whispering, his mouth wide with surprise.

"Roasted outside with the skin still on them," Blink and Miss answered triumphantly.

He's mouth stayed open.

"So are we still sleeping outside?" Kind Eyes asked as they neared the house.

"Who said you had to do that?" He answered quickly.

189

28.

GOGO J. HAD grown accustomed to hearing the men speak freely, without the pliant omissions they laid out in front of their wives—more honesty. It's why they came to her restaurant and the reason she had refused to marry. She needed honesty instead of smooth retellings. Life could be hard, so long as the words told what happened with no exclusions for her heart or state of being. Knowing had to be full or she was just a child.

The girl had left early to take a rest. It seemed she wasn't getting any sleep, her red eyes blinking constantly, so the old woman was alone for the night's serving. This is how she had worked for years, so she wasn't unprepared. But surprisingly she missed the youthful excitement. The girl marveled regularly at what she did successfully and the things Gogo J. did on her own. That way of seeing was new because Gogo J. had not let herself marvel in quite some time.

Raising a pot of pumpkin leaves stewed in a leftover rabbit broth, she scooped portions onto five plates for the men stretched out by the window table who had arrived on the late-night bus. She was out of bread, so she added rice to each plate, piling on mounds until she was sure there was plenty to satiate hunger and adrenaline. One plate received a little more because she liked the shape of his eyes and he'd kicked the dirt of his shoes before coming into the restaurant. She looked over the counter and saw him talking, arms folded, the other men's faces stricken.

"It was a thing that shouldn't be seen," he was saying as she sat the plates on the table. He thanked her with his eyes. "The kind of thing that makes rain stop because it will not touch the land where blood was spilled in that way. The kind that makes ants devour anthills and seek refuge in the rivers."

Gogo J. started wiping a close table, listening to the honesty she'd caught in its middle.

"Why did no one help?" someone asked.

"You know that town. Where even children work and everyone keeps their eyes low and feet busy. When they can take what you look at, they can take what you love, and you'll believe you never saw it."

"So they killed a family?" one man said, holding a spoonful of rice in front of his mouth.

"Two boys who had been walking home from the farms," Eyes said. "I heard they caught them in an alley and broke their ribs with their guns. Ripped open their skin with their shoes. Clawed at their faces and beat in their noses so they had to spit blood out of their mouths while trying to breathe through their teeth. And when they couldn't stand because their legs were broken, they held them up like a mother holding a baby learning to stretch and pulled their arms out of their shoulders. So they didn't look like boys who had grown and worked but faces that couldn't be remembered and bodies that couldn't be held."

"Why?" the same man asked.

Eyes shook his head. "No reason. The bus driver said they had taken care of each other like a family cares for each person and like two people committed to a life that works for both in the same way it does for one. They had lived like the old ones. Just family and love."

THE ONES WE LOVED

Gogo J. listened, unwilling to move away and return to her pots. She was thankful that the girl was upstairs so this story of death couldn't stray from its path around these five and build an altar in her mind. She would set herself on fire if she heard about these boys, Gogo J. knew it. One death had already wounded, two more, so closely twined, would pull the living out of a mind still struggling to stay among those who left footprints.

"Did they leave them where they died?"

"They did. Until a boy who was their brother found the bodies. He screamed like the first thunder to split the sky open. The bus driver said his voice rode over the night and swallowed the darkness so everything became thunder and everyone knew there would never be any rain because the boy became thunder and screamed at the sky."

Was he alone? Why did no one help? Gogo J. wanted to speak but knew the men would add softness if they knew she was listening.

No longer stretching out as they had been earlier, the men nodded in unison, not signaling agreement as people often do, but to show that they'd heard and would never forget. Their bodies took less space, growing smaller as the story grew bigger and the boys became any they would have seen on their way. Gogo J. sat down and thought of the girl. She also thought of the town with no rain and worried about the people who would now have no roots, and if they'd find their way to this town that started where the river ended. There wouldn't be enough for all who came. The woman felt guilty for guarding the peace they had and that she didn't think should be shared with people who had chosen to not see terror.

Eyes continued. No one asked him not to. "When the thunder stopped, the boy took the boys to their homes. He left one outside the house of his father and one next to the place his mother always sat, so she would find him before the rest of her family. They say he left after that. Took what he had and boarded a bus."

193

"But what could have been done?" mulled the man holding the spoonful of rice, who finally put it down, talking to a part of himself that was younger and knew a wrong was wrong and needed to be named for the wrong to become right.

"The boys could have been saved," said another one. "Protected."

"In what way? For how long?"

"Until they could leave. Go somewhere they could be safe."

"And those who helped them? What about their lives?"

"They couldn't have killed everyone," said Eyes.

Spoonful of Rice rubbed his mouth and pulled at the scraggly hairs on his chin. "It's not a matter of killing all the people," he began, "it's that we have given ourselves over to the idea that our lives are not worth enough to raise our hands and protect one person, two people, or a dozen. So, we have made them our killers because we have not decided to be our own protectors."

"What kind of protection?" asked Eyes, his voice tired from carrying his life that seemed to wish him ill, that forced him to grasp for kindness, instead of cupping in his hands as much as he could hold. He was tired of searching for beauty in the most barren places. Tired of trying to find it in the men he met who were so much like him that they offered a transient consolation, but who could not tell him about ease because they also didn't know.

"What kind of protection?" Eyes repeated. He knew there would be no answer. And still he asked.

The men were mute, refusing to lend words and certainty to what they all knew to be real—that the boys were killed because they had lived. It's what made swallowing their food so difficult. They were robbed of speech because they knew that some people had seen this living and only wanted it to be ended. This realization gnawed at their helplessness, forcing the men around the table in this restaurant to

THE ONES WE LOVED

silently question: What is there to do, to grow through, to reach for, if living is not the thing that is protected?

The only audible sound was Gogo J. rising to welcome some who had come in as the story finished. She ushered them to a table opposite the others, not wanting to put them close in case the hardened faces prompted them to ask for a reason, and the story was repeated. She couldn't hear it again. And yet the woman knew if it started over, after all that had happened, she had to be someone who listened. A family, a boy and a town all changed, because life was too easy a thing to not marvel at. The table of five ate vigorously and quiet. She wondered if this is why they spoke freely together, because they wouldn't be asked for answers. Or maybe they feared that instead of answers, their women would ask for their well-being. Ask if the story made them want to drop their hands and slump their shoulders. If it made their hearts twist. If their knees grew weak. It could be some things are not meant to be asked about, the woman told herself, only listened to.

This is why the men came here. To spill out an anguish they did not want to dig into the soil, and so their women wouldn't hear something that would cause them to wring sorrow out of their hands. This room kept their eyes from turning into cemeteries for the graves they couldn't visit. And tonight Gogo J. wished she was married so she would have received the softened story made up of a disappearance, a sky, a bus ride.

Here she was, alone in her restaurant hearing about a family, a boy and a town dead because life was too easy a thing to not marvel at.

In her young days, the woman had marveled often. Not in a girlish way like the one upstairs did, who was startled by her heart and was meeting her body for the first time as something that could be changed by more than the weather. Gogo J. used to marvel at the shifts

195

in the town of her youth, a place that at first had been a cave in the stories she listened to, only fitting two people. Until those two people built a leaning cabin that could keep two and one more warm. Leaning so the rain would always slide off and not settle on the roof. And later the cabin became four, and after that, nine, and then more. Gogo J. had marveled because the trees were far, at least three days away, and the hands that looked like her own were soft and wrinkled when they were squeezed, so how could they build one and four and nine and more from wood at least three days away? She had marveled.

Marveled at the shifts because the people were capable, so able. And when she began to change because of love, she marveled at the boy who made her feel like a charming stranger. Like someone who woke up with a smile not knowing if the new day had made it or if the night had kept it from the day before. Like a stranger who laughed at birds and smiled at wafting grass. Who cooked and ate with vigor and lust, serving her plate with the same care she served others. Gogo J. loved him like she saw her mother love her father, and he loved her like he saw his father his mother. Gogo J. had been girlish when she thought the love would feel new. The woman, then a girl, had wanted a love that looked like what she saw, fit exactly as it was needed and shifted like a cave that became a cabin and a town.

But it stayed the same. And the stranger, she grew to know. So there were no more surprises or smiling at precious, silly things. And she noticed while looking at her mother's face, trying to find a change, that the woman had always looked the same when standing next to her father—eyes wide, neither narrowing nor glancing towards a distance that was personal, the smile straight, without curving deeper or showing several teeth. So she worried about her own face and what would happen once she stopped marveling at the changes.

The town still pleased her, but her loving no longer did because the love among people is not like the love we have for our homes. We

THE ONES WE LOVED

love our homes like wind blowing past the same tree from the day it's seeded to after it's rotted or cut down. This is a long kind of love that lets you leave and return in the manner you feel able, as a full embrace or a quick caress. Gogo J. saw that the way people loved was different. There was no leaving to come back. It was like clothes that were passed on, already used. With the still-floating scents of the persons that had spilled water down the front, creased the fabric while wiping it between dirty fingers, dabbed eyes with the corner when bored and nervous or scared. The clothes we received when they were still large and had to wait to be stretched out into, for our limbs to lengthen just enough so the big spaces would not be as loose. Clothes we would start to reach for less because the small parts now tightened around the wrist, waist, shoulders, hips, chest and wouldn't fit over the head. Clothes are never new. The way people love, it's like clothes. It's always too big, and only gets smaller.

And those boys were passed on a love that didn't fit. Gogo J. realized—as her heart sent what it could to the two who had not been allowed to marvel—that she had probably left her own town so she wouldn't pass any love to a child. Because it wouldn't be new. It would be charming as it sliced past the days, then it would become blunt, bumping against life like an unsteady hand pulling a cart. It wouldn't change. And the wind would continue to blow, showing how little we knew of this thing we passed on.

29.

"ARE YOU READY?"

Clutching He's arm, She nodded her head, her feet tapping in anticipation. The bus would be arriving soon, and after boarding, they would become part of the people whose seated profiles would be briefly seen by those they passed in the countryside, while speeding along the road. She had left the restaurant and rushed to meet him at the bus stop, wearing a blue-of-the-morning dress dotted with white flowers and pretty lace around the collar, after taking a quick bath so these special clothes wouldn't smell of oil from her last service. Gogo J. had given her the dress after a day when her feet had moved faster than usual and all the orders left the kitchen as soon as the food touched the plates. She had squeezed her feet into flat leather shoes that were tight around the ankle straps, but that she was sure would loosen with time. Another gift from the old lady. In her free hand, she carried a bag with food for their ride and the money she had found wrapped inside a sock outside her room door. Gogo J. had really known she was leaving, even guessed right the day and time. She probably sent one of the children up to the attic, because there was no way the woman would have been able to climb up those stairs.

The girl had never lived in a place she had gone to by choice. Waterfall was Mama's destination, and this town had been a refuge directed to her by Kuda's grandmother. This time, He had asked if she wanted to go somewhere with him and allowed her to decide. She was leaving a place that had no landowners, and so now she knew that if this was here, there must be another. A town with no pews, because here wood was only the tables that were shined to lay hot plates and not rest praying hands. If it could be this way, it could be the same somewhere else.

I am going to take my time there, She vowed, imagining the place they would arrive. Nothing would be fast. Life would move slowly, each day taken in and released like a long breath after rainfall. It wasn't a good rest that made a day feel easy. It was the choices. To get up or sleep. To chase the sun or meet the moon. The place they were going would have to make her feel this way. She was going to choose it.

He was wearing the pants and shirt he had when he first arrived, which She starched to a blinding clean above the restaurant. The streaks of blood that he had brought with him were no longer visible, but looking at them, he could still point where the stains had been and how they had marked the material. He had on brown shoes that were given to him by the woman who had let him board, and a jacket he had found carelessly tossed and forgotten on the back of a chair, also at Gogo J.'s. He had wiped the oil off the collar until it looked like he thought it was supposed to.

We are on our way, He thought. And this wouldn't be like his parents. They were leaving this town with the same bent backs. Neither had a burden that would bury the other.

"Did you say goodbye?" He asked.

She shook her head. "It didn't seem right. Did you?"

"To the people who gave me the room?"

THE ONES WE LOVED

She nodded.

"I didn't really know them, so goodbye felt like a closeness we didn't have. I just left the place clean, my room and the room in front where everyone ate."

She felt guilty. She had forgotten to throw out the water she had used for her bath. It was still in that small tub. Everything else had been fixed: the bed made, floor shining, even the stairs on the ladder leading up to her room dusted over, every part of the restaurant cleaned, including the pots that looked to be black but were actually blue under the spills and oil castings. But she forgot the water and the girl almost started crying. How careless.

"I forgot something."

"What is it?"

"There's still water in the bathing tub."

He had been nervous, then relaxed.

"I'm sure she won't mind that. She'll just throw it in the sink and be done."

"But she'll have to climb up the stairs on her own and she might fall, and the water might be too much for her to carry, and it wasn't clean because last night's . . ."

He squeezed her arms and looked at her close. "You are not leaving her lonesome. You are not leaving her robbed. She was strong when you arrived and will be the same with you gone. Don't make her weakened, because although I didn't know her well or think fondly of her, I know she was never in need and would be upset that you imagined her in that way."

The girl choked back a sob and hugged him tight, then let go and pulled him along.

"Where do you think we'll start?" she asked, looking up at this boy who was now family.

"I don't know," he answered honestly, "but when it's the right place,

201

something will stop us." He lowered his head so he could place a kiss on her lips and look into her eyes. "Thank you for coming."

"I would never have stayed," she whispered, her eyes closed. The burning and stinging from the previous night had lessened. After her conversation with Gogo J., She had pressed her hands against her eyes in the afternoons and evenings, only stopping when she remembered that his face was one she loved to see.

"Are you afraid?"

"No," she replied without hesitation. She moved closer to him, and he lightly rested his head on top of hers. When the bus pulled up and they climbed the steps, he made a promise. "If there is a river close to where we'll live, I'll keep teaching you how to swim."

"As long as you don't let me go," she said, laughing.

"Have I ever?" he asked as they sat down and the bus made its way out of town.

After a few months, He would return to that stop and remember She's hand grabbing his own. And he would realize that the last person before her to hold his hand at a bus stop had been his grandmother, coaxing him to stand up, to trust her because she was taking him home. *I know the way*, he remembers her saying. He wouldn't be able to tell you the color of this bus that took She and him or the number of people on it with them. All that remained was that very first ride, the first escape that led to the first safe place. His grandmother had known the way. Could he find it too?

Later, She would think about the driver and why she hadn't looked to see if he was the same one from her first bus ride. She would remember the first bus she ever saw and how it was the one that carried the landowners' children in the opposite direction of her old home. She would realize that those children would never leave Waterfall like she did, and if the time came that they resettled, it wouldn't be loss they felt, but anger. She would realize that she also hadn't felt angry as she fled, only lost and tired. Why didn't anger appear? Was that also something she could not have?

And when they were underwater She told him
    About what she had, and all it meant.
    From the bubbles that left her mouth
    She told him about the voices.
    How they were all the people she knew
    And all that She could carry.
    Could he take it from her chest?
    He left her hands as they stayed
    And lifted her as she was.
    Lifting all the way up
    The voices She carried
    And pressing into her arms
    Those He could no longer stand to hear.
    He carried what She held.
    She kept what He gave.

30.

"I LIKE IT here," He said, his voice shaking like it was warding off tears. There was no sadness. He was afraid. Standing by a wall next to the front door, he watched her look up at the ceiling, scrutinizing the peeling and cracking, which looked much worse if she didn't think about how evenly he could rework it and make it better with paint. He saw her face moving strange while she chewed her tongue like she did when moments were only a little strained. This is how she settled into her body, he had realized. Seeing her hands against her dress, a part of him desperately wanted to curve her arms around his shoulders and urge her to see that this was their home.

They had been staying in a slim boarding house a kilometer away, where they had disembarked two weeks earlier.

"I've never been on a bus before," she had told him as their bodies gently rocked, his head pressed against the window, hers resting on his shoulder.

He had stiffened. "Yes, you have." And then cleared his throat, removing his arm from around her back before putting it back like he remembered that's where it had been. "When we met."

She had started to forget how she'd fled, so she forgot to remember how they first met. Outside of the water. The girl had wanted to laugh, but it wouldn't have been happy. When the bus came to a stop and the headlights lit up more than tarmac, she thought the geography ordinary. The boarding house was the only tall building on the long road that snaked into the flatlands. Those arriving could stop and sleep before moving on. Very few wandered further like He had, to see who lived in the houses nearby that were positioned on various plots without any sensible boundaries, like the town was made by a child who was learning how to clutch objects and turned their release into play. Some houses were very, very close, and some were almost in a straight line. Others just seemed to have been flung. No one had attempted to change it, and this pleased him. These people made decisions regarding their lives without caring how they would be perceived by those next door. He saw it in the look of the homes, which were made on land that best fit the plans and tools available to each builder.

"The Plains used to be a feeder town," said a woman at the boarding house who was perhaps the owner or a longtime guest. "The town that fed all the land around with enough workers to care for the fields and animals," she told them. "When the drought came and the river dried, the feeding stopped. People left, and the ones who stayed were tired of packing up. They remember what it was like when the water flowed, so they stay for the flashbacks that only make sense when they are here."

It was an extreme town. She and He would learn this. The sun was savage, unforgiving, and made leaving the house for work, stepping into the kitchen to cook or digging in the fields unbearable. Every breath felt clogged and condensed. Sweat dripped down, blotting shirts, skirts and pants with large, uneven stains. Sometimes it didn't drip. Its wetness held on to your skin, coating your body and making every touch slide, and any caress slip. When it grew cold, the chills burrowed into your bones in places small enough to be troublesome but too intimate to be warmed. The spring arrived, impatient and possessive, demanding

THE ONES WE LOVED

everyone be present to pick and pull the little that was offered. No time could be wasted because as quickly as it came, so, too, was its departure, and any time left was spent dabbing foreheads and failing to remember if the present haul was better or the same as the last. It could never be remembered, but somehow it was still known to be less. Autumn should have been the time of respite, when temperatures dipped without a bite and heat was noticeable without being suffocating. But after so much time spent trudging and groaning, when the leaves finally floated down, it was as if people had forgotten how it felt to touch without gripping or slipping. How to long for the most of something and still receive less. It was as if the weather didn't want them to touch.

Leaning towards the woman at the boarding house, She had quietly asked if there was somewhere people went to pray. "There is none of that," came the brusque response. The girl was too relieved to worry if the woman assumed she was seeking such a place. The next morning, He went to see what it was that convinced the people who remained that this life was enough, even if it was difficult. He saw that it was the type of town where people hung their private garments on the clothesline outside, pegged underneath their bathing towels so searching eyes could see they bathed well but not what they wore underneath the cleaned dresses, blouses, shirts and pants. They weren't being prudent, only thoughtful— redeeming the simplicity of their living with small acts of modesty that felt grand. Passing the butcher shop, he had felt some life. Seen the two men sitting outside a bar with bottles of beer and felt lonely.

Then the house. Sitting not too far from other homes but still a little detached from the clusters, it had called to him when he walked by on his way back to She. Like it had been waiting for him to meet its threshold. For him to come by and see that this was the place they had traveled three days to find.

He walked into what would be a better kitchen, once he was done tearing out the cupboards whose doors loosely pointed towards the floor, cleaning out the brown residue in the sink where a little water still trickled, and repainting the windowpanes that seemed to be a pale yellow but had become the aged colors of the cooking oil that leapt out of the pans when meals were being prepared, staining the walls with sprays and smells of unfamiliar food. "It's going to be just us, so we don't need anything that we won't be able to take care of with two pairs of hands. I could fix it. Make it look like a dream," He whispered as he walked over to her, unclasped her hands and brought them up to his mouth.

She saw a room for catching up on the day, a kitchen that was almost hidden so visitors would have to ask for what they needed instead of simply walking through their home, and a bedroom. A shack in the backyard kept the tub, and they would have to carry buckets of water drawn from a well in the front to fill it up. Some would land on the floor like it had in another home.

"I know you wanted a place with big windows, so I thought I could put that on this side, you see?" He gestured to where there was already a hole in the sitting room. "Once I break this down, I can make the window even bigger, give it more space. I could even put two, I think. Both of them big. Or we could do one on each side so the sun can come in from different places. That would be nice, I think." He was speaking faster than he wanted but he didn't know how to stop. Now he couldn't bring himself to look at her face.

"I don't want a dream," She said while meeting the new house with a guava tree in the front.

She didn't like it. He kissed her hands and pulled her against his chest. "I will keep looking."

Smiling, the girl looked at the rooms culled out of earth and cement. She shook her head. "I don't want a dream," she repeated, "because I don't want to live on faith. I want to make a life with you. One that we build and choose together. Here. There's no need for dreams, just us."

A big laugh cut through his face, and he grabbed her waist, lifting

THE ONES WE LOVED

her high enough so his arms were fully stretched, and her face glowed above his own. "I am going to build our home!" He screamed, and She laughed while they spun. The walls began to melt as the world turned until it was only his face, smiling, and his voice, laughing.

In this town, the homes matched in their washed-out white, dirty where the wind blew dust. Some had short walls in the front to keep those inside from being pulled out into the world beyond. Those that had walls would sometimes pretend that The Plains past their gates was what it used to be—full and restless. They imagined jumping into the river and drinking chilled water from their wells. These days, it was lukewarm. Behind those walls, entry and exit was a one-way path. Neither one could be done surreptitiously, and the way you left always mirrored the way you came back. Those without walls sat in their yards and left themselves open to being watched while perusing all those who offered a greeting, tilted a hat or quickly looked away when their piqued interest was noticed and returned. Nothing good stayed here easily. She and He would learn that.

Sometimes it was good to be in The Plains. The weather would settle, steadying itself for a little while. The extremes retreated to the perimeters, a kind of shimmering truce waiting for someone to exhale in quiet relief. The townspeople held their breath then, barely moving so as not to awaken the fire or invite the chill. When the quiet came, they all slumped down, slowly, carefully, gratefully. It wasn't too hot. It wasn't too cold. It was good. They stretched their bodies, feeling every nerve moving, every muscle bulging and each bone cracking. All this meant they were still here, their bodies loyal and moving, even in this place of extremes where trees grew but the fruit was sparse. Flowers bloomed but only for a short time. The ponds filled with rainwater but quickly became shallow and dry. There was a swamp, a persistent dampness in the place that used to be the river, where mounds of grass grew underneath the rocks and smells would rise that didn't push you away but instead made you stop, spend some

209

time and think what that could be. There were some dogs, but they never barked to warn, greet or cry. They slept, twitching slightly when footsteps got closer, and moving into the shade as the sun inched across the sky.

People turned to nothing but their own selves here, to bear the heat, to raise the crops. Nothing large had ever talked to those in The Plains and no one had looked up to listen. Everyone simply woke up and tried, each day, for as long as they were able. They could live here. His parents could have tried, too, the boy realized, feeling the thought swiftly then releasing it.

As he twirled her around, she let her eyes travel across his face and found her beginning in the joy she recognized. One that was his and not the other lives who sometimes told their stories through his body. Inside their home, right now, She saw herself in the middle of a chosen center, finally.

What would his face become if my story could be seen in its shadows and smiles? she wondered. Could he manage her past and his own? Perhaps, though, the past was likely a thing to lose like coins on bus seats. Who would notice them except the people who found them at the next stop? She would leave her past somewhere in The Plains, and if he found it, he could pick it up. If he chose to leave it, someone else could find it and know her a little better. He already knew that she ran. That a while ago, her feet had made circles at the bottom of the river and that her breathing sounded different when she was with him. She didn't need to be anything else in front of his eyes.

Her feet touched the ground, and she followed as he dragged her out to the backyard. Today, He's face was his. She kept quiet, and to her left, She saw a flash of red and knew this place with the guava tree in the front had called for her.

Here I am, she thought.

The silence began because of how they were.

31.

"Do you think we got enough for the frame?" She asked him, pausing to lift her knee and hike up the three logs that had started slipping out of her arms as they walked. "And for the stool?"

He kept turning his head back to make sure her arms didn't need rest. "I think we have enough for the bed frame, table and the stool," he answered, mindfully measuring with his eyes what they would use.

"I need to make another sweeping stick after we're done," She said. It had taken her a few minutes to say this aloud. The last had come undone because she had tried to make it while remembering and forgetting at the same time. Remember: *Choose twigs that are the same size.* Forget: *The twigs need to be the same size.* Remember: *Twigs should be hard but flexible so they can clean inside corners.* Forget: *Twigs need to be flexible.* Remember: *Make sure to tie them tightly with a thick band.* Forget: *Tie them tightly.* This time she would make it while her eyes stung.

"We would need to find more twigs for that."

"We have them already. Logs are just twigs that have grown too big so we can use what's left over."

"Do you need my help making the new one?" His question was

hoarse and there was a catch that could have been a gasp, but her ears turned it into a moment caused by the sun and the heavy loads.

"No, I know how to do it. I just forgot because Gogo J. only wiped her floors and so I didn't have to worry about it."

He nodded, not wanting to think of that town but also happy they had passed over the issue of the sweeping stick and the logs that are only large twigs. It was a funny thing that would have made him laugh if he heard it coming out of his friend's mouth. The one who would have said it, would have been quite certain and proud of his thinking.

"How long do you think it will take to make what we need?" she asked between long breaths. "I've never made anything." He had told her that controlling her breathing would quicken the trip back to the house.

"Two weeks, maybe more." She had insisted on only one trip, otherwise they could have returned the next day.

"Why so long?"

"It takes time to create things that will last. We can't rush it." He stopped and waited for her.

"I just want everything to be ready," She said, pretending not to see him and walking past while yelling over her shoulder, "Do you need to stop?"

"No, I'm enjoying my walk." He knew She was smiling without having to look at her face, and as she switched her gait so it wouldn't seem as if she was leaning too far to one side, he coughed up a chuckle.

In one hand, He held bundles of wood and in the other, the axe he had borrowed from the butcher's wife, Mrs. Clay, who had waved to him after he made his third pass by the butcher shop that afternoon.

"Welcome," she had greeted as he walked in, lifting herself from a seat behind the counter and offering her hand. It was very thin and almost completely covered by his large one, which hadn't expected to hold something it could so easily crush. But her grip was strong as he clumsily tried to shake it gently and then let go.

"You're in the house behind the guava tree?"

"I haven't seen a tree," He'd said before she continued.

"I've wanted to come by and give you some food from my garden, but I haven't quite been able." He looked down at her feet, which were swollen in her sandals. "Can I help you look for what you need?"

It had been a good spell since someone wanted to help him without cause, and for one breath, He'd forgotten what he had spent the morning walking to find. "We're building a bed frame and maybe a stool."

"So you need tools. Do you have some wood?"

"There are small trees I saw not far from here. We are going there today."

Mrs. Clay pointed behind the shop's door, where different-sized hammers and axes, a number of large nails and a chisel were propped in the corner. More help than he needed. "Take them, please. My husband wouldn't mind, and if he wasn't out delivering a large bag of livers to the neighbors behind our house, he would have come with you."

"Thank you." He wished She was beside him.

"Come back anytime. We are always here," Mrs. Clay said when he reached for the door.

"Thank you," He repeated. For offering to help. He hoped that was understood.

"Of course. And tell her I said hello."

On their way to the field with a grouping of trees that was right after the swamp, He had told She about Mrs. Clay. As the loaned axe broke open dry branches, he told her of their conversation and mentioned that it was probably best for Mrs. Clay to be the only one they got to know in the town, because people treated you differently if they thought you had connections with many others.

"What do you mean?" she asked him, impressed by what had been collected and ready to get home and start building. The girl also needed to step into her garden and touch her eyes.

"Well, if there's a time when we need more help, it's better to know one person who can give it readily than waiting on a whole town to lend their hands. One person is generous, people together are tightfisted."

"I don't think so. People help each other when there's trouble."

"No, they help themselves to avoid trouble."

"What about the person who gave us these tools?"

"That's why I said she can be our friend." He was confused because his words were simple, but She didn't seem to understand.

"What if we need other things besides tools?" She looked at him because help was not the only thing people could lend. One of these days they would need company. Not the whole town, of course, but people who could be their friends and who could talk to them about their own lives in The Plains.

"Is there something else we are going to need?"

She shrugged and looked at her feet. "We will always need things."

He didn't answer, focusing on the branches that now needed to be lifted. He should have brought a cloth for her shoulder so she could be more comfortable while she carried them. Perhaps she could hold them in her arms.

"I think we could also start to know ourselves better, once we know other people," She said.

She lifted what he had tied with the strips of a child's dress that he had pulled out of the swamp. She didn't consider that the dress was the lost piece of a bad event because the girl knew that if a child had been hurt, this town would have been broken instead of just being a place that was forgotten.

"You don't need anyone else's help to know me," He said. "Just ask me and I'll tell you." He believed it, and She knew he trusted her to ask.

THE ONES WE LOVED

But how could she tell him that even when people were asked to reveal themselves, they never shared all there was to know? Someone else had to be there who could see the person differently. And then together, the person who asked, the one who answered and the one who saw, would make a story that told more.

"Can I try to cut something?" She asked, a kind question, an easy answer.

He handed her the axe.

When they arrived home, they hoisted the wood to the back of the house, and she reminded him to offer guavas to the Clays when he returned their tools.

"We don't have guavas," he said, scratching his stomach.

"Yes, we do, in the tree outside. Just look up."

The house took time, longer than the two weeks, but neither noticed. While He worked on the wood, She pulled out dead roots in the front yard. He cut through the weeds; She scrubbed the walls inside. He chased the mice that headed for the doorway.

"They are just so curious," She said every day, following behind his shrieks of attack that made her sides ache. He made her laugh so much her eyes would water and wash out all the stinging that came from touching them regularly. So she did it often and still laughed.

"They need to leave now that we're here," He screeched, holding the sweeping stick.

On days when they sat in the sun, He taught her how to carefully run a razor over his head and cut only what was needed. She taught him how to cut meat off the bones without turning it into shreds. It wasn't a special place, here in The Plains. And nothing good stayed easily.

The silence began because nothing good could stay easily.

215

32.

He had forgotten the order of the three: Was it over, under, over, or under, over, over? He stared at his hand holding the loose strand, hoping the persistence of his glare would make it move, while replaying the directions She had given him in the morning. Feeling his hesitation, she tickled his foot and lifted her hand to the top of her head.

"See at the beginning here," she started, "just follow that pattern. If it's looking a little different, undo that section until you are at the part where it looks the same as the ones you've already done. Then start again and keep going." The afternoon sun warmed the nape of her neck where his hands were currently stuck.

"I know, I know," he answered without pause, maintaining the confidence that had begun this session, after he'd pronounced he could speedily get through her hair and save her the time she spent curled in a sharp circle, her legs in the shape of resting bird wings and her arms hovering over her head while her fingers deftly felt their way through the tight coils.

"I can weave, after all," he'd boasted, pulling at his fingers and stretching muscles that had flattened reeds into baskets and hats.

She had looked at the mat he'd made after they finished with the table and chairs, which now sat in their kitchen. "Are you telling me weaving a basket is the same as braiding hair?" she challenged, folding her arms, her mouth twitching.

"Are you telling me it's not?"

She then pulled her hair out of the two thick braids she usually did, eying him closely, watching to see if the hubris became humility, and offered him a comb and a plastic jar of thick oil. That's how they ended up sitting outside, he on the stool and she between his legs, arms resting on his thighs and patiently touching every braid. Every now and again, she would push her chest forward and feel her lower back sigh in relief. You would think her body would be used to this activity of discomfort whose outcome left her hair looking well-kept. He had been moving surprisingly well, until he started sectioning the middle part of her head, where the hair could not be easily flattened by any comb or sectioned by tender fingers searching for the scalp.

"This part of your hair is not like the sides," he said, pulling at her head so it was facing the sky and leaving a kiss on her nose. He would need to be less gentle if he wanted to succeed, but he didn't want to start yanking like he was pulling the arm of an errant child or clearing the ground of roving grass.

"Does it still feel like weaving?" she asked, her voice innocent. She squealed as his hands found the soft part of her waist and tickled the skin.

"I can't believe you learned to do this without a mirror or someone else to make sure the lines were perfectly straight," he marveled, pulling tightly at the three strands he held in his hand and reading the flinches of her shoulders to make sure he wasn't causing any pain.

"Don't worry, it doesn't hurt," she replied, reading his hesitation. "Your hands are actually very light." While holding a braid in one hand, he rubbed two fingers on the lid that seemed to have as much

THE ONES WE LOVED

oil as the jar. Every time She closed it, more would fill up the round space, even when scooped generously. He rubbed one finger on her scalp, as he'd seen her do, and kept the other raised. He hoped the oil wouldn't melt in the sun.

Mama's hands were also very light and the knees pressing into the lower part of her armpits would keep her from moving too much.

Her shoulders tensed, then she shuddered. It wouldn't have been noticeable had she been standing and moving. He hesitated.

"Are you sure?" He was convinced she was understating her feelings of pain to spare his pride. "I am really pulling so that I can get all the hair in the line."

His genuine concern lessened the tension and made her laugh. When she threw her head back, his fingers lost their grip and the nearly finished braid unraveled. His low scream made her laugh even more, and when she doubled over, she felt his hands pulling her up and placing her on his lap.

"Now look what you've done," he began, "I was so close to finishing."

"We have been sitting here for so long, I am going to be stuck in this position," she said and bent her neck so she looked like a bird. He refused to crumble, and so she bobbed her half-braided head up and down like a baby chicken.

He laughed, then clamped down on his tongue, but it was too late.

"You're very silly," he told She, cupping her face in his hands. Drawing close, she breathed the smell of hair oil that had found its way from his hands to his chin. She kissed him softly, running her fingers over his head.

"You should let me cut your hair," she whispered into his mouth.

"Trust you with a razor on my scalp again?" He feigned shock, and she gently punched his arm.

"I did well! And it's just like a knife," she responded quickly as they pulled apart.

219

"The same way braiding is like weaving," He exclaimed, glancing at her head apologetically.

"I told you that you were wrong!" she added, her grin marking her victory.

"Well, I lied to myself." He sighed, accepting the lesson and preparing his mind for a second attempt. He was going to finish.

"All these women you've loved," she began, pulling at his chin hairs, "and you never helped them with their hair."

He tilted his head. "What makes you think I've loved a lot of women?"

She mirrored his pose. "The first time we were together." He stayed silent, and his raised brows told her he was waiting for her to continue. She wiped her eyes awkwardly with the upper part of her arm, dabbing them so the stinging could dissipate. She raised her head and looked at the guava tree beyond their house.

"You were ready. And you were different. And I saw how the women in the town looked at you."

He mumbled under his breath, and She brought her eyes to meet him.

"Did you see how the men moved when you walked by?" He asked.

Her mind went back to what had brought her to that town where the men felt free to look at her with interest, without fear of divine retribution or the scornful eyes of praying women. She saw the smoke that had marked her departure, and squeezed her eyes shut, drawing shutters over the images that sometimes animated themselves with the laughs and looks that she recognized, but which often just stood, not breathing or dying.

"I was looking at you," She answered.

He released a slow breath, hoping that while her eyes were closed, he could compose his face and become someone who remembered how it felt when he first touched her skin. He wanted to remember

THE ONES WE LOVED

the connection and not the escape that preceded it. "There were no other women." He took his time with the words, carefully placing his answer between them so she could believe it. "I think it was different, because I had to change to love you."

The wind that had been blowing for most of the day now picked up the sounds from the bar a kilometer from their house, next to the butcher shop. It was not yet late enough to drink without embarrassment, but some of the townspeople had started walking by the house on their way to claim the seats closest to the window and farthest from the toilet. With each hour, those going to make room for more alcohol in their stomach would turn into men struggling to unbutton their pants before giving up and relieving themselves by the door, barely mustering the desire to even open it. So the smell was something to be avoided. When the early patrons looked over the small fence, it was the young lovers they saw, wrapped around each other so his arm and her leg looked to belong to the same body, both lean, one muscular and the other small enough to bend. The two didn't notice.

He often wondered, how much of this life, his life, existed because of whom he now chose to be, and not what She brought out of him. There was a lot that He no longer was, and what remained was this love, held not by time or blood, but circumstance and knowing. A knowing that he clung to because some things you know without needing to learn, like breathing and sleeping.

"What are you thinking?" She asked, trying to see his memories and covering her own with this curiosity.

She listened as He spoke, chewing her tongue until he finished. During that first time with him, She had thought herself to be the only one learning. She had assumed that the way He touched her was because a woman's body was already familiar to him, and not that he was hoping to know her own especially.

"I think I changed too," she said, after he finished, looking back at the guava tree.

"How?" he asked, following her eyes.

"I trusted you," she finally said.

"You trusted Gogo J. too," he said, kissing her shoulder. She turned to face him.

"But I chose to go with you."

He was quiet and she leaned into him, resting her head on his chest.

"Would you have still chosen me if I had braided your hair then?"

When they heard the full-throated chuckling, those walking by the house behind the guava tree wondered what had caused two young lovers to find enjoyment on a day of such heat, without any strong beers beside them.

The silence began because there were no beers beside them.

33.

"I FOUND IT! I found it! I found it!"

She heard him yelling through the kitchen window where she was peeling potatoes. She dropped the knife into the sink and ran to the back of the house while cleaning her hands on the cloth she had tied around her waist. She first saw him through the screen on the back door. He was bent over, and on his back was a big slab of glass that was as wide as it was long. It lay flat, held by two pieces of fabric tied on both sides that then went around his shoulders, so he could carry it like a pack.

"What is that?" She asked excitedly as he carefully set it down. Kneeling next to him she wiped his face, which was dripping sweat, and tried to dab at his eyes.

"Can you see it?" He asked, out of breath.

"Yes, this glass right here? Where did you find it? What is it for?"

He fell back to the ground and pulled her down with him as she laughed.

"It's your window," he said breathlessly, planting his lips on her nose, quickly on her cheeks, her nose again, and longer on her mouth before wrapping his arms around her waist.

"My window?" she replied perplexed, until his meaning was clear. She raised herself up and climbed on top of him. "For the sitting room?" She asked, even as his dancing eyes and smile proved she was right.

He had been looking for a large enough piece to fit the part of the wall that he was going to break and make the kind of room where light turned everything golden. There had been nothing in The Plains that could fit, and although she had told him it didn't matter, he was determined to find something.

"I can't believe you found it," She said, and before he could tell her where or how, she wrapped her arms around his neck and covered his face with kisses. She could taste the sweat on her lips. It had been one of those sweltering hot days that made lifting an arm feel like a chore, but he had walked through this heat carrying a gift for their house. Something for her.

"I promised, didn't I?"

"I don't remember that." She smiled, not caring that they were outside and anyone could walk by and see them.

"Well I did," he said.

She propped herself on her elbow and looked at the glass now lying next to them, reflecting a bright glare that made her squint. Looking back at his shiny face, she squeezed his cheeks and laughed wildly.

"I love it!"

He kissed her again and quickly lifted her up. "Help me carry it inside."

The lovers in the corner house with the guava tree stumbled into their yard, careful not to move too fast or hurt the other by letting one side go.

"How did you carry this by yourself?" She asked, incredulously.

He just smiled and steered them towards the tree trunk, where they gently laid it down.

THE ONES WE LOVED

"Can you believe this was just sitting by the road?" He gushed.

"Where?" she asked, wiping sweat from her forehead, which had already started to build, even though the girl had only been outside for less than five minutes.

"Behind Ma Dube's house. When I saw it, I knew it was the right size for that space in the sitting room. Can you see it?" He asked. "Can you see what the window is going to look like?"

"It's going to look beautiful, like you saw it."

They stood contentedly alongside each other, looking at the curtained open space in their house that would soon let sun into the room where they would sit and eat. It had been a few weeks since they'd arrived from the boarding house, and much more since they left the town. The Plains didn't feel like home yet, but it was slowly forming with every little thing they brought.

"Did you say you found this outside Ma Dube's house?"

"Yes, at the back."

"Do you think it's all right that we took it?" She asked cautiously.

"Yes," he answered, rolling his eyes and squeezing her waist.

"I just want to make sure they don't think we are stealing," she said. "We just moved here, and it would be a sour arrival if our neighbors thought we were thieves."

"All our neighbors know is that you go to the butcher shop and I go to the fields," he said, leading her into the house.

"Soon we'll have friends, and then they can come and see our new window and look at our new garden."

"What garden?" He asked.

"The one we'll put in the front."

"You have so many ideas for this place," He said as he closed the screen door behind them. "I'm excited to see what else you want to do."

"Maybe there will be flowers too," She said softly, her heart becoming tender.

225

"What kind?"

She shook her head. "I don't know."

"Well, it can be anything you want. Nothing now matters except what you decide. Your day is your day, and the flowers are yours."

He believed it, and She did too.

The silence began because the belief was not enough.

34.

"Do you want to know something I do that I think no one else does?" She asked.

"Chewing your tongue, I already know."

She was standing in the kitchen, trying to decide what to put in the pots. Would she make something that was stewed or fried? Perhaps both, although She didn't want to be on her feet that long. She put her hands on her waist and turned her gaze towards He, who was sitting on the floor in front of her with a woven mat draped over his straight legs. It was progressively getting larger as he added more tiers to its circular shape.

"You think there is no one else who does that?"

"I'd never seen anyone do it until I met you," He answered, looking at She closely and grinning as one side of her face started to move. She quickly stopped when she noticed his smile, dropping her hands to her hips.

"I don't even think about it when I do it. Because no other person seemed to notice, I just assumed people have made it an ordinary thing that my body does. Like sitting or clapping."

"Don't feel unordinary," He told She. "I love that you do it. It's only you. Tell me what you were thinking to say."

She leaned against the cupboard, then straightened to walk over and join him on the floor, watching his fingers as they moved across the reeds.

"When I sweep and take care of the house, I never want it to become clean."

He's eyes narrowed as he listened, not quite understanding what the girl was speaking. She continued.

"I clean and make the house look like a place that is good and right for eating and living, and also sleeping. And you know I don't stop until it looks that way. But I never want it to look as though there isn't more that can be done."

The boy looked around the rooms she had moved through that morning, the kitchen, the one where they sat, and reminded himself to look into their sleeping room where He knew it would look as the rest. Nothing out of place. Warm and safe. But She thought there could be more.

"The house always looks like a place I don't want to leave," He said.

"That's good," She answered, nodding her head.

He stopped weaving and found her hand, pulling her against his body so they were shoulder to shoulder.

"What else do you want to do here?" He waited for her to say what it was that she believed no one else did. The action that made her want to tell him so perhaps He could start doing it too? Or maybe to know if he had ever done the same?

She didn't respond immediately, spinning what she had uttered through her mind, wondering if it was sensible. If she couldn't properly explain what she did, would that make the action unreasonable?

"Even the food," the girl finally said. "I make it well. But not the best it could be."

228

THE ONES WE LOVED

"Now I am more lost than before, because what you make is always the best that I've had," the boy said, searching for her eyes, which She had kept downcast, focusing on the mat in front of him. He nuzzled her head with his face, feeling her braids rubbing against his chin. "You keep the house well, and you cook everything like someone who's discovered flavors no one else knows about. Anyone who eats what you make will never believe it's the same food they've always had."

She laughed softly. "You say that because you're always hungry."

"I say it because it's true."

"Because you're in love."

"That is also the truth. So now we've both said one true thing. You said one lie, so you owe me another truth."

She met his eyes, her body relaxing into his own. "Why do I have to do that?"

"It's what people do when they've told more lies than truth. There always has to be more truth so the stories can go on."

"I've not heard anyone say that."

"I heard it when I was a boy."

"From who?"

He shrugged and she felt tension in his chest that gradually receded when she clasped his hand.

"Someone who knew me when I was still a child. Tell me what you were saying," He urged, returning her to the halted confession.

"Whenever I'm done sweeping, before throwing the dirt outside, I'll take some between my fingers, only a little, and drop it back on the floor, then spread it around with my leg so it lands in different places."

"Why?"

Her laugh was uneasy, and he could see from the shape of her mouth that she was trying not to cry. He held her tighter.

"If I do my best thing, make my best meal, make this house really

229

beautiful, even make the windows shinier than anyone has ever seen, I think we would have to leave. I think I would have to stop cooking."

He still didn't understand but didn't ask why, because he didn't want to interrupt. The boy didn't want to get in the way.

"She won't be able to see how well I did," the girl finished quietly.

"Who?" He asked urgently.

She let go of his hand, and he found hers again so he could feel the sweat on her skin and hold her trembling fingers.

"Could you do your best thing if the person you loved couldn't see it?" It was a desperate question, but he couldn't give a desperate answer. So he spoke another true thing for their story to go on.

"You're the person I love, and you've seen all that I do. I do it well for you."

She looked at the kitchen and wondered again what she was going to make, and how it could be good without being something She needed Mama to also taste, so the woman would know how well her daughter had kept the things that had been taught about the ways we prepare what is shared and served.

"Do you not love me?" He asked cautiously, and She returned from the best thing of her past to the one that now needed to be enough.

"I love you every day," She answered.

He breathed it in.

"Is it your best love?"

"It's my only one."

He pulled her up to her feet and placed his arms around her waist, pushing her towards the open front door. As they walked outside, He led her to the small garden She had cleared and freed his hands only to pick up a little of the dirt that he put in her own.

"Use this," He told She. "When you're done cleaning, spread the dirt from your garden around the house. It won't be clean anymore, and it will also be filled with something that helps life grow."

THE ONES WE LOVED

The girl held him close, not releasing the dirt She had palmed in one hand while holding his own with her other, which she brought to her chest. She felt the steady tremor through her dress and around his palm.

"You're the only love," She repeated.

And still held on to the dirt. He had given her a small kindness. One that was old. Like the love that was her best.

35.

THE SOIL WAS white in The Plains, hard to look at when the sun was at its highest. When held, it poured through the fingers like the finest ground maize, and if it happened to become wet, the water rested at the top, like there was no room for it in the cracks and tracks below.

Wandering to a small plot, He saw three new stalks of maize, a tiny change from the first month, when nothing would sprout from the soil. He still had the seeds that were left in a faded yellow sack on the doorstep of their home. They seemed to be a sign of goodwill and a parting gift from those who had previously lived in the house. He didn't think they were a defeat, left by people who tried and failed to coax more out of the land.

The boy could see no reminders of the storm he heard last night. It had made quite a show with its arrival, the dull rumbling of thunder and a shift in the breeze rattling the windows and closing shut doors left ajar. He imagined the clouds darkening and large drops of rain falling. But the sand forcing its way into his shoes told the story of a ground only saturated by morning dew dripping off plants.

Rainfall would have to come every day, for much longer than the time it took to close a window or grab the clothes off the hanging line, if he wanted a good enough yield from the twelve rows he tilled.

Since they arrived, only five rows had given maize that was fit to sell or exchange for what they needed. His neighbors had been impressed, many having given up on the notion of farming and content to rely on the providence of Mr. Clay, whose seeds sprung to life wherever they were thrown in his backyard.

"Did you water them every day?" they asked He.

"No."

"How did you make sure the water lasted until the next watering?"

"I don't know. I tilled them closer to each other so they could share it."

He didn't understand their applause for the little he had to show. If they had asked him while he lived in Spilling River, he would have pointed to the sky that had listened and sent food. He no longer looked at the sky. Now it terrified him to only trust his hands.

The Plains was not Spilling River and that soothed his spirit. It also left him feeling aimless. That was the sense that hovered over his feet each time he left the house and didn't quite know which direction he was headed. Often, he found himself at this plot, with the large water jug in his hand, staring at what had once been a challenge and that now left him beaten.

He had to be a different person in this land of white earth, and he had known that when they decided to stay. That he would need a new way of talking to the soil without using any of the lessons passed to him by his grandfather and grandmother. He couldn't build their lives the way he had done in the past, with care that was slightly dampened by vigilance and that had shown itself to be far less than what was necessary. He should have been more watchful. He would be here, even

THE ONES WE LOVED

inside the safety of these people who moved slower than he was used to and lent a hand without their eyes needing to meet, and far from landowners. Coming to a stop on his walk, he felt the pain in his leg that demanded attention when he remembered Spilling River. What else would hurt him if he was forced to flee The Plains the same way he'd left home? The fear weighed on his back and brought his body to a crouch. He wished he had been there too, in that alley. The boy wasn't eager for death, simply seeking an interruption to the loneliness he knew his friends must have felt. His friends had loved each other, and he had loved them both. He wished he had been there too. Then we wouldn't be dying, He thought. We'd just be together.

The neighbors who had also risen early so they could take deep breaths of earth fed with brief amounts of rainwater saw his body and grunted in approval. This young man could make crops do his bidding. And he never stopped trying to do more. When he would leave it wasn't because there was no longer work to be done, but to rush home and see the young woman who kept their house.

He inhaled slowly and his eyes saw She and the small garden her hands had made bloom using water collected from the well. She had raised beds of garlic and another plant whose flowers were red as blood, with fruit that made his tongue feel naked and ragged. It had been there when they arrived, and from one stalk, She had grown over two dozen.

When the neighbors passed his plot and kept walking on, they would reach the small house with a guava tree in the front. They would think of the young woman who usually cleaned the yard before heading to Mr. Clay's or running her hands over the plants in her garden, feeling for spots carrying sickness. Not seeing her outside, they would once again think of He, and how easily both had fit into life in The Plains.

235

Unknown to them, that morning She had been woken by dread, smelling smoke so close it made her feel sick. Lying on her back, her legs failed to move and her heart felt as though it would leap out of her body and find a more deserving home. A better person to keep. Shallow breaths came out of her mouth, and her eyes, stinging, darted across the roof searching for the source. He had let out a small breath, and she remembered that she wasn't alone. She stretched her hands and felt his thin shirt on her fingertips.

She never knew a memory could leave you stunned. Her body was stuck, and She told herself to breathe deep, counting down like someone doing it for the first time. It was rattling, this knowledge that every day she kept herself alive by doing something that seemed so simple, but that right now took all of her effort. Her brain was counting, her heart was waiting, her body was alert.

One, breathe. One, breathe.

One, two, breathe.

One, t— breathe.

One, two, breathe.

One, two, three, breathe.

One, two, three, four—

"I am sorry," said the hand, who was now crying.

"I killed her," said She.

Her breath snagged in her throat. She could exhale next to He or hold back and sink into the bed that had now turned into a border, split between the past and the present. Breathe and slide your feet onto the ground. Or stop counting and fall. She waited.

The neighbors would have walked by after coming from the fields, admiring her tiny garden and coveting the clean homestead. Imagining her inside, they would miss her watching them as they returned to their homes, went to the bar or visited each other. She thought of the hand that had pushed her away from Waterfall and wondered if these

236

THE ONES WE LOVED

new people would ever grow to love her enough to do the same. Push her out of the nightmare so she wouldn't have to learn how to breathe while trying to stay alive.

From her place in the guava tree, they all appeared to be people who cared. Their words didn't reach her among the leaves, but they seemed kind from the movement of their lips and the glints of their teeth. Their feet could have been going to Eastern Farms were it not for the relief in their gaits, unhurried and winding, sometimes stopping to better accept a story being retold. She watched as they walked in groups and then focused on the one who moved alone. He had left early today, and even from so far up, she could see the frown on his face as he limped and the stiffness in his gait as he got closer to their house.

She watched from her branch and wondered how long she could sit here before she went back in the house and found him sleeping. Then they wouldn't have to talk, and she could forget that he no longer talked to her well. The silence began because he no longer talked to her well.

36.

THE SILENCE BEGAN because she wanted to have a meeting. Not a heavy one between people sorting through growing slights or those that happened with serious women who were never late and always devout. She wanted a meeting like at the restaurant when people would spread out between tables, hearing several stories at a time and becoming a part of multiple groups that, by the end of the night, were closer friends than family could be. Because a meeting with a well-made meal hoists people out of their mess and into a moment of happiness. She had seen it happen and wanted it here, too, in The Plains.

He had said a person could only truly know one person, and she thought he would understand after she explained that a town was not just the people who arrived, the things they brought and the one person they turned to when they needed small things. It was the neighbors who went to the same butcher shop, those who used a stick to loosen the guavas in the tree she climbed that shaded part of their yard and those who always sat in front of the bar, neither drinking nor buying but being a part of the rest, the sitting and the joy of others.

The silence began because she went to the Clays. On a day when He was in the fields, seeing to what he planted, and after she was done

239

working in her garden and touching her eyes. She had spent an afternoon with this small family, finding her way into their story without having to say too much of her own. They had let her ask all she needed, and when there was nothing else to say, they talked about the neighbors who came in. Their insight was not the kind that is serrated, just funny, in the way that people speak of those they have known long. He didn't ask to come when she told him she would be returning.

"Come with me," he said instead. "I can teach you what I'm doing with the plants."

"Can we spend some time in the fields and then pass by the butcher shop and see the Clays?"

"There's nothing we need right now. We have enough meat, and I don't need tools to make anything else."

"We can just talk to them."

The silence had started when Mrs. Clay died. And everyone in the town had gone to the Clays' home with food and intimations that all days start and finish. The sad ones too. They had left the house together, and she'd thought they were walking the same path until he turned towards the fields and she headed to the home behind the butcher shop.

"Why aren't you coming?"

"I didn't know her well."

"She knew us. And she's our neighbor."

"Tell him I'm sorry."

He had seemed unaffected by the death and assumed she would go to the Clays' less because Mr. Clay was now alone. But she went often, and He didn't understand. When the time felt right, she began to plan a meeting for Mr. Clay to come to their home and see what they'd made, and also for the neighbors to come together without grief as the reason. She made a meal for the meeting. In his shop, Mr. Clay had finally received what she had been unable to find since leaving

240

THE ONES WE LOVED

Waterfall. Even the old restaurant had not carried it. It was the only dish Mama had taught her without She having to beg or watch the process from the corner of her eye. A tripe stew. There was nothing else She had brought with her to The Plains: not her uniform, which she left at the restaurant, her friends' names or her mother. It was the thing that was still old, and in The Plains, she hoped it would become something new. The girl brought it to He first, wanting the boy she loved to be the first to try it before she made enough to feed more than just two people.

It was meant to be a gift, and when she took it out to the back where he was sprawled under the sun, she hoped he would taste it like the men tasted Gogo J.'s food and realize that more company would make the meal better.

"This is for our meeting," she had told him, smiling. "When Mr. Clay and the neighbors come to see the mats you made and the things we built. Taste it while it's hot!"

"What meeting?"

"For our neighbors! Go on and eat!"

He was now sitting up, arms draped over his knees. "We don't need the neighbors to come here. Why would we do that?"

She knelt on the ground and held his hands, feeling around a flower-like pattern of roughened calluses from long ago, next to the new ones that had sprouted between his knuckles and made him flinch when she delicately ran her thumb over the puffed skin. "Do you remember how people always came to Gogo J.'s looking exhausted, but when they left, it was as if their lives had been shaken loose and now they could not stop smiling or singing? Being the watcher and also the listener changed them in such a short time, and it felt so strange seeing happiness form in that way." She paused for a minute, growing softer. "I can't say it was the restaurant because that was only a building. And it could not have been just the food. I think it was all the people sharing the day so that everyone received their fill. No one got too much, and no one left with too little. There was a feeding happening and it wasn't just for the stomachs."

He didn't respond.

"Do you see?" She had asked, now holding his hands tighter.

"We don't need to do that," He finally answered. "No one needs to come here. To feed or relax or become an audience for stories that are not their own. This house is ours. We live here. That is enough."

"But don't you see—"

"No."

"It can be what—"

He had picked up the dish and tossed the stew into the weeds, splashes of sauce landing on her dress and feet. It was hot. It must hurt, he thought then. His mind went back to another house that had been for three. When a different person had cooked a stew that had made the room smell like decaying fruit before it became fragrant, making him have to swallow saliva every few seconds, hungry to try what had been made. His mind went back to the excitement. And back to the alley.

Her face had been confused, then startled, because he had never done something so barbed with fury.

"What is wrong with you?" She'd asked tensely.

"We already live here with them, why is that not good for you? We don't need any meeting." His voice had started to rise so that when he finally made the question a commandment, he was shouting in her face. The neighbors could have heard him.

He had run into the house and grabbed all the rest that was on the paraffin stove simmering, dumping it into the sink that slowly filled with water, where the smell stayed for several days. She had scooped out the food with her hands and thrown it in the front yard.

So he could see it the next morning, He thought, and remember

THE ONES WE LOVED

what he had done. Lying in bed that night, their hands—those that had thrown and those that had made—remained on top of their own chests, feeling and listening.

It was the closest their hearts had been since that day in the water, She realized. He also knew it. Their dual disregard of speech as a way through this moment—the thing that would take them around what had happened in the afternoon and place them on the other side of it the next day—bound them tight so they were elbow to elbow. She saw him. Someone who could flail and then quickly step back, triggered by an action and silenced by a memory. He saw her. Someone who could stand still, deliberately, while life happened past her feet. Someone who wouldn't move until they understood. They saw each other, better than they had in the water. The person who stepped back and the one who didn't move.

"I know you," she could have said.

"I see you," he would have answered.

It could have been another beginning. But no hands moved. No one's mouth opened. There were many times when the silence started. He could not remember, and she was quite weary. But the silences continued to grow and moved closer with each sunrise, not making any room for an apology that started as a feigned cough or an attempt at humor.

The silence was easier to bear when He became someone who spent much of his time outside, and She started to observe more than before, learning the town and making herself the third person in their home.

The one who knew the girl, who was close to the boy and who was now sifting through the silences wondering which of life's events had made them forget that He saw her on the bus, and She remembered him in the restaurant.

243

37.

"Where is the sweeping stick?" She asked, knowing it had been moved and only by him.

He answered after some time. "I don't know. Where did you leave it?"

She exhaled deeply, disappointment stirring under her skin. Not sleeping well had left her sensitive, and exhaustion sliced the ends of her sanity, leaving it frayed. He knew where she had left it. In the same place it had been since they started living here. And because he knew where she left it, he knew she would check there first. And so if she was asking him where it was, it was because she had looked behind the cupboard in the kitchen and not found it there. "Did you use it to kill the mice again?" she asked.

"Why would I use it?"

"Because that's what you always do. You see them outside and run after them." She rubbed her eyes roughly and thought of other places. "You could just leave them be. They never come inside."

"They could go into the front yard and destroy your garden," he said, hoping her ears would notice the concern in his voice.

"They are mice."

Standing in the middle of their small sitting room, she moved

245

her eyes from corner to corner, something She'd already done several times.

"Can you please look outside to see if you left it there?" she asked, her voice now milder, even though she never shouted. So now it seemed like she was muttering.

"Why would I leave it outside?"

"Because of the mice. You might have left th—"

"I told you, I didn't touch it. Not for the mice, not for anything." The intentions were clear in the bluntness of his response and the voice that was starting to wilt, every word thinning because he wanted this conversation to end—for her to stop talking. "If you can't find it, I don't know where it is."

On these slow days in The Plains—while the weather danced around hot and cold before deciding to be both depending on which side of the house you were in and, if you went outside, how close to the swamp you stood—when She approached He even slightly for an answer, he would grow quiet. His silence would cover them, and she would stand still, looking anywhere but at his face because she didn't want to recognize this person who had failed to speak to her well. Her eyes would focus on the floor mat by the door, find one woven thread and follow it through and under the dozens of other little threads he had pulled into a pattern.

She had tried to stop asking him for help when things were misplaced, choosing to replay their previous searches and act as two: the one always looking and the other who never knew anything was gone. But she missed his voice. And wanted to remember the sound of her own when directed towards him. When the missing grew too large to be contained, the internal dialogue would spill out of her lips and words would come out, barely audible. If he was in the room, his eyes would look in her direction and her own would find the mat. Like that it would continue. In the time they had lived here, not once had he

THE ONES WE LOVED

put the stick back where it belonged. When finished, he just dropped it, never asking himself how it always wound up back where he knew to take it from. That had made her smile until he stopped wanting to hear her voice or use his own.

She opened the back door and stepped outside, the morning's sun hitting her hard, almost making her recoil. Their curtains had stayed closed since the day he forgot to talk to her well, quickly turning her into someone who was unprepared for first light and surprised by its persistent attempts to make her eyes open wider, to creep past the threshold and make their house seem larger.

The girl let out a short breath. That ecstatic joy at being awake, having the sun wash your face and welcome you into a new day with a skip and a promise, was not a feeling she knew. She had heard about it. Some time and time past from her favorite teacher who loved to speak of "free mornings." Ones that were "easy as Sunday." She had listened, although Sunday was never easy, the same way she had listened to Mama speak about the ways of women, and nowhere was there mention of blissful mornings and rest. Mama talked about work. The work that She would have to do: She would wash. She would cook often. She would wipe, wring, rinse, dust, shake. She had been warned of what she would be expected to do in her own home during the day, and very few people had spoken of ease. Maybe if they had, She would wake up and greet the sun with a long breath in, out, and a smile.

Only later, living here in The Plains, did the girl realize it might all have been the same, her favorite teacher's lessons and Mama's instructions. Mornings were free because the routine was plain, simple to grasp and uninterrupted by choices. Perhaps that was the ease, she thought while straightening her shoulders. The bliss was in the labor, unchanging and plenty, offering something to begin and see to the end. That seemed like a joy. It also cost nothing of real value besides her own commitment. And it was what kept her rising and moving through the silence. The sounds of wiping, wringing, rinsing, dusting and shaking brought life into their stillness.

She found the sweeping stick behind some bushes by the rusting fence that circled their yard, close to a hole burrowed by mice. Picking it up, she tried her best to straighten the twigs, pulling out the broken ones and tightening the thin strip of bark and rubber that held the rest together. Out here belonged more to the wild than to the hands that cleaned and the face that went mute. They had planned to fix it up, rationed dreams of making it some type of relaxing place and using that tree stump at the left corner as an eating area. She would tell one day, and He the next. Never finishing the dream and always taking it into the next day so it grew bigger.

But the plants had refused to yield, and the mice were too determined with their visits. After a while She stopped trying. The tree stump never became a table they used regularly. Too much had happened out here. The food would taste bitter if placed on top of the fading circles that told of the tree's age before its death. Could it also tell her how long they would live as quiet neighbors? He still swung his machete at the weeds and whacked at the mice with the sweeping stick. There seemed no point, but he never stopped working on the yard, even after he stopped reaching for her.

"What are you doing?" he asked, leaning against the door frame, lending his voice to a face she didn't know.

She avoided looking at him and squeezed through.

"I told you I hadn't touched it," He added. "Why would it be outside if I touched it? You're the one who's always cleaning."

She started to sweep, going into the kitchen first. Knees bent, she moved slowly from one side of the room to the opposite end, her right hand resting above her lower back. Tiny bits of twigs broke off as she reached for the corners behind the stove, the temperamental cooler and the clogged spot behind the door that collected every piece of the

THE ONES WE LOVED

street their feet brought inside. As the dust rose and settled She hoped that this time He would grab a cloth and run it over the furniture. Like he used to do when they were wishing to make a home, and he would blow the dust outside even when he knew that wouldn't work, blowing with such force he started to cough. Each time she laughed until tears ran down her face. She would then remind him to wet the cloth, and while she moved through the house sweeping, he followed behind and wiped everything she pointed towards. If he felt light, he would grab her waist and sway like the trees when the wind was mischievous, while she half-heartedly asked him to let go. Now He was quiet and She sighed. Air stood still between them uninterrupted by anything, not a hand reaching out, a layer of dust or a smile made because eyes met.

Sometimes she wished he would try and wreck their home, tear through the mats he had made and, with three strong kicks, crack the furniture they had built. Then she would see there was still a need inside him that looked to her to make something beautiful from what was broken. This boy had loved her too much; now he couldn't talk to her well. She stole a look at him standing in the doorway to the backyard, his tall form blocking the rays. Thin lines of light came through the spaces where his body couldn't fill the entire frame, between his slumped shoulders and narrow waist, between his temple and softly shaped chin. The places she had touched and nibbled during their loving days. With his arms folded, it was hard to believe there was a time when she had begged they pull her closer and felt his hands gently cup her face. That they had impatiently reached for her body, wrinkling her clothes, and after, pulled at the threads that had come undone, swearing to be more delicate and patient with his desire. Through his dark shirt she could see the tightness of his back and knew that while she was reliving an old echo, this person blocking the door was festering on an injury.

"Are you going out this afternoon?" She asked him while she swept the sitting room.

249

He was silent and she held her breath, fearing he would ignore her question. So early in the morning.

"I don't know," He answered.

"All right." She kept sweeping.

"Are you going out?" he asked, turning to watch her adjust the green cushions on their sofa, which had once been in the boarding house and which She had asked for because those passing through the town only needed to sleep, while those who stayed needed somewhere to also sit. The light poured into the room when he moved from the door. She looked up squinting, shielding her eyes with her free hand. Her eyes were growing more sensitive. She touched them often these days, placing her index fingers under the wet skin and waiting until her ears grew hot and her stomach started to dip and swing. Then she kept holding.

"I'm still cleaning," She said, wishing he would say a kind thing, ask the right question, so she could answer.

He waited for her to finish with the sofa before sitting down, closing his eyes and stretching his legs as though he had just finished heavy work.

"I'm still cleaning," she repeated.

He didn't move.

She could have kept going, but what does it mean to try and work around someone who is doing nothing? If she kept sweeping, she would get dust all over him. If she stopped, the room would be half done.

"I'm going out," she said a while later.

He said nothing. Soon she left. Silently.

And the silence began because the first one, the earliest, said nothing to the one who asked about the things that made them say why. So the ones after said nothing, because they asked but no one knew, and so they had the question but no answer. And the silence began for the ones who had the question, maybe even the answer, but they didn't have a way to live with both. And the silence began because it had to continue.

38.

SHE HAD LEFT him sleeping or pretending. Part of her hoped He would finish cleaning, but it was more likely he would go and see to the land. She thought of Mr. Clay and the cuts he would have today. No one in The Plains had enough animals to rear for meat so he had to wait for the nearest town over to send leftovers. Mostly offal, it wasn't always the best, but it was enough for those who received, sometimes reluctantly. She was the only one who found herself pleased with what she picked up.

Her shoes were kicking up dust, and her dress played against her knees while the wind tried to rip it from her body. She was walking down the dusty road carrying a bag of guavas, her constant gift for the meat Mr. Clay gave them. That was the only fruit whose seeds wouldn't grow in the man's yard, so he was happy for the trade. It was also Mrs. Clay's favorite fruit, and after she died, She brought more for Mr. Clay, even when She didn't need anything.

The road was empty, and everyone was inside hiding from the heat or stealing a mercy underneath a tree. She liked walking when the outside was in its unbearable state. It made her feel purposeful, strong enough to take on the weather at its hottest or coldest and not look unkempt. Certainly, she was uncomfortable, and the sun pressing against her left temple was likely going to give her a headache that made her want to remove her head from her neck and place it to the side until the feeling of flames and sharp pins receded. But she wouldn't die. She would keep going when everyone else had stopped, and she would make it home with the same number of things she had left the house with, and the extra weight from the butcher shop.

She raised her hand to cover her face and red eyes. *I should have drunk a cup of water before I left*, she thought.

The wind continued to whip the bottom of her skirt up towards her knees, pushing the hem higher and higher until it was now moving against her thighs. On a quiet day, it was a respectable garment, but now she didn't look much different from the women at the boarding house, those who lived there long and those passing through, that she would see on Saturdays outside the bar, waiting for the men to finish their liquor before asking for their time. The women always made sure to not go with the ones who'd had too much to drink. They wouldn't have money left over to borrow, and it would be no fun lying next to a man who could barely hold his head up. They hadn't tried to talk to He when the couple first arrived. She had trusted it was because he loved her. If they tried now, He would be no different, but not because of her.

She saw the butcher shop as she rounded the corner and almost fell to the side while making the turn. She walked gingerly towards her destination, making sure to place her feet firmly on the ground, keeping herself straight.

"Almost knocked you all the way to the boarding house," teased Mr. Clay while he helped her with the door.

"I didn't see that wind coming! It was just a little flutter poking through my garden when I left the house."

THE ONES WE LOVED

"That breeze is always a danger on its own," said Mr. Clay. "Makes you forget that nature is a many-faced beast and each one could hurt you. Only a question of how badly."

Nodding while passing the guavas across the counter, She allowed this familiar exchange a space between them. The man talked to everyone, but she believed their conversations went deeper than greetings shared between neighbors because he never asked how she was. This would have given her a way to deny clarity, to herself and to him, with a quick "fine," "well" or "good." Instead he asked how she felt, and so it was much harder to be brief when someone wanted news on your feelings. In the beginning, nothing the old man said had been clear, but now it all landed very beautifully. When the meaning finally showed itself, all she could do was shake her head. These days she would think of his words, too uncommon to remember every day, but remarkable in how they fit whatever moment she was in. Standing behind the counter, arms full, he had an impish smile on his face, as if he had just listened in on something he shouldn't have.

"Did you get anything new today?" She asked.

He looked at her, trying to look passive while nudging his finger towards a small tray on the left side of the glass partition, between the chicken feet and slices of liver. Once it was roasted alongside thickly cut vegetables, it would have a snap and still be tender. Biting into it would be like sinking your teeth into a bubble of flavor, letting it all explode and run down your throat. She would have loved to share some with Mr. Clay, but she knew he wouldn't like the taste, although he did love pig feet, which she could not understand. Hers was a small and private delight that was going to remind her of a time when she was cared for and her heart was possessively guarded by the three people who knew her better than anyone.

"Should I pack it all up for you, or save some for your next visit? I don't think anyone else will come and buy this."

253

Although the tripe was rarely a favorite among his customers because of its cooking smell, a few other families still bought limited amounts. This type of meat, however, that he was currently wrapping up was the only one that would feed one person. It wasn't just the nickname that scared people off—"forget the relatives"—but the fact that a bad cleaning or a reckless swipe of a knife could lead to sickness. It was the kind of meat that required great care. When she had asked if he ever received any during one of her first trips to the shop, Mr. Clay had been surprised she knew about it.

"I'll just take it all now," She said. "Save myself the trip."

"It's always good to see you when you come by."

She smiled and looked at the man who gave her sweet memories with every visit.

"I'll see you soon?"

"See you soon," he said as he handed her the package in brown paper.

"Say hello to her for me," She said gently.

Mr. Clay nodded, grateful and always touched, as she pushed the door open, holding the packages tightly in her left hand and grabbing on to her skirt with the other. He lowered himself onto the stool placed to the right corner of the counter, where he could sit and watch people walking by and in. Mr. Clay prayed for the two young lovers in the house at the end of the street because he knew She and He did not pray for themselves.

When they had first come to town, he had seen them walking together, side by side, interlocked hands and heads bowed close while they talked. As they passed by the store during those early days, waving and greeting, Mr. Clay had understood their small circle. He had been in The Plains long enough to recognize any love that walked past his store, and the old man had prayed for them, then, too. Because as much as their love cloaked them from the world, it could shield

THE ONES WE LOVED

them from each other. It was surprisingly simple to love someone into silence. Treating the love as though it will claim us better if we say nothing about our guilt and floundering, and our hurt and deceitful calm. Thinking life needed to be clean and fine before a happy love could be allowed in and before its eyes no longer needed to be covered like a child's from seeing what made us persons.

When Mr. Clay had arrived in this town that stretched without a single hill, hump or valley, he had brought his own love. A love that had emboldened Mrs. Clay to leave her family for a new place with a man whose only dream was to feed people. That love had kept them when the store struggled to be everything it was expected to be. Mrs. Clay wanted it to be an inheritance for the children. The people in The Plains wanted it to make them feel like a real town, not a place for people to land after making flight. Only one of those things came to be.

Mrs. Clay had the children, but none lived long enough to know their parents built a store in a dry place. When the last one turned seven, an age the other three had never reached, Mr. Clay and Mrs. Clay clung to each other and thanked their passed people for finally answering the prayers that were sent. Then the fever came. The vomiting started. The body became smaller and never stopped. Their last child died curled up in Mrs. Clay's arms, weighing almost as much as he did when he was born. His wife stopped praying. Mr. Clay prayed harder.

They had laid their children in the back enclosure of their house, which had been an excess of soil when they moved in, with wisps of weeds that couldn't be convinced to spread farther than the edges and at least appear uniform. After they rested their last child, the ground started sprouting tiny patches of green. Four children, gone in less than a decade. And a garden that disgraced the drought in less than six months. Banana trees with leaves large enough to cover the table of

255

a family of twelve. Bright pumpkins, rambling strawberry roots, paw-paws that were unnerving in their yellow clusters and sweet potatoes. Nothing but dust and parched streams a few steps outside their house and yet masses of green in the Clays' backyard.

The pride of this land that now carried their children was a mulberry tree. Its stout trunk held up dozens and dozens of the small fruit that ripened impatiently, as if afraid to be forgotten. The leaves and droop-ing branches formed an umbrella for the children around town to hide under while they stuffed their faces with enough mulberries to change the color of their tongues and stain eager hands and greedy mouths.

"They took my children and now give me food to feed those of oth-ers," Mrs. Clay used to say while sitting under the tree. No rancor, only bewilderment. They stayed in The Plains because their love was there, inside the soil that whipped in a frenzy when the wind came, making it tap against the windows like their children had done when they played outside and wanted their attention. The townspeople's tenderness buoyed the Clays. No one asked what had taken their children. They just brought their own to spend time and hoped that their presence would separate Mrs. Clay's grief from her joy, because she no longer prayed but took care of the garden like it was all she now had to do.

"Will it hurt you if I keep praying?" Mr. Clay had asked her.

"How can I love you if I ask you to stop doing what you need?" was her answer.

His prayers didn't need a church because those who listened did not know of such a thing. He looked to the voices in the sky, the sounds in the wind and the messages in the ground after they buried their children. Mr. Clay prayed when he talked, and prayed when he worked, and prayed when his children became his people.

"What do you need?" he had asked his wife, who could no longer feel the presence of her own people.

"I need to remember them," Mrs. Clay told him, looking at their

THE ONES WE LOVED

garden that flourished after death. "I will forget how they were if I can't see them under all this green." The Clays had scratched the names of each child onto different-colored pebbles, marking the tiny graves that were now hidden from view. Fruit stalks would have to be cut and slashed for the graves to be seen, and neither of them felt able to swing a machete. "All I will remember is how they left me."

And so Mr. Clay talked about the children. Every morning when he woke up, while Mrs. Clay looked up to the ceiling, he pulled her into the room between his arms and whispered stories he remembered of their four, and how each had been. They stayed in that bed for an extra two hours after sunrise while Mr. Clay drew memories from his heart and let them find his wife. After a while, instead of looking at the ceiling, she would look at her husband and listen more closely.

"When did that happen?" Mrs. Clay started to ask when her mind began opening itself up to the remembrances it sought. "Yes, the boys were always so fast with the cutting," she shared delightedly when recalling their children's exploits with food preparation. "And when they ran after the bird and tried to fly after it," she wheezed, remembering the two girls. "Or when they all sat under the sun, asking for it to send its powers."

Their boys and their girls came back to her bit by bit, so by the time Mr. Clay got up to open the butcher shop, Mrs. Clay would be humming to herself while cleaning their kitchen and then the sitting room, and later when hunched over the huge metal tub in their washing room, rinsing water from the clothes she was washing. Theirs and the children's. While replaying all that her husband had told her, Mrs. Clay started seeing the boy who had smiled at her, back when he told his dream, and whom she had run with from the Tobacco Triangle to The Plains.

Grief was not what took his wife, heavy as it was. It was a knowing, delivered secondhand by the woman at the boarding house who heard it from a few who had sped from another place with such haste that their

257

shoes' soles stayed on the dirt road, left behind by feet that stepped so hard that the only prints they left were those that could not keep up. In the store to pick up her package of fatty gizzards, the woman from the boarding house told of a gardening woman who had been burned inside a church. She had been praying, those who were fleeing murmured, when another woman shot one bullet between her shoulders and another through the base of her bowed head. Then she dragged the body to the cross in front of the church, boarded the doors and lit a match using a branch from a piercing-spirit tree as the first kindle.

"Why would anyone do that?" Mr. Clay heard himself asking, his voice forgetting to disappear and allow the devastation time to stand and speak on itself. He couldn't wait for it to gather because his mind needed a reason. A road to follow so it could understand how such an act could be what happened to a person who had hands that opened to touch delicate things and stretched to free large things, who had feet that walked in search of home, a heart that curved and a mouth that trembled for happiness. Committed by a person who had hands that opened to touch delicate things and stretched to free large things, feet that walked in search of home, a heart that curved and a mouth that trembled for happiness.

Because of sunflowers, the runners had told the woman from the boarding house, who told the Clays.

"Sunflowers?" Mrs. Clay had answered.

"Sunflowers that grow under the sun, are fed by water, wither in the cold and return again when the warmth beckons. They had been tended to by the woman who prayed, and owned by the one with a gun," the boarding-house woman said. And the one who prayed made them a gift for a man who had complemented. And the one with a gun made them a crime.

"What of her people?" Mrs. Clay asked. "What happened to the praying woman's people?"

THE ONES WE LOVED

"She had only one child, and the tragic thing, the evil of it all, was that the child had seen the church burn after coming to give her mother a purse she had forgotten at home. A silly thing to do is to forget, a honeyed thing is to remember and soiled is what you become when you turn someone's forgetting and remembering into blood and smoke. When your hands make gentleness a terrible part of living. The child heard the gunshot, saw the smoke and went mad. She grabbed the gun from the woman and shot her."

Here, the boarding-house woman had stuttered, then held her heart, shocked that it was still where it was and hadn't sunk to some place where it wouldn't have to be the thing that made it possible for her to pass on such a story. A place it could just listen in on play and loving. The boarding-house woman continued.

"How could one day have been silly, honeyed and soiled?"

It wasn't grief that killed his wife, heavy as it was. It was this knowing of the others passing through town who had fled so fast they didn't have time to wrap up their losses and cries, bundle their shrieks and shorten their sighs. So that while they ran, they dropped pieces of luggage in every place they stopped, stumbling over their sadness while walking to their seats, misplacing their beginnings so they wouldn't have to think of where they'd been, but now not having anywhere to claim. And holding their joys in the things they had to pull apart to transport, so only the lid came without the favorite pot, one blanket from a set of three and a bible with none of the books except the one that began with E.

"And the child?" Mrs. Clay needed to know. The woman from the boarding house could not say.

"Maybe living, maybe dying."

It wasn't grief that killed his wife, heavy as it was. It was this knowing. Mr. Clay's love could awaken her spirit in the names of their children, but it couldn't take away this knowing of soiled hands and

259

bowed heads with bullets. Of a child that was maybe living, maybe dying. Sometimes love is just not enough.

Mr. Clay had seen all types of love walk by and move into The Plains. Love had brought him here. Love brought the women into his store looking for the juiciest cuts to feed their families. For each of them, he always tried to give the best for what they bought. The meat never arrived as they received it. The other town sent what they would have thrown away, and it was Mr. Clay who cut through the fat, the piles of discarded brains and stomach remnants packed in bags, and then separated the takings into edible pieces. Mr. Clay would wash them and make sure they looked good. Mrs. Clay never liked cleaning the meat, but would sit with him as he worked, and when a customer came by, she would make sure the wrapping was strong so nothing would fall out and it wouldn't tear. His wife had loved She and always found time to have a chat. Her packages, Mrs. Clay wrapped with double the brown paper and tied the string twice.

"We can't have your food blowing away," his wife told her every time, even on days with the slowest breeze.

It was Mrs. Clay who had noticed that the two had started walking alone, one without the other. She, with her hands held tightly against her chest. He, with his head low.

"They have forgotten to remember," Mr. Clay said.

"I don't think they forgot," Mrs. Clay had mused. "I think they are finally remembering, and it's all too much."

Tiny rocks beat against Mr. Clay's windows as the wind blew its way through the town. A man whose grief had taken more than a meal and a night's sleep, but who still reached out to the people he knew.

"She says hello, Mrs. Clay," he said to the empty room.

260

39.

HE USED TO squeeze her hands and thank her shyly for cooking. The pleasure she took from it embarrassed him and also made him feel small. Not like something that could be easily taken away or abused. But a thing that could be held discreetly without courting too many questions on origin. The first meal She made for him reminded He of his mother blowing on his porridge so his tongue wouldn't burn. It wasn't a dish that she had seen Gogo J. make but one she created from her mind. That moment in Gogo J.'s kitchen had felt much larger than the time it had taken to turn the raw food with its dirt and leaves, blood and slippery skin, into something that spoke of care before either of them were ready.

"It's very good," he'd said, carefully stepping around love. "What is that flavor?"

She smiled in relief. "I was worried."

"What did you put in this? I taste something sweet."

"It's those round red seeds the hunters gave to Gogo J."

"They are a little sour on their own. I've tried them."

"Yes, the taste really tunnels into the back of your teeth if you eat them without any other food. That's why I put them in the dough, so they can work with the sugar."

After a while, that sensing and talking became what they did with every meal She cooked.

"What's in this one?"

"Those plants we saw growing next to the river with the petals that look like caterpillars."

"I didn't think they could be eaten."

"Me neither, but then I saw one of the hunter's children chewing on a stem. So I tried it."

"What did you add in here?"

"The small, fat bananas I got from the woman at the boarding house before we left. She wanted us to have some food while we settled. Isn't that kind?"

"She probably didn't want them to rot because that would have been a real loss. The sweetness is not too much at all."

"It's even better with the soup."

"This is very different."

"I picked the guavas that weren't quite ripe."

"What's new in this one?"

"It's the lychees from Mr. Clay."

"He has lychees?"

"Mr. Clay has everything."

"And there's something bitter too. I think I know it, but I can't be sure."

"What do you think it is?"

"Lemons?"

"Grapefruit," she said, her enthusiasm making her almost jump off the seat.

"Does Mr. Clay have oranges?"

"He might. There's so much in that garden, I'm sure there's food he hasn't even found," she said.

He reached for her shoulder to play with the strap of her dress, which had been sliding off with every move.

THE ONES WE LOVED

"Maybe I should cook for you wearing this dress," He said, playfully.

"It's hardly a dress," she answered.

She had been wearing one of the gifts that Ma Dube sometimes gave away to the women in The Plains. Their neighbor had been a performer in her younger years and had traveled from town to town, bringing entertainment to rooms of men and interested women who chose to watch. Now older, after having stopped in The Plains merely to lift her feet but winding up burying her shoes, Ma Dube sold pieces of her wardrobe. There was never an announcement, yet the women in The Plains would arrive at different times of the day, the timid ones later than the others, to receive what was available. *Payment is whatever you can afford within reason of the change that will occur in your life once you buy the clothes.* Those were Ma Dube's words.

You couldn't choose what you wanted—she asked what time you woke and slept, and then handed over folds of fabrics. When She bought her first pieces, they soared above her low expectations and challenged her commitment to be different. There was a long purple dress that raised her breasts and jealously circled her waist. She had held it up to the light and then against her body, wondering if she could be a person who wore this dress and still move as herself. The second was sheer, held together by thin straps with tiny pearls at the ends. She'd almost thrown it away, then remembered the bag of guavas and two maize cobs that were traded. She put it on and was looking at her reflection through the window to their backyard when He'd come home early.

"What is that?" He had asked, running his eyes over her body and returning to her face. He was standing in the doorway watching her with a look that made the lower part of her abdomen contract.

"I don't know, really. I bought it from Ma Dube today." She hadn't known how to stand in front of him while wearing that dress. It had felt like the morning after they were first together in the attic, when

263

she couldn't figure out how to be in front of the boy who had heard her act out of herself, when the darkness made it possible to come undone. A part of her, then and now, wanted to stay exactly where she was so he would keep looking. But she also wanted to grab a blanket and cover her body. He dropped his bag and came towards her, wrapping his hands around her body and pulling her close.

"It feels nice," he whispered close to her ear.

Her breathing wavered. "Do you like it? I feel strange wearing it. A little ridiculous."

"You look beautiful," he had said and then kissed her neck, trailing to her shoulders while his grip left prints on her hips.

"I was going to wear it while I cooked for you," she whispered, barely able to get the words out as she closed her eyes and felt him draw near.

He brought his lips near enough to kiss. "Please wear it."

"Can I wear this outside?" she asked teasingly.

"Is there someone you're cooking for out there?"

She laughed, slapping him on his shoulder.

"I do want to cook for you too. I know how," He said.

"I like doing it. It feels good to show you how much I love you."

"So if you cook for me, you love me?" he had asked, with a half smile.

"Yes," she answered, looking in his eyes and holding his face in her hands. "The day you starve is the day you find yourself alone in this house."

"But I can cook," he answered, his eyes only slightly open.

"Not like I can."

"I watch you. I'll remember."

"No you won't," she insisted.

It had been some time now since She'd told him about the food.

THE ONES WE LOVED

Even longer since He'd asked. Or laid a hand over slippery fabric draped on an arm. Today he watched as She moved in the kitchen, her hands flying from one pot to another, dipping and tasting, cutting and washing. When cooking, she seemed to grow several pairs of every body part, and He could recognize the girl from the restaurant because of how unflustered she was when a pot of oil sat too long over heat or water splashed into a hot pan.

What are you making? He could have asked. The question was one She would have answered because it didn't require anything except facts. After responding, she would have become silent again, He thought. Or she could have also asked him if he wanted to help, and he would have said yes. Then He would have stepped into the kitchen and taken the knife from her hand to cut something, or walked outside to grab the garlic she needed, and a little more. After, She would ask about the crops in the fields, and he would have told her they were as fine as they had been yesterday. Then the silence would grow longer because He couldn't ask about her day. He knew she had been at the Clays. And he knew that when she thought of them, she remembered the meeting she had wanted to have, the way she had tried to talk to him and the dish he had thrown away. So He didn't ask a question. And She didn't have to answer.

He had been thinking of the splashes that landed on her feet after he had tossed that tripe stew when she placed a plate in front of him. It must have hurt, he thought again. He quickly bit into the pork chops, letting the gravy spread across his mouth and licking the corners of his lips like a lizard. The aromas of meat and vegetables made him shut his eyes, and he wished she was sitting next to him so he could hear about the things she put inside that he could guess.

She was now washing the used pots in a small dish to save water. Her meal she would enjoy after he was finished and had returned to their bedroom. Everything had changed, he thought. He looked at her neck that he had once covered with kisses, leaving tiny bite marks. He looked at her back, which he'd once traced with his finger from her shoulders to the lowest part. He thought of her stomach, where he'd rested his head and listened to her breathing. He remembered worrying if she was in pain from the weight of his body.

40.

THE LEAVES RUSTLED, rearranging and dropping off as a breeze half-heartedly made its way through because it, too, didn't want to be creeping across The Plains at this hour. She was sitting in her spot, between two branches in the guava tree, with a clear view of the house and enough shelter to be unseen by a passerby. She reached for a large, misshapen guava hanging above her head. Biting into the thick, pebbled pink flesh, she leaned back and wondered if She had been wrong.

Living in The Plains was a choice She had made because the town did not hold too tightly to the temperamental reversals of the weather. If it was hot and then cool, all in the first hour of the morning, life continued and the day's plans remained with little disruption. Unlike in Waterfall, where one truly hot day inevitably stoked fears for the rains that would come after, in The Plains, a hot day was simply that.

Certainly, there were moments in the town when a balance between the people and the outside seemed like a truly distant desire, especially when the sand twirled itself into a frenzy around the feet of anyone walking outside and it appeared as though people were not welcome here. As though the first person to have landed on this ground had to bargain with the weather for room and still somehow lost, but chose to stay because a lost bargain was better than another relocation. Bargaining needs patience, and this She had spent her life reaping so her life could hold a measure of relief. Landowners didn't have patience. She had known it then and recognized it when they stepped into the boarding house and learned of this town that had probably survived because of a bargain. There would be no landowners in The Plains. They could not survive here. And so when He and She decided to stay, all she saw was a home.

Had She been wrong?

She had counted their days living here in bus rides. When she was happy, every time she heard the bus, she was reminded of how they'd arrived and what had changed. The first time the sound of the engine came through the windows, they had just finished cleaning the dust off all the floors in the house, wiping layers brought in by the previous people and their lives, and those discarded by the wind. The next time she heard it, He had finished building their table and was beginning to weave the floor mat. Sometimes she would miss the sounds and only knew it had come when she saw a new face sitting outside the bar or walking out of the butcher shop as she walked in. On those days she was surprised by how busy her life had become—her days so full that she could miss the sound of wheels scratching on top of the gravelly road.

The bus had come and gone fifty times since the silence began. She swallowed the last of the guava and looked at their house through the trees. The sun had set a few hours earlier, and the day had passed without a word shared between them. If he happened to wake from his slumber and notice her absence from the bed's left side, She wondered if he would care to know where she went. She was never far. All he had to do was look up at the sky.

"Are you hungry?" she'd asked him that morning after the silence began, squinting, after waking to touch her eyes and press her fingers deeper into the spongy inside.

THE ONES WE LOVED

"Not now," he had grumbled out of the corner of his mouth while he struggled to raise himself.

"Do you want something to eat?"

He had been silent before lifting his head to meet her eyes and then turning away. For a second his coldness made her body stiffen.

"There's food on the table."

She was used to silence. Had grown up piecing the lives of those she loved from the things they didn't care to share. It was a way of being She understood, so it unsettled her that in this moment, she felt as though she had been cracked and left to slowly break. The cracks with their thin lines were traveling under her skin, and she worried that soon people would be able to see them and wonder about the cause. Her eyes burned, so she closed them and saw his face in the itching haze.

When she got off the bus with the oil stains and the ripped-out headrest, some pieces of her life failed to follow. If someone asked her now whether she'd ever touched a gun, She would answer without hesitation. No. And yet she still knew how Mama had left. And how the red-hatted landowner's wife had died.

Her geography had receded as the bus moved, so that when she climbed down the steps far from home, all she remembered was Kuda's grandmother. And all she wondered was who buried her mother. Did someone put out the fire? Or did they wait until everything was ash, making the cross just the same as the bones and the blood, and the leather shoes and the suit that had once been part of a set of three? She had never wanted Waterfall to be her beginning, but she left knowing more about the town, while her past and future rose to the sky as smoke. Who was cleaning the house? Had they burned it too? What did Mama see while her eyes were closed during that final prayer? Was it her daughter's face or that of God? She hoped it was neither. A God had allowed hell to enter where she prayed. And my

269

face would never bring her comfort if she thought about me while in church.

The memories that stayed were no longer simply her own—Reverend Mr. Shoko, the boy who was shot and who cried, Kuda's grandmother, the woman who held him and made him stop. Waterfall had spilled all its torments into her mind, and all the girl could do was leave. Where would she put her town's geography? She still remembered Kuda's grandmother when walking through The Plains and thought of the life the woman might have created if she'd stayed on the bus longer, passed Gogo J.'s town, and landed here. The girl always preferred to think of the possibilities and not the truth. She preferred to imagine who Kuda's grandmother could have become every time the woman let Waterfall fall back. Instead of wondering about the change that could have happened if Waterfall had chosen to let Kuda's grandmother stay, and become the town she needed, with neighbors that pulled her in and didn't close her out. Where she wouldn't have to decide between being the mother of a reverend or that of a boy who was shot. The guardian of a child whose parents died, or the mother of a boy who had survived.

The girl could have stayed in the other town, working with Gogo J. and living in the room above the restaurant. But this was the town she'd run to, and you cannot live where you escape. You learn to breathe again, make yourself one of the patterns on the new fabric, and only when the strands could hold and the thread had enough length to keep feeding into another do you unravel and become your own fabric. But you can't live in a medicine room. You take what you need and leave the rest for others. If you stayed, how would you ever know what it was that hurt and if you've healed? How would you stop looking at the ointments without believing you needed one for the pain that only came after you saw there was medicine? The town was medicine for Kuda's grandmother, and she had come every time she needed a drink or a spray of fronds. But the town alone could not make her better.

THE ONES WE LOVED

Kuda still mourned a grandmother she could have had, and Reverend Mr. Shoko was so ashamed of living, he spoke nothing of the woman who had raised him. He prayed, and he preached.

She had thought about returning. Once when they were happy and She wanted Gogo J. to feel pride and meet the man She knew. But their house was not quite done, and if Gogo J. had decided to return with them, She couldn't have her see an unfinished house. Now the house was done, but it was no longer a home.

She spent more time sitting in this guava tree, thinking about the woman she tried to be and how she had failed to truly settle into a good life. Mama had been a woman of faith, holy and terrified. Calling on God every Sunday, looking for him all the other days, and She can't say that happiness was something that filled Mama's life. So the daughter chose to become a woman who was loved easily. But as easy as the love came, it turned when she became part of a memory. Was easy love not lasting love? Had Mama loved her father viciously and hard? Had Kuda's grandmother loved selfishly and quietly? She should have known better. Studied all the geography and seen what love could do to anyone who came seeking its warmth. Love had turned Kuda's grandmother into a shadow and made She a child without a father. Kuda's grandmother kept leaving because love would not let her forget, and Reverend Mr. Shoko preached because love told him to shout. There had never been lovers in Waterfall, only believers. Here in The Plains, if She couldn't be the holy woman or the loved woman, what was left?

Mama would have told her to pray. Gogo J. would have reminded her of the warning she gave. And Kuda and Joy would have listened, then told her a funny story. Was she not meant to love if all those she'd loved would fail to help her understand the state of her life?

Sitting in this tree, hour after hour, it hurt her to realize she needed help to understand the girl who had run. Her geography kept changing and now she was starting to feel like the smoothest rock below the

271

water. No edges, no friction, no imprints or markings to speak of the journeys or the forces of the waves. Just smooth sides that could not be properly held and slipped through unsteady fingers.

The holy woman rose in smoke and the loved one watched from the trees. Neither came close to touching the sky. Maybe if they had, they would have left some signs. Like the streaks she would see while sitting in the classroom and looking at her first tree. So that when people looked up, if they ever did, they would see thin, tiny signs of commotion. Signs that a trying life had passed by here, and things had shifted as that life got older and older. Was there any commotion somewhere when Mama burned? And if She returned to Gogo J., would she be the girl who was an orphan? Or the one who killed them all?

She could no longer be the one who was loved because there was no answer for where the love went after he stopped giving it to her, and she didn't feel the need to search. Mama should have said more about love. She didn't know enough.

"I don't understand this change," she said of her geography. She waited for an answer—from the woman who taught her about living to match the environment and learning to live with lack. *I never listened to the wind in Waterfall*, she thought, swinging her ankles over a sturdy branch and placing her back into a carved-out opening that had been the home of something much smaller.

She thought about Mrs. Maynard, her Numbers teacher. What had she said about rapport? *A close relationship where people understand their feelings and live well.* She always made sure to understand. Talked and listened and was quiet when others needed silence to grow closer to the chatter of their internal disturbance, deciding if they should speak it or respond with eyes carrying resurrected pain and burdened sleep. She, too, wasn't sleeping well.

THE ONES WE LOVED

"I could just leave," She said to the wind and massaged her shoulders. During the days she had gone to school carrying her notebook,
reading book and lunch in her bag, she had felt her shoulder muscles tighten and had sometimes longed to have her back pulled apart,
so the skin could be slapped against a tree like Mama did with the
blankets that needed a little refreshing. There was nothing to really
carry anymore. But her shoulders continued to tighten and her back
hurt more. She thought of Mama and the type of loved people she
had left behind when she arrived in Waterfall. That's something She
should have asked before. Had the love been enough to last through
an absence or did they give it back when Mama left because love was
nothing without the person who gave it? Did she take it with her to
give that same loving to other people?

Pressing her fingers against her eyes, she leaned into the tree, feeling
the dry bark needling through her dress and poking her skin. Where
had she picked up this floral garment? Must have been Gogo J.'s.

"I don't know what to do . . ." she confessed, then stopped. A light
flickered in their house from the lantern that could be seen through
the sitting room window. The flame went out, and She knew he had
blown it. They had passed lots of hours planning the placement of
their furniture, so he knew how to move in the dark without causing
injury.

"He probably moved to the sofa," She said, which they had moved
four times. The last time, he had joked they should just return it to
the boarding house, because it seemed to fit better there than in their
house. It had been missing a woven rug on the floor to match the one
he made for the kitchen. Then it was perfect.

What had she told Mrs. Maynard? That rapport did not make
sense and harmony was an inheritance, not a choice. She could choose
harmony because of the rapport she had built with him, but if

273

He didn't choose it, too, then all She had was a relationship that caused her shoulders to tighten and her back to ache, even when there was nothing she carried.

The door opened and she heard him let out a cough while cracking his back. It was darker now, so his outline was barely visible. She waited, not like in Waterfall, but like He did in the restaurant, waiting to find the right words before speaking, and also looking through the window, hoping not to starve.

41.

HE HAD PLANNED on walking by the butcher shop and not stopping, but something in the window drew his eye and pulled him away from the road. The boy's feet briefly hesitated before dusting off on the entry mat.

"This is more surprising than the roses growing beneath my tomatoes." Mr. Clay spoke first, smiling broadly from behind the counter. "She was in here only a few days ago."

"Hello, Mr. Clay," He said, politely looking past the man at a spot above his head, close to the shelf with some of the objects that the man had found and picked up around the town. A green stone shaped like a bird's beak, a creased-up can, an empty snail shell, a button too large for any piece of clothing. The boy had not seen Mr. Clay since the time before Mrs. Clay died, when he had returned the borrowed tools and found them both in the shop. It had been hard to talk to them together; now it was difficult to see the man alone.

"Where did you get that?" He asked, pointing to the half-finished basket holding flowers from Mr. Clay's garden.

"Ahh, I just started working on it," Mr. Clay answered proudly, lifting it up and placing it in He's palms, which were already waiting.

Leaning forward, he continued, "I found some particularly pliable grass underneath the shade of the mulberry tree and decided to try a different kind of work with my hands."

"Something that didn't involve dicing," He said, each word clearing his throat and adjusting to the necessities of conversation.

"Only folding and patience. If anything, it's my hands that have been sliced. No one told me how dangerous weaving can be."

"Why did you start this?"

"Mrs. Clay always wanted to learn," Mr. Clay answered gently. "There was never anyone to teach her and so I decided to teach myself. Learn it for her."

Running his fingers across the basket, He felt slanted ridges that brought a smile to his face. His first attempts with his grandmother had felt and looked like this, too, his eager fingers unable to loosen and work. Mr. Clay came from behind the counter and looked at He, whose eyes had closed as his fingers continued to feel the basket.

"It made you think of something," the old man said kindly.

Opening his eyes, He lifted up the boxy shape and held it in front of Mr. Clay. "You see here?" he began. "You need to fold the edges down like this, so they don't poke out when they dry. If that happens, they won't hold. They'll also scratch and cut if you try to move them. And better to fix now because once the grass dries, they'll just prick your hands."

The instruction was fast, easy and confident. A former student recalling the words of a missing teacher.

Mr. Clay's shock was so apparent, He almost laughed.

"You can weave?"

"My grandmother taught me when I was a boy." He paused. "It helped keep the ghosts away."

"The ones you didn't want past the threshold?"

"I don't think there's any I would have wanted to come across. Too much comes with them."

THE ONES WE LOVED

"Some are good for the soul," Mr. Clay said, turning his head to face the direction of the mulberry tree. "They don't all come to haunt you. Some just want to become a part of your life in a different way."

The boy thought of what to say, before choosing silence as the response that was safer, and inevitably honest. Mr. Clay chose it, too, and for a while, the boy and the old man stayed by the counter, one looking at the basket, the other listening to the creaks and sighs of the nearby garden. The store's shadows lengthened as the sun rolled through and the town seemed to free a tremor as it noticed a change—a small light trying to stab its way through a fog.

"So the weaving made you forget?" Mr. Clay finally asked.

"No, I never forgot. But when I would weave, all I thought about was making sure the lines were straight and my fingers were moving as they were supposed to. It somehow became the way I told time. Instead of seeing days passing in the things I remembered, time moved through the baskets I made and the ones that were good enough to make my grandmother wake my grandfather so he could see how well I was doing."

"A true gift," Mr. Clay uttered, almost to himself. "So that's what brought you in here. My little basket."

The boy sniffed it, not quite certain why. "It smells like the sun."

Mr. Clay, who was watching, didn't ask for an explanation, but He felt bound to give one. "When the sun touches grass, or any plant, there's always a smell. The plants have their own scents that help us recognize them, but they also have one scent that's the same, and when I was young, I didn't know what it was. Then a friend told me it was the sun. He always had odd answers for everything, and they made sense, so I believed him."

Mr. Clay bent his head slightly and sniffed the basket, still in the boy's hands. "The sun," he whispered.

277

Smiling, He placed it on the counter. "There aren't that many places here with good reeds. That's what you really need. But those you have seem to be working."

There wasn't much left to say, and too many words had already filled up the shop. He started to feel nervous, fearful of this nearness that seemed to have sprung between them and that could not be trusted. Pushing back the basket, he walked towards the door before stopping abruptly.

"I would try going by the swamp. I've seen some reeds there that could be good. They are the only thing that sprout from that stiff water."

"Could you teach me?" Mr. Clay asked, tentatively. Turning back, the boy looked at him curiously.

"Well, you're the only one who knows how to do this," Mr. Clay responded to the question on his face. "I think I would very much enjoy it."

He was quiet.

"And I think you would enjoy it too," the old man added.

"How do you know that?"

"Because you still remember the first steps."

Heading out, He reached for the door and Mr. Clay lowered himself onto his stool.

"Tell She I send my love."

He turned back and nodded before leaving. A decision was made before the door clicked shut.

It lay where it was remembered. The sweeping stick and its split parts. Sometime in the days someone would pick it up and run its bristled edges along a floor. Another would pick it up and use it to clear a place filled up by time and absence. This would keep happening. Some hands would pick it up, others would leave it down. Until the bus arrived again; then one pair of hands would add more sticks next to those that were loosening out of the grip and needed to be regathered so they could be closer to the others, strengthened now by the extra support lent by new branches with stronger cores and sharper ends. In time it would become flexible enough to handle. Then so flexible that it was not useful for work and clearing. Until one pair of hands added more sticks. So the sweeping stick wouldn't bend so far it caught nothing. So far it broke.

42.

THE BOY HAD watched Mr. Clay receiving bags of meat from the next town four times since he started teaching him how to properly hold and fold reeds so they could make the right shapes, and the old man was making progress. He would come to the store and Mr. Clay, like a keen child, would be ready with the tools they needed—a small, sharp knife, some wires of various sizes, scrounged scissors, the reeds—each assigned their position in front of their hands. The old man had even gone down to the swamp on his own, something He had already done because he didn't think Mr. Clay could walk so far at his age. Now they had more than enough to use for as long as they worked together.

Mr. Clay's daily events had been habitual for so long that the labor of practice was something he looked forward to every week. If a customer came by, they would have to call out loud, and he would rush to greet and send them on their way with none of the inquiries and conversation they had become accustomed to. When the man was learning something particularly difficult and was interrupted, he would shut his eyes and click his tongue.

"I don't think I have ever seen you look annoyed," He had said the first time.

"I wasn't annoyed," Mr. Clay responded.

He had looked at him knowingly and then let out a low chuckle.

"That was the second time Ma Dube came in today," Mr. Clay said defensively and glanced at the boy before breaking into a smile.

"What's wrong?"

"I don't think I've ever seen you laugh," Mr. Clay answered.

Now self-conscious, He turned his attention back to the mat he had been making. These had been good moments for him. As good as life had possibly been since their beginning in The Plains. On the days Mr. Clay had lessons, He would wake up in their house and remember the new student, a memory that preceded all the others despite having less time to claim his mind. Today they were sitting under the mulberry tree, hiding from the sun.

"Look at this!" yelled Mr. Clay with delight, holding up two hours of work. "I made a handle!" the man added, raising up the curved piece that would be put on the side of a bag. Having moved from mats to something more challenging, the student was learning quickly and He was impressed.

"That is very good!" He said, examining it. "Very good," he repeated. "Remember to hold them tightly, but not to pull too hard."

"You know, soon, I think I'll be able to work just as fast as you do," Mr. Clay said, his brow furrowed in concentration as he started another.

"I know you will," He answered, proud and amused. He had been the same.

As Mr. Clay folded the reeds, one on top of the other and under and back again, the old man looked at the immaculate rows on He's side. "Did your grandmother start teaching you when you were quite young?"

He nodded his head. "Yes, she did."

"And did your mother know how to weave as well?" Mr. Clay asked carefully. The old man didn't want him to feel any sense of urgency

THE ONES WE LOVED

from the questions. He wanted the boy to be willing to speak without feelings of duress.

"I don't know," He answered, frowning. "Some days I think she did, and I can remember her weaving, but then other times I don't know if it was her or my grandmother."

Mr. Clay was quiet while the confession lingered.

"Does She know you are weaving with me?" the old man asked after a time.

"I haven't told her," He answered.

"Why?"

He shrugged.

"Why don't you ask her? She might want to learn too."

"I don't think she will."

"Have you asked her before?" the old man prodded.

"No, Mr. Clay, I have not."

"Then you should ask her! She might want to come and learn with me. And when I start selling my meat and baskets, I will need a lot more help than you to serve everything quickly."

"We are selling now?" He asked, another chuckle escaping.

"Well we can't just keep them for ourselves," Mr. Clay answered.

"I see."

His mind traveled back to his house, as his hands moved deftly and quickly, twisting and shaping the reeds. Something was happening to his heart the more time he spent with the old man. It was still too precious, and if he told her before he could recognize it, it could leave and never come back. If he told her before it became part of his bones and spirit, it might disappear.

"I'll wait," He whispered.

"She might not," replied Mr. Clay.

He hadn't answered out loud, but the old man had dropped the anxious thought that had been spinning in his mind, and that often

283

woke him up in a panic. He would turn over, and her back facing him would be a relief and a guilt.

"I know you love her," Mr. Clay started.

He needed Kind Eyes and Blink and Miss for this discussion.

"She's hurting, because you're hurting. It's fine to hurt. It keeps us from dying every time we lose something that was loved. But you're not telling her what you lost. Neither is she. And so now she thinks you hurt her, and you believe she hurt you."

"I don't," He answered, while his fingers gripped the mat in his hands.

"Then what are you doing? What are you holding on to that has made her a stranger?" Mr. Clay was pushing him now, and He could have risen and left. But he stayed. He had the answers. He knew he did.

"I think I have been unwell. I might have always been, but I would just look to the sky and then the sickness would just leave my body."

"The sky . . ." Mr. Clay repeated, not quite understanding the boy, but hoping he would continue.

"All I did was look up, and I felt comfort."

"The sky gave you that?"

He nodded. "I stopped looking, and when I did, I met her. It felt right. As if my friends had sent me something I could see face-to-face."

At this point He stopped and began to fold and unfold in his chair.

"Then somehow everything returned. The alley, the house, the fields. And I still couldn't look at the sky." He leaned forward, and Mr. Clay thought he was readying to leave, but he only reached for his leg, which had started to ache. "And I can't tell her any of it."

"Why?" asked Mr. Clay, confused.

"I don't want her to know that I couldn't let it all go. She makes me so happy, and it's still not enough for me to only remember our joy." His hands were shaking, and the mat he had been clutching fell from his grasp.

284

THE ONES WE LOVED

"And the sky's gone, so there's no one to tell me what to do. No one to listen. No one to tell me about the next day."

"Why can't you look at the sky again?"

"I told the sky about all the things that mattered to me, all the people I loved, and it took them all," He said after a pause that felt like it would turn into a long silence. "As if I didn't deserve them, and like they were people I was only meant to know and not love."

He pulled at each word and his leg hurt even more. "If I look up now, what else will it take? She's the only one left." He got up quickly and walked towards the door back to the shop, before he stopped and crumpled to the floor. Mr. Clay slowly moved beside him, and placed his hands over the clenched fists. The boy raised his eyes.

"I know she has questions. I do. But I can't speak until I have something to say that will be enough. Do you understand?"

Mr. Clay looked in the direction of the mulberry tree and thought of his late wife. He thought of their children. He held on to all their memories.

43.

"So she would take the big knife," She continued.

"The curved one?" Mr. Clay added for clarity.

"Yes. And when everything was skinned and piled together on the board next to the sink, she would bring the knife down and hack away, banging the meat into chunks and moving it to the side with her hands at the same time."

"She never sliced her fingers?" Mr. Clay asked, both startled and awed, imagining the loss of his own clumsy ones.

"Never. Not when I was there and not even before. I asked her. And she would never lie about that."

She had gone by the shop, and when she noticed that Mr. Clay had rabbit legs behind the counter, she couldn't help but think of Gogo J. She had only meant to share a line about a woman she knew who could cut and skin a rabbit better than anyone, but once she started, the stories linked themselves to another and came out of her mouth like a chain. The smells from the restaurant had come rushing through her nose, and laughter climbed up and around her mouth, forcing her to let out guffaws and bellows as she told Mr. Clay everything that had made her smile from the woman in the town with the strange name.

287

"I should be working for her," Mr. Clay said, impressed.

"No, she likes to work alone. You could sell her your meat, though. Only the best cuts because she will know if you try to give her anything less," she warned.

"You worked for her," he said.

"I did," she answered plaintively.

"No, I mean, you said she likes to work alone. But you worked for her. So she can't like working alone all that much."

She looked at her fingers tapping on her lap and laughed dryly.

"I guess that could be right. I don't think I gave her much of a choice."

"I can't see you demanding that anyone give you work. And from what you've told me, she's not the type of person to deny herself choices."

"Gogo J. is certainly not that."

They were sitting in front of the window dappled in sunlight. It wasn't too hot and the air around them was crisp and light. Mr. Clay's shop was never overpowered by the smell of raw meat and smelled like the leaves he secretly placed in all the spots of the store that were open to the wind. When it blew through, no matter how briefly, so, too, did the leafy scent, unknown to everyone but the owner. An idea from Mrs. Clay.

She looked up at him and saw that his eyes had never left her face but were waiting for more of the story.

"Gogo J. knew I needed to work. That I needed something to do so my heart could feel something other than what I had been feeling."

"How had you been feeling?" he asked.

"Like I was carrying death."

He didn't look away and she was grateful.

"She gave other things for your heart to carry."

She nodded. "She gave me a place to stay. I cleaned with her. I laughed with her."

"Leaving must have been quite painful," Mr. Clay answered softly.

THE ONES WE LOVED

"He was with me," she answered quickly, before she had a chance to think about it, and stop herself.

The wind blew against the door. She glanced up just to make sure it wasn't raining. If the sky had opened up just as she started speaking about leaving Gogo J., she wasn't sure she would be able to hold back all of her stories.

"Is that where you met him?"

"Yes," she said.

"What was He like?"

She looked at Mr. Clay and tried to raise her shoulders, but it just looked like a shiver.

"Have you thought about returning?"

She nodded.

"With him?"

She started to chew her tongue. Her eyes stung.

"I don't know."

Mr. Clay reached for her arm and held it tightly. She shut her eyes. *I must look ridiculous*, she thought.

"I'm waiting for us to be better. To be like we were," she said, before her eyes opened to focus on a spot on the ceiling.

The door swung wide and He stepped in carrying reeds from the river. He didn't see She sitting in front of him, wondering what he was doing. He turned and found her face.

"You look tired," She said, looking at his arms, which had a few cuts on them. "And you're bleeding."

He looked down. "It will dry."

They looked at each other. She remembered Mr. Clay and looked at him questioningly. It was He who answered instead.

"I came by to drop off some reeds for Mr. Clay."

"Why?" She asked, turning back to He, who was starting to fidget.

Mr. Clay waited, looking at them both.

289

"It's for his lessons. For weaving."

"Mr. Clay, you can weave?" she asked the old man, who shook his head, and waited. She looked up at He, her mind racing. He looked back, his heart quickening. She turned her eyes towards the reeds, then back to He, who didn't look away.

"Are you teaching him?"

"I am."

"Is Mr. Clay good?"

"Getting better."

The questions came fast, as if they wanted to share all they had to say before something happened to make them stop. Mr. Clay was still there, yet the old man stayed silent, not drawing any attention and feeling Mrs. Clay demanding that he make little sound.

Let them talk, he heard his wife say.

"Are you buying something?" He said to She, looking at the counter.

She shook her head. "No. I just came to see Mr. Clay." And they both turned around to look at him.

It was silent while all three waited for someone to begin.

Mr. Clay cleared his throat, and both She and He expected him to speak, but the man remained silent. Simply moved the reeds to the back of the store.

The walk from the swamp was starting to settle into the boy, so He sat down. Looking at She, he took a breath.

44.

THE LEAVES ON this tree fell readily. They turned the ground into a covered place, carpeting where the neighbors put their feet, spat, lost their things and met their lovers. The heat was on its way out, and again it would be good to be in this town. Then she would slide onto the ground, feel the leaves beneath her and see the branches above, naked now that the heat was leaving and autumn stretching. She could reach for him, and maybe she would find a hand now that the sun was gone, and because there wasn't any sweat, his fingers wouldn't slip through her own. She heard a tiny crack in the branch that supported her leg and moved her body only a bit.

There were fewer guavas now that the leaves were lessening, and this one that she was eating was not as soft or sweet. The seeds were getting stuck between her teeth, and because the guava was hard, they weren't coming out as easily, no matter how hard she pressed her tongue into the spaces where she felt discomfort.

He could talk to Mr. Clay. And he could speak to the land. But he couldn't talk to her. She nodded, hearing the words as though they came from someone else's mouth and she was just lending her ear while sitting in this tree reaching for the last guavas. She had climbed higher because the guavas were disappearing, and because she needed to almost touch the sky if she wanted to be hidden behind the last leaves of the season. She wouldn't be climbing for days, weeks and more days until the first bloom appeared. They would be paying for what they needed with his maize, which seemed to remain even if it was not as much as he wanted. She remained, too, even if He was less than She needed. Is that what he told Mr. Clay?

When she saw them at the butcher shop, she was happy. Then she was angry. Then she was guilty. He was here talking to her friend. He still hadn't started speaking to her like he used to. Mr. Clay must have said something that made it easier to speak. Hearing another crack in the branch, she raised her arms to pull herself onto another that was stronger and also closer to several guavas that looked like they were ready to hit the ground. Once the leaves fell and she couldn't climb anymore, She would stay in their house more regularly, and cook, sweep, wash what needed to be cleaned and wipe off the dust that had collected around things they didn't touch. There was a lesson here, about dust finding room if things were not lifted. If they weren't used and only left to be still. Mama would have known it. Or perhaps Miss Bride. Things needed to be moved.

She hadn't thought about her Geography teacher since getting on the bus, the first time. And the time after that. But she'd noticed her geography change. And she had shifted too. Not because she could see it, but she knew from their lessons that everything, including the ants and the flowers, the people and the soil, changed with the shedding of time. It was how the world began. She wished there was someone who could tell her how she had become different. When the soil changed, it was the people who lived there longest that noticed. When the flowers turned into seeds, it was those who picked them most and the animals who scurried under the petals and stalks that missed the colors and fragrances. She was different. She had to be.

THE ONES WE LOVED

What was it that Miss Bride had said? That she would belong
wherever she was loved. In the place where people saw her change
and still chose to hold her close. They would remember her there and
recognize the love they gave, even while her face shifted. She loved all
of his faces, the ones that retreated and those that used to come into
the restaurant and wait to speak to her. She knew she was different.
She wished He would tell her how.

She had waited for him to say another word in the butcher shop.

"How long have you been doing this together?"

"Not long."

"What colors are you using?"

"No colors. I am just showing him how to make strong baskets."

"Only baskets."

"And other small things."

She had left when she started to feel that another voice was going
to jump out of her skin, and instead of asking simple questions about
weaving, swamps and mats, She would scream about the silence, the
discarded dish, the easy coldness, the leaving early and returning later,
the never looking up to see her so close. Her walk home was quick.
Like a girl who didn't mind sweating. Someone who had no one to
mind if she looked unkempt. She had changed. She knew it. When
she saw the gate, her feet had moved faster until they led her to the
spot in the garden where she had planted the mhiripiri she had first
seen in the back part of the house. Pulling it off the stalks, she rubbed
it on her hands, covering her palms, her fingers, and rotating around
the knuckles, then raised her hands to her face and pressed them
into the eyes. The stinging and the burning made her cry. She wept,
not because of what she had lost but because of the stinging and the
burning. And while her eyes fought to clean what she put inside, She
thought only of whether she'd go blind and what would happen if she
did. She squeezed her eyes shut, the burning and stinging taking her

293

mind away from Mr. Clay's butcher shop. Away from Gogo J.'s, where she had also made her eyes sting and burn.

All she thought about was the pain. Would she finally go blind? It had been three days and he hadn't said anything about his time with Mr. Clay. She had waited. He came home to sleep and left. The next day, She cleaned and He left. The day after, She placed the food on the table and he ate. She had waited. Her eyes kept stinging and burning.

She looked up and saw more guavas. These were brighter and bigger than those on the lowest branches. They were the guavas that would usually rot without ever being eaten because they were too high up to grab. Firmly trapping her foot between two branches that were close together like praying palms, she pulled herself up, preparing to reach and lightly tap the fruit. As her arm lifted, she felt her leg slide out of position, and the other searched for a ledge that could keep her upright. She saw the ground as she slipped and felt the leaves brush by, and she saw a hand reach out like the hand under the water. Pulling her in. A hand finding her through the church smoke. Pulling her forward.

It looked like the one that saved her life.

Acknowledgments

WHILE WRITING THIS book, I spent an outrageous number of days and months in solitude, moving from the bed to the sofa in Toronto, Harlem and Harare—yet, for the times when I stepped outside, I am inordinately grateful to the people who surrounded me.

I want to thank Aeman Ansari, an inimitable and supremely tender force whose eyes were the first to see, recognize and fall in love with She and He. You changed my life.

I tip my cap to the team at HarperCollins Canada who've wondrously rallied behind this book: editorial assistants, public relations mavens, designers and all those who make up the machine of book publishing, down to the drivers whose vehicles will transport boxes of this book to stores. To Alan Jones, an intuitive and gifted art director who left me astounded and giddy and saw my made worlds so clearly from inception. To Natalie Meditsky, our production editor, who kept this dream looking good and on track. And to Catherine Dorton, my copyeditor, who reintroduced me to the characters I love and made certain that all their voices carried as much weight as their hearts.

While on this stretch of remembering all the adaptations and alterations, I want to thank Jennifer Lambert, my generous editor. I

ACKNOWLEDGMENTS

am so lucky that we shaped this book together, that you listened with great care and patiently joined me in the reimagining, editing and endless revisions. Oh, the endless revisions! Jenn, I am forever sorry for going back into a draft with all the calm of a golden retriever thirty seconds after I told you it was done. You must now absolutely loathe the phrase "by the way."

By the way, I just thought of a chapter I could revise right now, but I'm also very content leaving it the way it is, and I think that shows sublime progress.

Thank you to Kamal Al-Solaylee, whose classes were the most fulfilling and clarifying, and whose guidance helped me make sense of all that writing could encompass. To Mrs. Gwati, the first teacher to call my stories art. Hanah, Vinnie, Mariani and Jess, my first readers and my soul family. Thank you from the bottom of my wildly besotted heart. All your advice, encouragement, voice notes, opinions and memes made this journey an unforgettably sweet one. Alyssa, thank you for always lifting me up during our annual get-togethers. Reva, for being so true and so brave. Zoé, I adore you for always putting our Zoom writing dates on the calendar, and more importantly, for always leaving enough room for me to judge. Xi and Adrian, y'all don't know this, but the group chat brought me to the finish line.

And lastly but always the beginning and my first storytellers, I want to thank my parents. And all of our ancestors who courageously lived and profoundly loved so the two of you could be the people who raised me. Mama—your speaking and loving is an honest gift and blessing. I would not be the writer I am without your boundless imagination and even more immeasurable support. You are the most tender part of my soul and the place my faith takes shape. Daddy—with your optimism, curiosity and enduring interest in all that I love, you have given me my most treasured inheritance. The journalist I became is because of the man you are, and I will never have the words to magnify my gratitude.

ACKNOWLEDGMENTS

To Thandi, my closest half, Tata, my years-apart twin and Thandeka, my older-than-me baby sister, I am grateful for our shenanigans and to this universe that made us siblings. I minded sharing pork pies when we were younger; I no longer mind sharing this life with you all by my side. Thank you for being my witnesses.

And to Zimbabwe, my home and my heart whose earth remembers me constantly and calls me its own. Tapinda, Tapinda Madzitateguru!!

29th book of 2025
Started: Aug, 25, 2025
Finish by: Aug, 31 2025
Sept 4